# DEEPEST,
# DARKEST EDEN

# DEEPEST, DARKEST EDEN

## EDITED BY

## CODY GOODFELLOW

Miskatonic River Press

New York • Florida
2013

Dedication —
For CLARK ASHTON SMITH,
Sage of Auburn, Savior of Atlantis.

For information, contact Miskatonic River Press

Published in the United States by:
Miskatonic River Press, LLC
944 Reynolds Road, Suite 188
Lakeland, Florida 33801
www.miskatonicriverpress.com

ISBN 978-1-937408-02-2

# Contents

# Wider Than The World: A Door To Hyperborea

*Neither by ship nor on foot would you find the marvelous road to the assembly of the Hyperboreans.*

—Pindar

Just beyond the highest mountain, just before the dawn of history—everywhere out of reach and beyond knowledge, there you will find Hyperborea. There you will lose yourself in a dream of a simpler, more dangerous past in order to face what you could otherwise never accept as your own reflection.

To the ancient Greeks, the place beyond the home of the North Wind was a paradise of eternal sunshine, "far from labor and battle." Homer located it north of Thrace, the extent of the settled Greek world; Pindar supposed it lay somewhere near the Danube. Plutarch and the Romans pushed it ever further north until it vanished beyond the Arctic Circle.

To a modern age that has mapped the world to death, the need for Hyperborea is still so great that we must bury it in the prehistoric past. In her ambitiously mad metaphysical exegesis, *The Secret Doctrine*, H.P. Blavatsky posited, among a pageant of forgotten rulers of the Earth, a race of yellow-skinned creatures that reproduced by budding like polyps, known as Kimpurshas. Though they left no biological descendants, the residents of the lost continent they called Plaksha enjoyed a Golden Age of tropical plenty and esoteric enlightenment until they, like the Lemurians and the Atlanteans, fell from their height of achievement and spiritually devolved into brutish, bestial monsters—namely, us.

Theosophy flourished among an explosion of pseudo-mystical philosophies in the early twentieth century, but those who most effectively spread its gospel never pledged their faith, but swiped the crazier ideas to spice up their pulp fantasies. Foremost among these plunderers of the dubious new gospel was Clark Ashton Smith.

For those unfamiliar with Smith's phenomenal weird fiction (put this book down immediately and rectify this lapse; if you must, go to http://www.eldritchdark.com/, where all his short fiction may be found), Hyperborea was but one exotic setting among many for the self-educated poet and romantic iconoclast's fancifully grotesque fables, all of which shared his celebrated lapidary prose and a sardonic wit to rival Ambrose Bierce or John Collier. Using both the theosophist and the Classical Greek visions of Hyperborea as base pigments, Smith created a panorama of weird fantasy unlike any other in a mere handful of lush short stories. Indeed, if they had a clear, inarguable fault, it was that there were far too few of them.

Smith's flurry of weird prose output lasted less than a decade, and it came at the height of a period largely lost and forgotten in the long shadows of Conan and *The Lord Of The Rings*. An outgrowth of the fin-de-siecle Orientalist and Decadent movements, pioneer fantasists such as E.R. Eddison, James Branch Cabell and Lord Dunsany devised lavishly foreign settings and bizarre schools of sorcery to supply new thrills for pulp aesthetes burnt out on the Arabian Nights. Escapism so pure it often ran out of air and became suffocating contrivance, but pre-heroic fantasy was unburdened by the all-too-familiar sword & sorcery conventions that have come to define high fantasy, and also refreshingly free of the reactionary constraints that would later hamstring the genre—witness the lush, carnal and presciently trippy illustrations Frank C. Papé, Hannes Bok and Virgil Finlay did for them.

If for no other reason, Smith's fantasies continue to thrill long after most of his contemporaries have been forgotten because they were the antithesis of Howard's alpha-machismo psychodramas or Tolkien's grand tapestries of valor and faith. In escaping into Smith's primeval Eden, we find the first humans to be all too much like us, the Golden Age to be a thin coat of gilded paint. Frolicking in the forest primeval, we find a cruel and exacting moral code at work eons before the first mention of sin and Hell. Greedy, deceitful, lustful, larcenous, cowardly and mad with preposterous ambition, Hyperborea's gnomish proto-human buffoons snort at us from the fossil record, mocking the polished modernity of a technologically omnipotent empire brought to its knees by trivial scandals and imbecilic media circuses.

# INTRODUCTION

The literary adepts who gathered to bring you this anthology were not instructed to create counterfeit CAS stories, but were instead presented with an even more daunting challenge—to expand the canon of Hyperborea's extraordinary mythos with tales told in voices out of time, yet uniquely their own. More, they were hounded and harangued by your humble editor to insure that these tales would be pure escapism—wild, ripping yarns with no cynical axes to grind. Therefore, be forewarned: any resemblance between the beetle-browed subhuman misbehavior on offer herein and your own is entirely coincidental.

Cody Goodfellow
Burbank, California
April, 2013

# Hostage

## By Nick Mamatas

The north winds fell silent. The blind man at the bottom of the boat actually had some idea of where he was. North of Thracia, he reasoned. That was why the wind had stopped. The craft had drifted, crewless, past the realm of Boreas, who was the North Wind. The blind man would have laughed had he could. He had been taken hostage for a reason he didn't even understand—the men with spear points at his back and throat spoke only in the *bar-bar-bar* of strangers, and dragged him onto a triaconter, then set off, the thirty banks of rowers grunting and singing as they worked. Then the ship had come upon a sudden storm. The blind man could smell it in the air, but when he tried to speak he got a fist in the mouth and lashed to the mast. That's what saved him when the great wave hit. Anyone who hadn't gone overboard was either dead at their station or unconscious, perhaps drowned in a puddle. The blind mad had squirmed from his ropes when the mast had snapped, and hung on as best he could.

All the water was salt, but the blind man had salvaged a skin of wine, some bread that had gone to paste. Even a fish, raw and bony, that had been swept into the boat. It hardly mattered—a hale man with two eyes couldn't navigate a ship such as this himself, and all the oars were broken. He briefly considered throwing himself, belly first, onto one of the shattered oars and ending it all, but the blind man was a storyteller of sorts. He was curious—what would happen next?

That night was colder than he had ever known, though the night came late. The blind man had never experienced such a strange night—he shivered under the scraps of sail he could find, and it was so cold he thought he felt salty water freeze on the hair of his arms. His limbs went numb, and his nose, always so sensitive, closed. Waves spilled over the prow of the triaconter, littering the bottom of the boat with fish. The blind man tore one to pieces, alive, with his hands and teeth, drank its blood and spit out the bones as best he could. To choke on a bone after everything—that was an irony not even the gods would dare.

*The gods*, the blind man thought. He was far north now, where most of the gods he knew were strangers. Even the waves upon which the blind man sat were not Poseidon's. There was only venerated on the edge of the world. He raised his arms and begged the sun for mercy, but sleep took him first.

He dreamt of warmth, and of the smell of musk, and when he awoke he was warm and under the skin of a great beast. The blind man opened his mouth, but his throat was too dry to speak. So he croaked. And in return, the people gathered about him—and there were several—also croaked, then murmured in the language of barbarians in a way that the blind man knew to be tinted with curiosity, and perhaps even a little joy.

The blind man was given water, and he finally could speak. He remembered hearing that the barbarian tribes of the far north knew a certain form of magic that depended on, and was empowered by, knowledge of names. So he croaked out what he was, what he had been—a blind man, a hostage. In the language of his people, those words were near-homophones. *Hau-mohr-uhs.*

The blind man was bathed, and fed—though the food was slimy, and gamey—and even masturbated by a slim hand, and slowly he regained his strength. He did not know whether he was being kept in a tiny hut made of skins, or a long and twisting cave, or in the belly of a leviathan. In his dreams, it was always dark, and the world was a great pulsing thing, squirming and twisting around him, a dragon from the muck. But one morning he realized he hasn't been dreaming.

The boy spoke to him in his own language, though one heavily accented—aristocratic and foreign both at once.

"What is your magic?" the boy said. An older man bar-barred something, prodding or correcting the boy somehow. "What do you have that brought you here?"

"I don't even know where I am," the blind man said. "Or how I came to be delivered here." The boy repeated the words, his voice lilting and excited, in his own language. After a generalized murmur the boy tried again:

"What gods brought you here? Do you know the truth of *Zho-thaqquah*?"

Zhothaqquah. The blind man guessed it was a name—the name of a god. He had heard it before, during his recuperation, in his waking hours and in his dreams, where it was sang by the slow beating of his heart.

"Cruel gods," the blind man said. "Capricious gods." The boy grunted in confusion. "Gods who are like children, smiling one moment, weeping the next, then dancing and singing," the blind man explained. The boy seemed to like that better. He petted the blind man's hairy arm.

"Zhothaqquah has no such flaw," the boy said.

"Then why are you blind like me," the blind man said. The boy gasped, there was some *bar-baring* from the men, the boy answered them, then asked the blind man, "How did you know?"

"The way you reached for my arm, as if you did not quite know where it as, or, when you touched it, where it ended." The blind man said, "Just because you are blind does not mean that you cannot be an observer of the world around you."

"I mean..." the boy said, his voice tentative. "How did you know that it was Zhothaqquah who blinded me? With his tongue, that snapped out from the darkness to mark me as his."

The blind man realized that he should stop speaking before he said something foolish. Hospitality was always tentative in barbarian lands, where the virtue of *philoxenia* was all but unknown. And, if the boy wasn't just a lunatic and surrounded by the same, the gods here seemed rather closer than the far off game-players of his experiences. For a moment, he thought to pray, but the blind man had little to sacrifice. He hummed a hymm he knew, for the only god who could be found this far north. Perhaps the boy would think him a lunatic, and leave him now to rest.

Instead, the boy sang. Like a native of the blind man's country, in words unaccented by the barbarian tongue, free of grunting and growling. It was the blind man's turn to gasp. Then, an epiphany—for the first time in his life, he was glad he could not see, because whatever these barbarians were hiding, he did not want to know. The other barbarians shushed the boy and entered into a lengthy, acrimonious, ten-way conversation with the boy. It sounded to the old man like a pack of angry dogs coming across a newly dead goat.

The old man realized that all the voices were those of men, and some youths, like the boy. Unusual that there were no women, as there was the smell of cooking food about, and the blind man's bed was made thoroughly well. Perhaps this was a group of pederasts? *Well, there's nothing wrong with that…* But no. Too many men to too few boys. Was this a military outpost, or an all-male mystery cult? The argument with the boy continued, and the blind man drifted off to sleep. He hoped to dream of the boy and his paean to the sun, but instead dreamed again of a sticky, pulsing dark.

When the blind man awoke, his limbs were bound together, and he was being carried on a litter. He called out for the boy, fearing that he would only hear the *bar-bar-bar* of the older men in return. There was the laughter of self-satisfied men, but the boy did speak.

"We're taking you to meet a god," the boy said. His tone was casual, as if discussing an unremarkable tide. The boy, blind, was holding one of the poles by the hostage's feet, as if he were the guide. The blind man was full of questions, but there were rocks in his stomach. What if he said the wrong thing, and was dumped onto the rocks, the crawl about this frigid, foreign land till he starved?

"Oh, how lovely," the man said. If the boy agreed that it was lovely, he did not say. The blind man strained his ears to listen to footfalls, to the exhalations and murmurs of his bodyguard. There were no birds in the sky, no insects buzzing about, even when the rocky hill over which he was carried, the litter swaying like a small boat drifting from shore, turned to swampland. Finally, some time after noon, the litter was lowered into the muck.

"Am I to be sacrificed now?" the blind man said.

"No," the boy said. The blind man could hear the other litter-bearers, and the rest of the men, shuffling away. They hadn't stopped to eat or rest. Perhaps he wasn't as far from the place with the fire and the bed of animals skins, as he had thought. A ritual march through a labyrinth of some sort? A path designed to confuse him? "I'll even stay here with you."

"Because you are blind."

"That's right."

The blind man relaxed. The god was probably nothing other than one, or more, of the men, who'll circle around the swamp once time and come back, wearing masks and lighting flaming powers and affecting strange voices. As gods do. He vowed to thrash about and grovel and beg convincingly, like an actor, to please the locals. He had some questions for the boy, but the boy only spoke a prayer in the grunting of his tribe. Then the blind man saw something. The trees of the swamp parted somehow, and light poured into the clearing. The black behind the blind man's eyelids blazed red, then white, as when he was a boy and turned his face up toward the sun, in the hope of seeing some of the chariot behind the great and fiery wheel.

Someone said his name. No, sang his name. The song penetrated the blind man's bones. In the distance, he heard the boy shrieking *Zhothaqquah Zhothaqquah Zhothaqquah!*

The blind man said *Apollon!* and Apollon, the only god of his people known to dwell north of Thrace, answered.

Apollon knew of the blind man. He had seen him from his perch in the sky.

Apollon appreciated the blind man. He knew of the man's wiles, his stories.

Apollon assured the blind man. He would leave this place one day, and perhaps even sing of what he learned.

*Zhothaqquah Zhothaqquah Zhothaqquah!* the boy shouted. Then more barbarian jibberish. The blind man felt that the boy was far away. The blind man was floating on a cloud, in the immanent presence of a god in which he hadn't truly believed since he was a boy whose eyes burned.

The boy thrashed about in the mud, in an ecstasy of his own. The blind man nearly called out to him, but what would that mean to Apollon, to turn his attention toward a worm of a boy, and a barbarian besides?

But...the boy knew Greek. He must have learned it from the god. The blind man swallowed hard and dared ask a question. It was well-phrased, practically a hymn, with meter and rhyme. It encompassed many subjects—who were the men who impressed the blind man and took him hostage? How did he come to be the sole survivor? Why did the boy know Greek? How could Apollon live half a year among such savages, with a dark and filthy thing Zhothaqquah as his only divine company?

And Apollon spoke: Oh. It was all My will.

That the blind man be dragged from his home. That he face death at sea, and that his captors all die in the roiling water.

That the blind man live, but only barely, kept alive by his curiosity. It amused Apollon to see a blind man aboard a rudderless ship.

*Zhothaqquah Zhothaqquah Zhothaqquah!*

There was a poetry to the notion.

That the blind man hear the boy's words as Greek.

And Zhothaqquah was just the guise Apollon wore in these lands. *Zhothaqquah Zhothaqquah Zhothaqquah!*

And Apollon was just the guise Zhothaqquah wore among the olive-pit spitters and squid-eaters and the boy-rapists. Death through the plague of frogs, or death through disease and arrow-points, it is all the same.

*Zhothaqquah Zhothaqquah Zhothaqquah!*

But Apollon also has the power to heal. Should he heal the man, or the boy?

*And if you heal me,* the blind man thought, *which divine visage would I lay eyes upon?* Then he understood that someone had already been healed.

"Boy! Look out to the sea!" the blind man cried out. "What is it?"

The boy gasped, then gurgled. "Dark," he spat out finally, "dark as wine!" And those were the last words of Greek the blind man would hear from the boy, who chanted *Zhothaqquah Zhothaqquah Zho-thaqquah!* till his tongue swelled in his throat and he died in a frenzy of thrashing. The sun finally set after long hours rolling through the sky.

The blind man made his way to the sea, on his hands and knees. His flesh was shredded, and only the blasted landscape kept night-beasts from pacing the streak of blood he left as his wake. The appetite of the mad god had consumed nearly all life on these shores. The blind man threw himself in the water, hungry for death.

But he would not die. The blind man bobbed like a piece of drift-wood, though he dove deep and swallowed salt water by the bellyful. His limbs were broken sticks, but still he floated, and paddled against his own will. At dawn, a ship of Thracians encountered the deranged, blathering man. Two little specks in the endless black sea. It took weeks for the blind man to find his way home; months for the blind man to regain his senses. Why Apollon compelled him to live, he knew not why. More caprice, more fatal whim. But lived the blind man did.

And the blind man plotted his revenge. A tale of gods, cruel and changeable, bedeviling even the greatest heroes of the world. Who could not hear the long song of war and blood and fail to raise arms against these beings from the sky? The nations of men are not enemies of one another—we have only one foe, and we are fools to worship him. But we are many, and the gods are few. Indeed, fewer even than we think. The blind man's song would be timeless, a magic message to the future. *Men of the world, cultivate your intellects and use your minds to free our world from the caprice of the gods! We need not be pawns of the gods, hostages of fate!* Even if Apollon had manipulated the blind man into singing his song—to eliminate the hold other gods have on the tribes of men, to taunt men with visions of terror—what could Apollon do against the weight of the human race?

It might take three thousand years, but surely all who heard the blind man's song would join together and cleanse the languages of the Earth of the very word God.

Any day now.

Any day…

# To Walk Night... Alone...

## By Joseph S. Pulver, Sr.

*(for Cody Goodfellow... because he's crazy)*

B ig moon. Wind forging things in the trees.
      NIGHT-SOUNDS. Sorties.
     Things that are. Not there.
Clouds pushed from their climb toward East.
at the base of a hill
under a sky not painted black
cold
wind tearing chunks from skin
still WET
mud-and-bog WET
(a whole day in the marshes. fell twice. cursed the mage's charge a hundred times.)
Small fire climbing among the ring of ceremonial rocks. Risky.
Dry
or FREEZE. Attha is searching for dry. After dry he'll try for warm. Then he'll try to kill a grey-pig.

Chews on the blood-root. Sour, but here where the rough-grass scratches and cuts, food is food. The energy transfusion swims, each little arc promises. Bitter, the tongue wants to go away from the task of the mouth. BITTER. Only the stupid refuse to partake.

Attha adds two more chunks of wood to his fire. Builds another layer on risk.

They might see it. Could smell it. And if they did, would come, on their bellies, cutting through the tall grass and the dirt. Come with their black eyes and black talons. Come—COLD as any device of war—with arms to clutch. Come to eat flesh and gorge on blood.

GREENandREDandBLACKanddirtBROWN, some striped, some blotched, the Snakemen. Long flat heads and long arms and long snake bodies.

Lifts his fingers. Bite. Chews.
Looks at the
moon.
Looks at his
sword.
Both
sharp as the cold.
Then his axe.
Sharp as the
cold.
Moves closer to his fire.
Dry.
Dry can kill the cold god.

Attha stands. Stays close to the fire. Rearranges his clothes on the sticks. Some parts are dry. Some soon. Won't be long he can put his shirt on.

Not long.
Good bed of coals now. Adds more wood. Stands close as he can.
Dry.
The naked side facing his fire warm.
His naked back burns with cold.

The conviction of an owl cuts the moon. Attha knows his hunger. Wishes him luck. Good to honor likeminded, might
find
it returned to him.

He's dry. Warmer. Not warm.
Shirt's dry. Puts it on. Covers his arms, torso, almost down to his knees.
Dry.
Warmer. Not warm.
Thanks the owl.
Wishes him well again.

Looks at the pouch he carries, the pouch marked with the shape of Sisyph. The pouch he carries to Vwidlen the Enchanter. Looks at his sword beside it, the sword never far from his scarred hand. Knows which is more powerful.

East waits o'er this
   titan hill of bramble and black sores and struggling green.

Vwidlen's black and dusty keep sits there.

Vwidlen waits—

Over the sheer hill and through the sizable address of darkening trees and parched grass when the sky opens its mouth and shouts light.

No clouds. They've gone. Flew east. His day-walk will be dry.

His pants are dry.

Puts them on.

Warmer.

Blesses the owl again.

Drier
   and no Snakemen. As soon as his boots are dry he'll put his sword into a grey-pig. Eat.

With a full belly he can make it through the long day to Vwidlen's keep.

It will be warm and dry there.

Warm and dry like the Hall of the Toad.

Drier now. Warmer now.

Over the hill there are no Snakemen.

Over the hill there is a long day's march and the keep.

Cloak and boots are dry.

And now on.

Warm grows.

Light comes.

The Snakemen that crawl and eat men do not.

Attha fixes the pouch to his belt, presses his palm to it, feels the small mound within. Sheltered and safe. He is pleased. Takes his sword in hand. Slings his axe over his back. Moves away from his fire and into the tall grass.

Deep in the affairs of flesh his sword bleeds a grey-pig. A small one. No joy, but a blossom dressed like relief comes over him. He blesses the owl again.

Puts a chunk of the grey-pig on a stick over the fire. Puts a few strips on other sticks. Hears them sizzle. Puts two more chunks of wood on the fire.

Before the sun is up and full he will eat.

Looks at the sky above the trees, hopes the owl will, as well.

Under the sky he faces, no taverns burning with ales and wine and plump wenches that offer their bottoms to loins as they bend to pour from frothy pitchers—Savage every season is this house of death. No past battles lie here, the half-men, the Snakemen, enter not into battle, they come, they slay, they offer no time for reply. And after they take living's ambition from blood and bone, leave little trace. Six days in this kingdom with his sword in his fist. Six days, a flood of thrusting and goading nerves, his blue eyes cutting every sound, and still carrying his skin . . . Walked and walked and walked and kept walking . . .

*Charged by the mage Messtisl. Left the bane-hung halls.*

*Left the alleys of migrant cats and pickpockets. Left the chasms between torches that often outlived the hurried strides that were broken by danger beneath them . . . pieces that take up space and don't float . . . Left the scaffold-phobias of timid Us crossing and recrossing the thirst of the huddled and hidden in their dark places. Afflicted, pontificating Us divided by the brute deposits of They/middles of squiggly-scandals/ naked (to their dirty ankles) candles hissing for thrills/another and another, one fancy, one nervous, judged and used/fetish/guilt/scruples/"It was not." . . . Left, as if hurled, for the freezing tongue of darkness.*

*Left flaunt and frail. Left a world, every gesture of ploughed field and tower, called civilization.*

*Outside its thick dark walls, walked, hand on his scabbard, by the field of dead tongues.*

*Walked*

    *over wind-carved slopes*

    *through ragged knots of ebony trees the ages could not devour*

*Heard*

    *bats sing of their achievements*

*Smelled*

    *migrating vines of rain coming to moisten meadow and sky*

                *and efforts . . .*

*Walked*

    *and diminished,*

    *grew tired.*

*Climbed*

    *go on*

    *muscle. next step. wet boots. resist the slow sink-mouth of mud.*

*go on. wet.wet.push*
>*for the steady and sharp of fire.*
*Curse the dripping sky. Curse the ground.*
*Curse the oarsmen pushing the porcupine wind hunting the skin in his clothes.*
*wet. wet.*
*Slogged*
>*mud tugging . . . go on . . . MUD hamstringing every left . . . right . . . left . . .*
*Cursed*
>*the chains of the slavers who came to his village and bought him from his parents and sold him in Uzuldaroum to a guild wizard who served Zhothaqquah. Cursed the wizard who bought him and then sold him*
>*cursed and kept on*
>*and*
>*vowed by all Elder Lords that song of the worms could not corrupt he would not*
>>*fall.*
*Rope bridge over a river whose swift blue hands carried the voice of the mountain to the cold sea.*
*Rain*
>*gesture and claw of splayed castanets rattling*
>*—epic if you could remain inside incommunicado—*
>*biting every itch and edge.*
*Swollen*
>*by the stacked WET thorns*
>>*scalp*
>>>*to*
>>*knee. RAIN . . . Dyeing blood and bone—*
*Go on*
>*as the wind forged.*
*Walked, shouldered the on to,*
>*as the sun*
>*bled to death*
*in*
>>*the arms of the*
>*horizon.*
*Built*

*little fires singing with flame*
*that*
  *streamed*
*and*
*smoked.*
*Slept*
*when he could. Ate when he could. Watched.*
*a day*
  *dead leaves scattered, flapping*
*and*
 *another*
*Noted the grey-black turns of the meshed sky, and walked*
*over*
*rocks*
  *with customs*
*that had nothing to say . . .*
*and*
 *another.*
*—tired*
*—sword poised*
*ready for skulls*
*ready to outlast*
*—brooded*
*—shivered*
*—slept*
  *in a small cave*
  *outside*
 *the wind carried*
  *the scent of*
  *blood*
  *to*
*night-things*
  *that laughed.*
*Walked*
 *where death walked*
  *where death—slow or frenzy or tangled—turned living into cadavers*
*blue and black until small creatures and black deathbirds and contagions*
*of insects and null finished feasting.*
  *Attha walks the day*

*night comes*
*makes his camp, makes his fire in a heavy stand of trees*
*he is dry*
  *this night carries a small chill*
  *his fire stretches its warm*
    *he has food*
    *and his heavy cloak.*
*On... In... Over...*
  *the brown-bog*
  *and the long marshes*
  *mud*
  *and pools*
  *wild grasses*
*treeless*
*fell when the dirt-water was knee-high*
*the wind laughed*
*splashed him with COLD*
*Walked fast as he could.*
*Fell again. WET clings to the bone-clinging chill of WET. And the*
*wind laughs . . .*
  *Needed trees.*
  *Needed FIRE.*

Bends closer to the snarls of his fire. Warm his god. Smoke curls
from the altar.

Night-sounds.

They comfort him.

He eats four strips of meat. Cuts strips from the chunk and wraps
them in a skin for the march. Drinks his last from the skin-pouch.
Warmer. With his sword tip spreads small coals on the dirt. Stirs them
around in the dirt. Buries some. Lies down with his sword in one hand
and his long-blade in the other.

Dreams.

Big moon. Its noiseless whole in the woods.

Wind laughing in the trees.

The smell of a fire. Not his fire. A fire roasting pleasing fare, meat
among herbs. A woman's fire offering ripe. Turns. Through a thin in
the trees he sees smoke and light in the small window of a hut.

Stunned he looks long.

Here?

In the Empty Land? None rest here. Legend and map and tavern-talk agree none live here. Death will send his giant cloud here to remove any settler and, most often, traveler.

The door of the hut opens. A woman comes out. Young and robust and naked, prettier than any pretty tavern-girl. Eyes as bright as the moon. Hair the color of soft moonlight. Breasts round and full, soft in tone and firm, twin perfect moons white as the inside of a coconut-fruit from the shores of the deep South Islands. She steps into the moonlight. Gliding white-dove hands stroking the moon above, she begins to sing and dance.

He clears the trees. Walks to her. Stand and watches—watches her curves arrange the future—watches her legs beckon the stars to come down and unfold red poppy music, come down and bejewel her seeds of living.

She turns and stops.

Proud. Open. No downstream of fear breaks on her face.

Smiles.

Center and deep he is warm.

Voice convivial as the gleam of a jewel. "I offered all for you to come," she says.

Offers her hand. "Come inside and I will show you."

Awake. Shivers. Blinks at the full light. Shakes with *be quiet now* to the clinging mist of his dream.

Too many days without warm food. Too many nights without honey and ale and the warm gleam of an agreeable girl in his soft bed. Curses the hard lot of a soldier-servant.

Stands.

Another day has been uncovered and thrown before him. He has his sword in his hand.

Begins to mount the hill.

Up the hill.

Down.

Onward. No mud. No snakemen . . . A butterfly crosses his path . . . A field with charms. Chews a strip of meat as he leaves morning for mid-day. Fills his skin-pouch in a clear pool.

Marches on . . .

The trees thicken and become a forest. Night's black sails will soon suck up the sky.

Hoping for the wide face of the moon, he gathers wood. Is pleased with the fire. And the tenor of night-sounds.

Eats from his chunk of meat.

Pulls his cloak tight about him.

Sleeps.

Woken by his caretaker owl.

Big moon.

The smell of a fire turns him. Not his fire. A fire roasting meat. A harbor of honey and heartening herbs sings in the air. A woman's fire offering ripe he thinks. Through a thin in the trees he sees smoke and light in the small window of a large hut.

Stunned. Looks long.

"How can this—"

The mage and his sworn master tested him when he was a sapling. Too keen for the stables or the kitchen, yet not drawn to the systems of scribes. The boy was rooted to the relations and aspects of worldly matter, no vision, no further or sense of motion in the windows and blacknesses of the Beyond called to him. Labeled him, "Soldier." Put a sword in his hand. He trained hard under the swordmaster and the guard captain, and when he was ready and promoted stood ready at the enchanter's doorway. All day while the wizard slept. Soldier, marked by his master's eyes and word as not one to peer into the charnel cloudstream of the Tolxian vapors and the mirror abyss of Phreinalor. He is a soldier, nothing more. Without the gift and the journey of wizard-craft he could not create this.

His master said he could never see tomorrow, he was no visionary, no dreamer.

Yet he had.

Stares at the door of the hut.

It is the door. The same.

"This can not—"

Opens.

Gasps as the dream-woman steps through it.

"She is . . . *Her.*"

Pure and young and full-bodied—no girdle or robe.

Unashamed.

Prettier than any appealing tavern-wench. Eyes as vivid as the moon. Hair the color of pure velvet-moonlight. Breasts round and full, soft in tone and firm, twin perfect moons white as the interior of a coconut-fruit from the exotic South Islands. She steps into the moonlight.

Gliding white-dove hands—the ascension UP! UP! Measured by charity never quarrel—caressing the moon above.

Begins to chant… and dance.

Attha clears the stand of trees. Walks toward her. Stands.

Watches—

watches her curves divine—

watches her legs beckon the stars to come down and unfold red poppy music, come down and bejewel her seeds of living.

She turns. Stops.

Considers him.

Proud. Open. Fearless face
and set of form.

Offers him her smile.

Skin to inmost he is warm.

Rose-soft voice. "I offered all for you to come," she says.

Offers him her hand. "Come inside and I will show you."

Follows.

There is a warm fire. A bed lush with furs and feather-filled fabrics. Seasoned meat is in her hearth.

Rouged red and black and blue primal masks made of wood and autumnal husk hang on the walls. Brass charms and silver charms flare in the flickering hearth-light beside them.

On the table stands the swift and terrible mêlée of a yellow-jade dragon and a green-jade snake.

She pours wine into a fine-wrought silver mug. Hands it to him.

Warm wine.

Seizure. The wicked bite of poison that crush a man's constellations, choke all the wings and spires of his hours.

*Witch.*

Witch-woman. Black beast beneath. Full of worm-cavern secrets and the black delvings of rat-filled halls where the dust of Yohk and the disquiet of pale stars are moist with underground things. Witch-woman. Who does not flinch when blackness bulges with the Zhophek's terrible signs, and his retinue's unpleasant wings flutter from the unwholesome places to consume the cycle of light. Hand and mouth devoted to dreadcraft, each full of rite-spun errands obstruct the good fortunes of men with reasonable habits.

Witch. Masked. Scented for soft cascades of glissando affections.

Seductress. Fake the molten sweetness of connection she offers.
Sword up. Poised. Ready for her skull or heart. Ready to outlast.
"I will not fall to your witchery."
"Good Sir, I am no witch. I am only a hand of the Good Mother .
. . A healer."
Sword tip pressed to her white belly.
It's sharp, ready
       to open
       and mark with RED.
"I saw this place . . . And you, *in my dream*. All was faithfully this."
She looks at the sword. Shows no fear.
Bell-soft: "The Good Mother offers comfort to travelers."
"You think to put down my steel with wine. Believe breast and
green cunt will exhaust me, send me off to the coils of sleep."
"I seek only to refresh you—"
His grasp is ice.
Deep is his sword.
Deep is the laugh of His Master.
Hand flees hilt.
Backing away.
No girl.
Before him stands His master, the wizard Messtisl.
"You serve me faithfully, Attha."
On his knees.
Head bowed.
"My Lord." Eyes asking questions.
"My messenger could not be trusted without being first tested.
This was your test."
"Master—"
Future-slanted hand raised to silence him.
"You carry a seeing stone. It allowed me to gaze upon you.'
"I had to know if you would truly walk in death to perform the
task I set before you. Your next journey is no less dangerous, and no
shorter. Here is the ring you will deliver to the Oracle of Balon'Marr,
and the map to guide you to her. You must arrive before the moon
of Red Sulmanopses sits like a leering skull low in the sky. Complete
this task for me and upon your return I will give you jewels and long
health, and the girl of beauty and perfume and unvanishing glamours
will be waiting for you.

"Now rise. The ribboned gardens and viper-jawed cemeteries of your task await."

Stands.

"It will be done, My Lord."

Bows his head deeply.

"Drink this potion, Attha. It will bar fatigue for seven days and nights. Ride hard and firm, phantoms and night's balesome wolves will be at your heels."

As commanded he drains the cup.

"This locket contains a lock of the girl's hair and a simple enchantment of mine. It will keep you warm when the storm-bloated winds croak and bark. Take it. Place it about your neck. Your blade will keep the journey's lesser harms at bay."

As it rests upon his broad chest warm spreads within him.

"If he comes to you, heed the owl's advice. Allies are hard to come by when darkness weaves. Now go."

Rides
  deeper into
the West . . .

                    Scent of glut . . .
                    Brute-worm, shaking their silent,
                    eyeing blood and bone . . .
                    Wood thick with beards of open
                    mist, riddle and ghost . . .

The sun recedes . . .

He has gathered wood.

A small fire.

A chunk of meat on a stick sizzling.

Touches the locket.

Fixed on a silken image of
  the girl of beauty and perfume and unvanishing glamours . . .

Stands.

Gazing into the blackness.

Its gleam, vertical as any Immortal,

cast shadows long in Night's bodiless tempest.

Black stormy eye and

whirlwind-blade in his hand

stormy-decorum READY

he listens, stretches his eyes

into the realm of bat and along the road
for the bite of forces that plot to end life.
Baleful things that were abed waken—
Strange stains, rising from inhabitants of the lightless under-
ground, flavor the shadows.
Night winds snarling with hunger are upon him . . .
MOON
in a place without walls.

Alone.

Attha
   his heavy-cloak tight about him
   listens
for the owl
   in autumnaltrees . . .

(*KEW on my mind again*..........)

(*Joan La Barbara Shamansong, Morton Feldman* Rothko Chapel,
*David Diamond* Night Dances for orchestra, Opus 114~ ~~*looped
and intertwined*)

# In Old Commoriom
## By Darrell Schweitzer

Paliphar Vooz met the tempter at a routine orgy in old Commoriom. This was, indeed, in the old days, long before the city was abandoned in an ill-described hurry and given over to nameless horror. It was in a time when the decadent nobles still lolled away long, sweltering, jungle evenings seeking the extremes of pleasure and pain, some new sensation which might yield, at least, a transient spark of light, like what you see when a smoldering log is bestirred in darkness; some new thought or experience desperately hunted out. *Something.*

On this particular night, Paliphar Vooz lay sated. On the couch next to him, lizard-headed demons devoured a corpse with great relish, their heads wriggling as bits of flesh and splatters of blood flew everywhere, but no one seemed to pay them any mind. The air swirled with smoke and incense and the strong-smelling vapors of opiates and far rarer drugs. A bat-like thing, but with the form of a man, flew from one end to the other of the great, palatial hall, swerving around the sputtering lamps that hung from the ceiling on golden chains.

Somewhere someone screamed, whether in ecstasy or terror it was hard to say. Vast, naked masses of bodies still writhed on the floor and in the alcoves, rising and falling rhythmically, susurrating like an ebb tide.

It was under these circumstances that a gentle hand touched him on the shoulder and shook him, and a soft voice whispered, "Will you come with me? There is more than this. Many are the wonders left to behold."

And Paliphar Vooz turned blearily, and beheld rising before him what seemed at first to be a column of black, gleaming smoke, but which then resolved itself into the face of a beautiful young man, like an exquisite marble mask floating in the darkness, and then he made out a slender figure in an iridescent, sparkling black robe, like a patch of starry sky torn from the heavens.

This apparition reached out a hand to him, and he took it. The grip was firm and warm, almost burning. He allowed himself to be hauled to his feet, and joked under his breath, muttering, "Well, my calling calls at last."

It might have been one calling or another, for Paliphar Vooz fancied himself a poet, though he'd never gotten around to writing much verse, and he wore a philosopher's gown, though he'd not done much philosophizing beyond the sort of rote recitation that impresses the dull masses and earns one the requisite copper pazoors which make further meaningless existence possible.

Now here was, perhaps, something more, for the stranger was reciting what sounded like, "Behold, the gates of birth and death are open, and the clockwork of time has paused in its turning," or words to that effect, to which he, if he'd been a bit clearer-headed, should have been able to respond in kind.

Instead he slipped and fell splashing into a puddle of something foul. It was hard to tell what. Once more he was helped to his feet, and the other whispered again softly, almost seductively, "Will you come with me?"

The other's face floated in the darkness like a gleaming mask, whether a youth or perhaps a maiden, he could not tell, or some kind of demon, he could not know . . . and yet he allowed himself to be led into a dark place, a space between spaces, where creatures like luminous, skeletal fish or serpents wriggled by; and then the darkness parted like a curtain, and he stood before the great king of Commoriom, who lay unconscious in his vast, golden bed surrounded by his wives and concubines, dreaming dreams of blood and splendor. Paliphar Vooz saw those dreams flickering like shapes of flame.

He was impressed, ultimately, by the ugliness and pettiness of the king's mind, and he made to go, when the other nodded and guided him gently by the elbow. The two of them walked in darkness again, through solid walls, in and out of rooms and houses and towers, in spaces between spaces, where the senses could not quite follow.

He saw the great multitudes of Commoriom, many of them in their slumber, some in night time duties or seeking pleasures, or amid the commission of crimes nefarious or petty; for though the king and the great ones of the land might seek an escape from ennui in one endless debauch, there were still the common folk who drove the carts and baked the bread and repaired the aqueducts, who carried messages and patrolled the city's walls against marauders and retiled the roofs. These respectable folk he looked upon now, dreaming their mundane dreams, or performing such mundane tasks as are performed in the darkness, no more remarkable when a purse was lifted or a throat slit than not.

Yet he hesitated, half afraid. It was not the vision itself which troubled him, but the suspicion that he, like his companion, was a spirit, that he was a ghost, carried off from his body – perhaps it, too, now devoured by the crocodile-things while he lay absolutely insensate – already dead and bound for some nether hell yet undiscovered by genuine philosophers, let alone shallow frauds like himself.

His companion reassured him that this was not so, arousing adventurous expectancy within him, and bade him continue on their journey.

Once they passed like smoke through the walls of a certain private chamber where lay his own young, exquisitely beautiful mistress, who had missed the evening's festivities, claiming she had a headache. Now she slept blissfully in the arms of some other lover. This did not move him. The lover might have been a baker's boy, or might have been some blue-skinned, beast-headed thing from out of the swamps beyond the city's edge. It hardly mattered now. His perspective had changed.

He remembered, how after a perfect night with her, when he was very young and filled with expectancies, and those expectancies had just been, it seemed, fulfilled -- before he had the imagination to yearn for anything more -- she had finally shooed him out of the bed, given him a peck of a kiss on the cheek, and dismissed him, saying only, "Leave the door unlatched on the way out."

Then, this had merely filled him with obsessive desire, and his every moment's thought was filled with visions of her flesh, until such a time as he could be reunited with her. But now the scene replayed itself, and he went through it again, like an actor well-rehearsed in his role, and when he came to the end, he merely left the door unlatched and once more took his companion by the hand.

"If you should find yourself afraid," the other said, "take this." He pressed a stoppered ivory phial into Paliphar Vooz's free hand.

"I am not afraid."

"Nevertheless take it, and when you wish to end these visions, and behold only the absolute and unelaborated truth, drink from it."

"No, I want to go on," said Paliphar Vooz, for there was awakening within him some genuine desire to know, to see what lay beyond the perceptions of the everyday, to plumb those depths to which poets and philosophers are supposed to pay more than lip-service. As for the exact nature of the miracle which was unfolding before him and affording such an opportunity, he did not inquire, for the philosophical part of his brain was, he knew full well, like a flabby muscle and unused to the exertion.

He would do better to take this a little bit at a time.

They passed, then, beyond the human realm entirely, drifting in the night like huge, lazy moths on a hot wind. They soared among treetops, through the teeming jungles beyond the city's wall, and there he beheld and shared in and became a part of the dreams of beasts, as his subtle passage disturbed the contentment of some monstrosity that split the night one more time with its howling until it sank down beneath the mud again, with only its fiery eyes visible, blinking open and closed, slowly, like lanterns. His only conclusion was that the feastings and fornications of the beasts were not appreciably different from those of human beings, and of as little interest.

He looked skyward now. His companion led him up, off the earth entirely. He did not gaze back as the city of Commoriom and all of Hyperborea fell away beneath him. One of his slippers came loose and went tumbling away into space.

Now there was before him, far more immense than he had ever seen it before, the horned Moon. It filled the sky, blinding him. His sense of up and down were completely confounded as he and his companion settled among the mountains of the moon, amid great cliff faces of sheer gold and silver, which, he had always heard from the speculations of philosophers – on the rare occasions he bothered with such things – were valued about as much by the inhabitants of the Moon as common mud is on Earth.

This was more solid than any dream. They walked a long way through the mountains of the Moon, at times battling or evading immense and ravenous moon-beasts shaped like enormous worms or insects, though sometimes with human faces screaming in outrage at the intrusion of these two outsiders upon their pristine domain.

Since he'd lost a slipper, his one bare foot was soon sore and bleeding from the sharp rocks. He limped, leaning on his companion, whose shoulder felt solid enough, but whose whole body seemed a slender thing of sticks, which he feared might collapse under his own more gross weight.

In this somewhat disheveled state they came to the palace of the King of the Moon, and there found welcome, and dwelt for what may have been days, or months, or even centuries. All sense of time left them as they reclined upon cushions of soft, somehow pliable stone, and the bejeweled and fantastically-garbed moon-folk gathered around them (or above them, for some were winged). He drank the ambrosia of purest moonlight and discoursed as a true philosopher should, to the enrapt audience of the lunar court. For the first time in his life, perhaps, he rose to his calling, as he expounded upon the deeds and works of mankind, describing kingdoms and cities, far voyages across remote seas, treasures discovered, and the knowledge accumulated by terrestrial philosophers. This the lunar king and his courtiers took in with a polite nod. It was only when Paliphar moved on to the *wisdom* of mankind and attempted to demonstrate the beauty of human artistry, reciting lines from the greatest of human poets, that his audience broke into howling, grunting, barking laughter, loud as thunder, and as cacophonous as that of a pack of baboons. They hurled refuse. The lunar king sent his guards with flaming whips to drive the impostors forth from the palace.

It was in considerable pain, much the worse for wear, that Paliphar Vooz, now in rags, and having lost his other slipper now in the resultant mad scramble, limped with his marble-faced companion to the top of a lunar peak and gazed out into space, at the distant stars.

The other turned to him and said, "Perhaps it is time to go on."

"Yes, it is," said Paliphar Vooz. He took the other's hand in his. He still held the carven, stopped phial in his free hand, but he did not open it.

Once more his sense of direction was utterly confounded, and they leaned forward and fell upwards, into the sky. Now the blackness and terrible cold of space closed around them, and they fell for what might have been a thousand years, while he, dreaming, lived out what must have been a hundred thousand impossible lives on other worlds. Every once in a while he would awaken in the night with his head upon a pillow – if there were such things as pillows, or if his form possessed even the most rudimentary accoutrements of humanity and could be said to *have* a head – to wonder if he really was as he seemed to be, in the midst of life, or merely a mind invaded, or worse, yet, *dreamed into existence* by a crazy speck of a pretend-philosopher tumbling through interstellar gulfs. Most such creatures dismissed the notion as too absurd for further consideration. A few sought the counsel of doctors or shamans. One alone founded a religion based on the visions of the Tumbling Philosopher – this was not a success; it caused revolution and ruin on a world of three sapphire-colored suns – while several more went mad and a few committed suicide.

Then Paliphar Vooz and his companion dwelt for a time among the intelligent, but profoundly malevolent fungi on the black planet Yuggoth. Later, the two of them rose skyward, streaming light, to escape the ravenous fire-jungle that covered the entire surface of a dying, blood-red star near to the rim of the universe. They conversed long with vast beings that swam like whales in the darkness beyond the last suns, in the truest, outer abyss, where the thousand-light-year length and immeasurable bulk of these creatures was no more or less a speck than a single mote of dust.

Yet everything might still have been a dream – as he attempted to convince himself that it was – when he came to dwell in a place of the gods, and not just of the familiar, anthropomorphic gods of Earth, either. They were there, to be sure, but so too were the countless gods other worlds, monstrous things in more shapes than his senses could grasp; and though some of them were sentient gases or existed in dimensions beyond the usual three, he moved among them as an equal, for he had become a god of sorts on that war-wracked world of the sapphire suns. With all gods, even the strangest, he held converse, until he concluded, in great sorrow, that their comings and goings, their strife and fornications, were of no greater interest than those of the beasts in the jungle outside Commoriom.

Then, ragged as he was, burnt almost black by the heat of ten million suns, he climbed slowly and painfully the highest, jagged peak on the world of the gods, the axis of All at the very center of all things.

Somewhere, far off, demon-pipers played mindlessly, shrilly, madly, but their sound was like the distant susurrus of waves at ebb-tide, and he did not allow himself to be distracted. He attained the summit, and there found a pavilion of purest crystal, wherein, upon a dais, was placed a single, thick book.

There he dwelt for an aeon – or perhaps only a few seconds, for his sense of time was completely confounded – while he and his beautiful-faced companion, who seemed completely unsullied by their adventures, guided him as he turned the pages of the book. He came to understand that it was that very book in which the names of gods and worlds are written, so that when he turned to a new page, he called a new god or a new world into existence; but when he turned to another page, that former god or world passed away, like day over-taken by night, light and dark, dark and light, life following death and death following life. Sometimes in a waking dream he heard the cries of gods and of the myriad peoples of the worlds as he extinguished them. That they called out to him and worshipped him as he brought them into being was of little import. It was over in an instant. He could have gone on forever, drunk on the wonders he beheld in that book.

At the very end, though, he turned one more page, and came to a portrait of himself. He could only look on it and ask himself, was this the picture of a god, or of a philosopher, a poet, or a fool?

Was there any difference?

He could only sit and stare and ponder and desperately hope that this might somehow be a dream.

Then his beautiful companion reached over with a hand like living, carven, purest marble, and closed the book.

"It's time to go," he said.

~*~

And suddenly Paliphar Vooz awoke with a shout. He sat up, streaming sweat, all the more bewildered to find himself not on the couch among the orgy-hall, but in that humble, private bed with his mistress, who seemed in the dim light to be as she had always been, soft and beautiful as he had known her in his youth, for all that he was now a scraggly, naked old man burnt black by the fires of a million suns.

Or at least that was how he thought he saw himself. His senses were confounded. Perhaps he was still that boy who had come into this bed for the first time with such expectations and the sun-blackened old man was no more than a delirious nightmare. Perhaps nothing had happened at all. Perhaps nothing ever would, and he was trapped, like an insect in timeless amber, in this single moment of illusion.

He sat up on the side of the bed, weeping, trying to recall in his mind something he could not quite grasp, something he had seen in the book perhaps, the one perfect image or idea or phrase which expressed precisely the summation of all his visions, from which the philosopher might derive complete enlightenment.

But like some detail in a fading dream, he could not remember it.

His mistress sat up beside him and put her hand gently on his shoulder.

"What is it?"

"Nothing," he said. "I suppose it is nothing after all."

He got up. He wrapped a cloth about his middle, although in Commoriom there was no particular taboo against going naked.

His mistress kissed him gently on the cheek. "Leave the door un-latched," she said.


Outside, his companion waited for him. They joined hands, and once more the scene changed. They were in a vast cavern, and some-how he knew – for surely he had learned something in the course of living so many lives, of sharing so many dreams – that the bubbling, shapeless protoplasm before him, an oily mass like a living, formless ocean susurrating at ebb-tide, was none other than *Ubbo-Sathla,* the Unbegotten Source of life not merely upon Earth but throughout the entire universe, without mind, without entity, yet, in the end, the only true thing in existence.

This he had read about in the book of creation and un-creation, on the only page which did not go out of existence when he turned it.

He saw that his companion was sinking down, fading into the mass of *Ubbo-Sathla.*

For one last time that beautiful face like living marble, which might have been a boy's, or a maiden's, or a demon's spoke to him, and told him how sometimes a bit of *Ubbo-Sathla* splatters out among the worlds, an inchoate mass that takes on shape and even the illusion of consciousness, and fancies itself man or monster or god.

The beautiful one shrugged his shoulders and smiled wanly and said, "But it's all pretension. They're only fooling themselves." And then he added, "Oh, by the way, you've still got that phial I gave you. Now would be a good time to use it."

Then he was gone and Paliphar Vooz got out the phial in one last frenzy of terror and despair or even, just possibly, absurd hope. If he drank from it, could some incomprehensible magic still cause him to awaken yet again in his mistress's bed and find that nothing at all had happened and no time had passed?

He pulled out the stopper with his teeth and spat it away.

But the phial was empty. He put it in his mouth and sucked desperately, but there was not even air inside. Nothing.

That was when he realized that he could not feel his legs, because he was standing knee-deep in the mass of *Ubbo-Sathla* and he too was no more than a splattering of that oily mass, which had learned to delude itself with pretentions.

After a moment, he knew nothing more.

# Yhoundeh Fades

## By Ann K. Schwader

Her inquisition chambers wait
In vain.  Too silent, now; too clean,
Exquisite blades & pain-machines
Teach no more innocents the fate
Of heresy.  The high priest's gate
Sags webbed in ebon silk, pristine
As dust upon his chalice green
With verdigris & mithridate.

Throughout the fanes of Mu Thulan
A strange & bitter incense burns
Once more to desecrate its sky
With daemon-rites not meant for man,
Unless to herald the return
Of Him who squats in dim N' kai.

# Coils Of The Ouroboros: The History Of Avasquiddoc The Apprentice

## By Cody Goodfellow

ockingly do the fuligin shades recount the tale of Avasquiddoc of Cerngoth, the feckless apprentice who abandoned wisdom in his greedy quest for arcane knowledge; and of his master, the renowned sorcerer Varka Zhom of Commoriom, who held his vaunted wisdom too dearly to spend it to save himself.

Though it was not in his nature to share with others the fruits of his eldritch delvings, and all those previous acolytes under his stewardship had met one or another obscure fate by disobedience or misadventure, yet did Varka Zhom eagerly accept young Avasquiddoc as his ward. His reasons for doing so were hardly altruistic, for Avasquiddoc was himself a learned and erudite adept, having studied for three lustrums under the venerable Squarvash-Yun, the foremost conjuror of Cerngoth, who had only recently perished under a cloud of ill rumor.

Herein did cynics believe lay Varka Zhom's ulterior motive for taking on Avasquiddoc; for so notoriously miserly was Squarvash-Yun with his own secrets, that Varka Zhom himself had never succeeded in prying out the least of them by bargaining or stealth, and hoped to extract from the student what he failed to glean from the master.

The same jaundiced idlers who tarred Varka Zhom thusly also speculated that Avasquiddoc had been totally unsuccessful at mastering Squarvash-Yun's hermetic practices, and had poisoned the ancient Cerngothic necromancer to absorb his close-held knowledge by other means, which even their cynical musings dared not frame, even in darksome whispers.

On the first day of the Year of the Red Serpent did Varka Zhom take into his home the moon-pale Avasquiddoc. He arrived afoot, clad in road-grimed rags and bearing only a curious bag made of the cured carcass of a giant toad. Though the first meeting was cold and almost wordless, it was a giddy occasion for both, as each hoped to learn more from the other than he might be forced to teach.

Avasquiddoc was quartered in a closet in the cellar of Varka Zhom's tower, a singular edifice hewn out of the fossilized shell of some colossal Cambrian mollusk, which loomed out of the Jungles of Zesh, just beyond the edge of the capitol. Though the closet was too short for a man half Avasquiddoc's stature, it was richly appointed with a myriad of creature comforts, which had belonged to one or another of the master's previous apprentices, of whose manifold fates the master was brusquely dismissive.

For his part, Avasquiddoc proved a quick study of his new master's niggling lessons, so much so that he soon became disdainful of the Commorian's arcana. Thereafter, he shirked the toilsome chores his new master heaped upon him, and tumultuous clashes were often heard from within the sorcerer's cloistered retreat.

Frequently did the heated exchanges of venomous words escalate into salvos of wantonly destructive sorcery, the defiant apprentice retorting only with his new master's easily mimicked defenses, which inevitably died in stalemate, and betrayed nothing.

Avasquiddoc bridled under Varka Zhom's taciturn instruction, which beat him down under a torrent of menial labor, yet edified him with only a trickle of gnosis. Not allowed to observe Varka Zhom's nightly conjurations, he was instead consigned to wander the jungle until sunrise, harvesting specimens of night-blooming fungi and carnivorous orchids from an endless list of chores which trailed off behind him most of the way back to the tower, and by which he learned to find his way home.

Varka Zhom distilled the nocturnal blooms into a noisome concoction, which the apprentice supposed was the source of his master's prolonged longevity, though the subtleties of the purification process were performed, naturally, well out of sight.

Returning home from his harvesting chores a little earlier each night, he would skulk up the spiral corridor to Varka Zhom's inner sanctum to discover the means by which the master worked his most potent arts, yet he was ever disappointed to discover the sorcerer waiting for him outside the bolted door, a mordant scowl creasing his beetling brow.

By the end of the first fortnight of the apprenticeship, Varka Zhom had abandoned his awkward attempts to civilly draw out his new apprentice's knowledge of the peculiar arts of Squarvash-Yun, and commanded Avasquiddoc to perform the Voorish Sign or be turned out. Thus commenced a new round of sorcerous sparring, which ended in yet another uneasy stalemate.

Brooding upon this insalubrious state of affairs one moonless night as he hunted down ingredients from the list, Avasquiddoc reflected on how best to extract from Varka Zhom the knowledge he so jealously guarded and move on, for Avasquiddoc was nothing if not ambitious. He had resolved to study under all the greatest sorcerers of Hyperborea, collecting the various schools of conjuration and necromancy, and of one day becoming the wisest, most powerful mortal in the world; then he'd see about working his way up among the ranks of the immortals.

Patiently had Avasquiddoc toiled in the house of Squarvash-Yun, gleaning only crumbs of his grim arts, which the Cerngothic master had himself pried from the antehuman tombs of the Voor, and learnt at the knee of brutish shamans of Thulask and Thuria. When the acolyte had, by his own reckoning, suffered enough, and delivered himself of his unrewarding bondage, the gods remained silent, which Avasquiddoc had taken for approval.

After Squarvash-Yun, Varka Zhom had been the most learned and fat of fame, and Avasquiddoc had appealed to him hard upon his old master's passing, subtly proffering some illumination of the Voorish practices Varka Zhom had so long coveted in return for his apprenticeship.

Varka Zhom's renown sprang from a single feat committed in his youth, well over a century past, which had earned him the eternal gratitude of the kings of Commoriom. While only a year older than Avasquiddoc, Varka Zhom had somehow contrived to destroy—nay, to utterly abolish—no less an enemy than the Citadel of the Ouroboros in the shadow of Mount Voormithadreth, that infamous sanctuary of the last and most skilled wizards of the serpentfolk race which ruled the earth in the ages before humans arose from the primal slime.

Exactly how this impressive feat was accomplished varied in the telling from one city to the next, but all agreed that with one spell, the Citadel and the pestilential ophidian warlocks within, and the whole valley in which they abode, were struck out of the grand design of creation, the volcanic peaks to either side of it closing together as if the dreadful place had never existed. Avasquiddoc, bent to the breaking point by his master's recalcitrance, had come to suspect that only this last bit of the tale was not an outright lie.

Since that storied day when the Citadel vanished—if ever it was, he darkly mused—Varka Zhom had confined himself to less peril-fraught pursuits, practicing divination and necromancy for paying customers from as far as Tscho Volpanomi and barbaric Atlantis. Each night, he collected the demands of his clients and retired to his sanctum, emerging each morning with answers, inventions and new arts inscribed on sheets of mammoth-hide parchment with the ancient ink of a kraken, which he kept locked up in a trunk of adamantine, and retrieved only at the summons of copious djals.

Because Varka Zhom had never turned away a client without vouchsafing some cryptic yet precious morsel of knowledge—plucked, seemingly, from the lipless mouths of the dead, or from outer spheres beyond the Rim—Avasquiddoc dreamed fervently of acquiring not only Varka Zhom's arcana, but of using it to divine all bodies of magic forgotten or yet uninvented by men, and so realize the end of that relentless geas which inscrutable fate had set upon him at his birth. Resolving this day to break the stalemate and seize that which he felt was merely destined for him, Avasquiddoc collected the ingredients for a potent, yet tasteless, soporific brew in his basket.

He returned to the tower not long after moonrise, and was gratified to discover the verdigris-crusted copper door to the master's sanctum locked, and he nowhere in sight. Faint murmuring from within met his ear when he pressed against the door and spied with baited breath. He made out the master's voice sleepily intoning an alien incantation, as if deep in the throes of a trance. It might have been his imagination, but Avasquiddoc believed he heard a susurrant, whispering response to his master's voice.

Avasquiddoc hugged himself for delight at his good fortune and superior cunning. Hastily, he decanted the night-blooms into their respective urns, then brewed the soporific and decanted it into the crystal retort from which Varka Zhom would draft his morning tonic. Satisfied, he retired to his closet and an early breakfast.

Hardly had he crawled into his cramped quarters and commenced making his evening ablutions, when the low bronze closet door slammed shut behind him.

With a clangorous shooting of bolts, he was entombed by a cackling Varka Zhom. "Now, insolent whelp, you will teach me what you have learned from Squarvash-Yun, or die most painfully where you lie."

"Are you so eager to have me for a master, dear Master?" Behind the shield of his prison door, Avasquiddoc freely vented his spleen. "I have victuals within, and potable water. We could be at this for a long time indeed, or have done with it in no time at all. Let me out, and I'll teach thee a lesson, indeed."

Varka Zhom barked a death rattle of acid contempt. "Would you be blasted from the tablets of the Unbegotten, rebellious bastard? Would you be consigned to the gray limbo, whereto I cast the Citadel of the Ouroboros, when your grandsires were yet unborn savages, inimical upstart?"

Avasquiddoc laced his reply with poisoned honey. "Master, such exertions would no doubt tire you. Perhaps first, you should have your morning tonic. Then I would be most eager to see you work one of your legendary higher arcana, even upon my most unworthy self."

Varka Zhom gave no response, but he must have taken his apprentice's advice to heart, for Avasquiddoc heard no sounds for several hours. He passed the time eating and meditating upon the lessons he'd learned from his departed Cerngothic master. Because of the unique manner in which he had learned all that Squarvash-Yun had to teach, his memories were as yet unsettled, like the sediment in a rashly decanted flask of palm-wine. A last remnant remained yet unabsorbed, that tempted him still with uncanny promise of power, but he dared not, for there were risks even foolhardy Avasquiddoc would not brave.

Presently, a better notion possessed him. Flashing the Voorish Sign as a prelude to still more abominably potent gestures, he conjured up a mephitic entity from Outside—a nameless starveling from an empty dimension, all mouth and yawning cavities yearning to fill itself and make a body out of any matter it found in this sphere. Avasquiddoc made a minute blood offering from the back of his hand and smeared it across the bronze door, then performed the incantation he'd learned from Squarvash-Yun, and shut his eyes tightly against what was coming.

Presently, he felt a brisk, icy wind as a tiny door into nothingness opened and disgorged an angry emptiness that emitted a keening whine of absolute hunger. Drawn to the blood offering, it devoured the door and part of the surrounding wall before Avasquiddoc could stammer out the incantation of banishment.

Only when the wailing devourer was gone and the last echo of its extradimensional caterwauling had died away, did he open his eyes. The door lay in savaged shreds on the floor, more thoroughly destroyed than by any acid, and insanely looping cavities had been gnawed out of the walls by the devourer before it vanished. Avasquiddoc shuddered at the awesome implications of turning such a force loose upon his master, whom he discovered asleep in a chair in his library, halfway up the tower. A goblet lay spilled on the floor beside his dangling hand.

Too exhausted at present to conjure up another devourer, Avasquiddoc contented himself with a gnarled dagger carved from the jaw of a labyrinthodont. When he approached the master, however, he learned that the deed must go undone for the moment. A piebald smilodon stalked out of the shadows behind Varka Zhom's slumped form and lounged at the master's feet. The tawny beast chuffled amusedly at Avasquiddoc's puny threat, its lambent amber eyes dancing with preternatural sentience.

Most likely, he could dispatch the tiger with a lesser spell, but this might awaken Varka Zhom. Conversely, killing the master would insure his own swift death on the saber-fangs of the great cat, and he lacked the confidence in his stolen arcana to believe he could destroy them both and emerge unscathed.

Varka Zhom was irretrievably incapacitated, and would remain so for some hours; better to take advantage of the unguarded library now, and use some newfound wizardry to destroy the master at his leisure. Snatching up the key from its place beside the library door, Avasquiddoc bounded up the winding tunnel to the uppermost floor, and the locked door of the master's sanctum.

Avasquiddoc's glee threatened to throttle him where he stood before the door, but he reined himself in and painstakingly unlocked it, disarming defensive contrivances both mechanical and thaumaturgical woven into its intricate bulk, and threw the portal wide.

Inside, a palpable miasma of bitter stench assailed his nostrils and soiled his palate. Smoky shadows swarmed the passageway with such implacable density that Avasquiddoc hesitated, fearful that they were another familiar, more subtly lethal than the tiger. He steeled himself against the risk by reminding himself of the esoteric treasure trove sure to lie within, and, laying one steadying hand against the cold fossil-wall, crept deeper into the sanctum.

Presently, he came into the deep cobalt glow of a weirdly smoldering lamp, which depended by a chain from the low ceiling. By its azure-shrouded light, Avasquiddoc could discern only a bewildering maze of shelves, trestle-tables and alchemical apparatus filling the chamber, between which ran narrow alleys along which one must needs move crabwise. Even so, Avasquiddoc's every least movement provoked some calamitous avalanche.

Set into the far wall and sheathed in moldering, moth-eaten curtains were the doors to the balcony that projected from the apex of the tower. With both hands outstretched, Avasquiddoc fumbled around the perimeter of the cluttered sanctum to grasp the curtains and rip them open with a gasp of relief.

What the light revealed as it stormed the shadowy enclave stole his power to draw another breath for some time to come.

The sanctum was crowded with every conceivable description of conjuror's equipage, stacked or piled haphazardly upon and around the maze of furniture, yet the center of the chamber was cleared to form a circular zone in which one item reared up alone. Only this object was not coated with fine, scholarly dust, and it was the only thing the apprentice did not recognize.

Avasquiddoc made his way to it with greater trepidation than he had in near-total darkness, for this, he intuited with much trembling and palpitations, was surely the repository of his master's innermost arcana.

It stood only a little shorter than the apprentice himself, and was in shape a globe of apparently solid obsidian, inlaid with shimmering bands of platinum and silver, and etched with sinuously tangled glyphs of a wholly alien nature. Its water-smooth surface was broken around its equator by corrugations like the gills of some submarine leviathan, from which leaked wisps of noisome steam.

The globe rested in a cradle of age-blackened bronze, which was in turn bounded by concentric rings of the same odd glyphs painted on the floor. Avasquiddoc recoiled when he saw these last, for at first he mistook them for a carpet of writhing serpents, a last ring of defense round Varka Zhom's ultimate treasure. Even in the mundane light of day, the symbols did indeed seem to move with a preternatural vigor most unbecoming in written characters, as if some invisible scribe were forever erasing and amending them.

The ebon glyphs frenziedly transformed themselves into ever more complex forms as he knelt before them, twisting and mingling and begetting offspring characters, so that the looming obsidian globe was the eye of a cyclonic storm of automatic writing.

How to dispel such an enchantment? Avasquiddoc wracked his ambition-mad brain for answers, but Squarvash-Yun had never encountered anything like this ward, and so in the end he experimented with a pitcher of ordinary water, spilling a cautious amount over the characters beneath his nose, and was gratified to see the whirling vortex of snaky characters lapse into stillness and fade.

Reaching out a palsied hand, he found the surface of the obsidian globe hot to the touch, and vibrating with pulsations like the unquiet gullet of some great sleeping sauropod. Streams of condensation wept from the seams of the metal bands encircling it, and a puff of acrid vapor escaped from the gills.

Avasquiddoc fought to put down his awe at the barely contained vitality of the unknowable artifact. Surely, this was the source of Varka Zhom's knowledge, his power, and now it belonged to him.

But what was it? A scrying glass, perhaps, with which the sorcerer spied upon the tablets of cosmic wisdom which legend claimed lay about the divine idiot protoplasm of Ubbo-Sathla, in the infancy of the universe. Or perhaps it allowed the enlightened user to astrally project to the court of the Outer Gods and hearken unto the cacophonous madness in which the story of all that ever did or ever would occur in the universe was eternally blasted out in a stream of warring, unbearable piping by the larval servitors of the blind idiot gods who ruled all creation.

Consulting the uncannily absorbed memories of Squarvash-Yun, he decided it might be a necromantic prison, wherein Varka Zhom trapped the souls of demons or departed magi, and thereby pried out their secrets. Whatever it was, he had best work to possess its secrets in haste, before his master awakened and undid all his careful machinations.

Then, it seemed quite suddenly to Avasquiddoc, as if the face of the obsidian globe itself did open up like a maw more ravenous than that of the devourer, and swallow him whole.

~*~

For a time without measure, Avasquiddoc fell through darkness and heat and noxious vapors with only his own screams of unhinged terror for company. As his throat grew hoarse and raw with no perceptible terminus in sight and his fear gave way to curiosity, he left off his ululations and strove to explore his most unnatural predicament.

Of light there was none, yet air, though foul in extremis, was abundant enough. Roaring winds tore at his tunic, though he had no feeling in his bowels or inner ear of falling, and when he struggled against the rushing air with his extremities, he touched, then dragged himself down to embrace something that, though hardly of the earth he knew and pined for, was at least solid rock.

The moment he seized it, the rock seized him also, and Avasquiddoc plummeted out of the prison of wind, coming to rest upon a bed of volcanic stone, warped and contorted by the fury of the molten inner earth, and blacker still than the stygian abyss from which he'd lately escaped. After a suitable period of desperate rest, the lost apprentice hauled himself to his feet and began, haltingly, to make his way in the new world that had claimed him.

Whatever manner of place this was, yet his mind and body survived intact, so he might yet learn its secrets, and perhaps win his freedom. His spirits soared as the field of rock declined in a treacherous downward slope. The path to supreme gnosis was ever fraught with peril, or it would be crowded with fellow travelers. All alone in this hell in a bottle, the rash apprentice was certain he journeyed toward a pearl of such great price that Varka-Zhom himself had been too craven to seize it.

The pestilential mists swirled about him on all sides, obscuring all but a few paces in any direction. Avasquiddoc fumbled over the broken hinterland until he found a promontory of rock that rose up from the plunging slope like a looming raptor. Scaling it with much difficulty and no inconsiderable discomfort, he stood out on the edge of the aerie and willed his eyes to penetrate the swirling cauldron of seething mist below.

It was as if he looked down into a vast crater forged by some falling trans-sidereal stone. The walls were chains of jagged peaks and slumbering volcanic fumaroles and kettles of scalding water, all jumbled like the waves of a heaving sea cast in blasted basalt and jagged obsidian spires.

Through the thinner corona of vapor doming the valley, he could just discern the mountain chain upon which he stood arching away to either side, only to meet on the other side, at a distance that could be crossed in a few hours.

But in this place, an hour's measure was itself a matter of guessing, for there was no sun or moon by which to gauge the passage of time. The dim light seemed to be shed by the mist itself, which blotted out all semblance of a sky and bathed the grim demesne in eternal, murky twilight.

Below his perch, the mists thickened about the floor of the valley, rising up the sides like steam from a slowly smoldering concoction in one of Varka Zhom's retorts. About the base of the basalt cliffs, he could see verdant jungle flora among the fractured rocks below, thickening into a dense arboreal zone where the slope softened.

Out of the floor of the valley far below, where the mists were thickest, there arose the ebon fingers of a cluster of cyclopean towers of the same basalt rock that he stood upon, though shaped into forms most unnatural, if not necessarily by the hands of men.

A moment more to contemplate, and Avasquiddoc might have discovered then and there where his reckless quest for gnosis had led him, and might or might not have sought to repent and turn back, but his choice was made for him when a hurtling rock struck him upon the temple, toppling him from his vantage point to the unforgiving slope below.

Head ringing, fighting oblivion, Avasquiddoc took shelter from further volleys of flying rocks, bones and less pleasant missiles. The air was rent by a cacophony of bestial hooting, howling and growling. The apprentice was set upon most savagely by a pack of shaggy troglodytes whom he noted, without a trace of relief, were at least familiar to him.

The despicable Voormis pack encircled Avasquiddoc and redoubled the ferocity of their attacks, though none closed in to subdue him when he made no resistance. Their loathsome visages, a brutish amalgam of the least lovely features of simian and canine, mocked his own otherworldly wisdom, for their animal assault so stirred up his brain that he could call no cantrips to mind to retaliate.

Hapless Avasquiddoc fled the hostile barrage in the only direction left open, descending the precipitous slope in a desperate gait that was more tumble than sprint, and finding a respite beneath the shroud of mist that canopied the emerald maze of the primordial jungle. So deranged and panicked was he by his rude reception that he stumbled blindly through the thickening stands of cycads and towering ferns, thinking only of reaching the towers he'd seen from above.

Wherever this place was, his senses told him he hadn't left the earth, for the tortuous terrain had the unique traits of the Eiglophian Mountains, which he'd glimpsed from afar while traveling to Commoriom from Cerngoth. The degenerate Voormis still thrived in the shadowy warrens that honeycombed the skyscraping peaks of Mount Voormithadreth, despite the best efforts of men to scour the land clean of their repulsive scourge.

Plainly, he was still in Hyperborea, though the vegetation, to his trained herbalist's eye, was of a cruder, more primitive sort, such as flourished in the strange days before men rose up from among the beasts to tame the land, and which lived on only in benighted corners of the continent that the gods, or their unspeakable thanes, claimed as their own. Perhaps this was some forbidden abode of the Other Gods, whom Varka Zhom had taken to spying upon to steal their secrets.

Yet where was the sun, or the moon? No slightest stirring of the air had he felt since he came to rest atop the valley's mountainous border. Could it be that he, and this entire valley, were trapped inside the sphere in Varka Zhom's sanctum? No, far better to imagine that this was all a dream.

Avasquiddoc had just caught a glimpse of the towers through the trees, when he tripped over an enormous root and sprawled in the road. Still sprawled on the ground, he strained to see the base of the citadel through the mists, which were thickest here.

The towers—twelve in number, pyramidal in shape—seemed to rise up out of the bubbling black water that filled the valley floor. A most formidable natural moat, the black lake was fed by the steaming runoff from the geysers and calderas above, and teemed with unseen life. Avasquiddoc quickly dismissed the notion of swimming it, and he could see no sign of a bridge.

Now charged with a task that required cleverness and patience, Avasquiddoc was in his element, and squatted in the middle of the jungle, scratching his head and cogitating so furiously, that he never took note of the root he had so recently tripped over, until it began to move.

When he did take notice of the obstacle, he dismissed it as a prodigiously thick vine or fallen log, and when it displayed unlooked-for ambulatory properties, slithering across the trail at a speed most disquieting for so large a specimen of vegetation, the apprentice was only passing interested, as it fell well out of the parameters of his embryonic schemes to traverse the lake.

He was left with no choice but to take notice when the obstacle reared up above him and revealed itself to be but the merest tapered tip of a monstrous serpent, longer even than the chore-list of Varka Zhom. The mailed head of the giant viper hove into view through the overgrowth—or, one might say, the heads, for a second, smaller, serpentine visage sneered down from above and behind the head of its giant cousin, which it rode as a kind of steed.

Most thunderstruck was Avasquiddoc as he met the malevolent golden eyes of the serpent-rider, seeming to fall into a trance as it became clear what Varka Zhom really did to the Citadel of the Ouroboros to earn his fame, and where he, Avasquiddoc, in his vanity and lust for power, had let himself be led.

As the enormous viper encircled Avasquiddoc, the apprentice did belatedly reclaim his wits and commence to scheme bold new schemes for extricating himself from his present dilemma, but they were none of them beyond the daydreaming stage when the serpent unhinged its jaw, swooped down and swallowed him whole.

~*~

When next the light met his eyes, Avasquiddoc had cause for both celebration and dismay, for while the problem of crossing the lake to the citadel had been resolved for him and he seemed to have gained a reprieve from the abominably prolonged ordeal of ophidian digestion, the circumstances of his arrival made it plain he was less than a welcome guest.

He awoke from his peristaltic slumber as the serpent regurgitated him out onto a floor of triangular flagstones, having been dosed with some explosively potent emetic, which Avasquiddoc had fed him while interred among the other contents of the serpent's commodious stomach.

Before he had half recovered, he was rudely seized by hands which, to his grateful, tear-blurred eyes, were at least good, fleshy human limbs. Though they dragged him to his feet with the rough indifference of a headsman, he took comfort in their presence, for it meant that men could perform service here, and, after a fashion, learn. Varka Zhom must have some such arrangement with the serpentfolk, else why keep them alive, in this hermetic prison?

"It comes before it was sent for," one of the serpent mages hissed in its native Aklo tongue, which Avasquiddoc had learned, along with so much else, from Squarvash-Yun.

"He has demanded much of us of late. Perhaps he favors us with more offerings." The sardonic tone of the serpent's sibilant speech told Avasquiddoc whom they meant.

The devious apprentice swiftly deduced his master's gambit, and under any other circumstances, would have saluted its ruthless beauty. Varka Zhom fed his prisoners human sacrifices in the form of apprentices, in return for the serpentfolk's oracles and arcana. Avasquiddoc's ambition had only hastened his stumbling into this place. But he was not so shaken that he didn't believe he could turn this dire tribulation to his own ends.

By now, he had regained sufficient sight to dimly see the array of serpent mages all about him: savants of the bygone ophidian race, clad in monastic robes made from the hides of their own saurian cousins, imprinted with the sigil of the Ouroboros in cracked, black mammal-blood. The thorny outgrowth of their scales, the palsied twitching of their talons and restive, painted tails, bluntly testified to their epochal decay.

They skulked in a great hall crowded with a metropolis of glass and metal apparatus such as would have stupefied the most puissant human alchemist. Great arcs of blue-white lightning shot from one great vessel to another, vivifying the superheated fluid with the primal energies of captive demons and stranger creatures, whose supernatural properties were harnessed to some incomprehensible experiment.

Only when he had taken all this in did he chance to look upon the human whose harsh yet reassuringly familiar hands had extricated him from the maw of the incontinent serpent.

Hands there were in great profusion, but little else, for the creature was some sort of homunculus. A veritable thicket of twisted human arms, far too many to count, sprouted from a wriggling serpentine body which had no eyes or other features, but only a silently gnashing mouth to feed itself. Human the abominable thing might once have been, but the perverse vipers had made of it a frightful, squirming engine, and a fit demonstration of the only capacity in which humans might serve them.

Flat on the moss-furred flagstones did he prostrate himself before the lords of the citadel, and his eloquent speech in the Aklo tongue stunned them to rapt silence, despite the lamentable shortness and rigidity of his tongue and snout.

"O illuminated first lords of Valusia and of Hyperborea," said he, "I beseech thee, look upon me not as provender, nor as a sacrifice, but as a humble and intrepid scholar of the transmundane arts, even as yourselves, though my mastery is, as my race, in its infancy. I bow to you and pray you accept me as your devoted apprentice, and I will endeavor to teach you, in return, of the arts which I did learn from the greatest human sorcerers, which might edify and distract you, even in this most unworthy prison."

For a long while did they deliberate in silence. Then they hissed in unison and rattled their wattled throat-scales in the closest approximation to laughter of which serpentfolk were capable. "It considers itself our equal," one rasped, and, "It would teach us," sulked another, to fresh susurrations of venomous amusement.

"The greatest human sorcerer is but the greatest thief," a blind serpent-mage wheezed. "Your magic is our science. Even as your rodent ancestors stole our eggs, you steal our knowledge, and cloud it in mysticism to hide your crimes. Odious scavengers, to the last specimen."

Only by sheer will did Avasquiddoc reign in his overflowing vitriol. "O wise and enlightened ones, how then, did you come to repose in a bubble?"

"Your master stole the art of the Demesne from us, as ever your kind has stolen that which it could not beg. You would learn our arts?"

Avasquiddoc trembled, doubting that such an offer could be sincere, yet incapable of imagining that his destiny would have it otherwise. "I would, O terrible and secret masters! I would carry the light of your gnosis into the new world, and in your name, grind my own hated race beneath my heel. I would even kneel before the sublime majesty of your lord and creator, the lord of all that crawls, Yig."

At the uncouth mention of the serpent god's holy name, the magi coiled and reared and spat venom that sizzled upon the stones at his feet. Avasquiddoc feared he had pressed too far, too fast. The handservant groped for the frantically backpedaling apprentice, who tripped again over the prone body of the sickly giant viper.

One of the serpent magi advanced and loomed over the hominid blasphemer's cowering form. By the elaborate runes and glyphs carved into its scales and the dazzling assortment of knives and cleavers hanging from its robes, he recognized it for a haruspex—a diviner of the future by the examination of fresh entrails.

The eager haruspex craned its emaciated neck and unsheathed a blood-rusted cleaver. "You have nothing to teach us by your unforked tongue, yet we could still learn much from you."

Claws traced the serrated fangs of a scalpel under Avasquiddoc's trembling chin, but he held himself as still as death. "I only came here to learn from you, O indomitable ones," Avasquiddoc pleaded.

"It jests with us," one bitterly aloof serpent mage sneered. "It parrots the words of that other warm-blooded worm who was our apprentice, in days not long gone, who made us this prison, by those arts which it stole from us. Does it truly believe that its race rose to its current height so quickly, where we toiled for hundreds of millions of years, because it was wiser than us?"

"O insurmountable masters, I make no such claim. As a lover of knowledge, I know well that all human knowledge flows from the primordial wisdom of your celebrated race, and for that gift, I and all true adepts do love thee."

The regal serpent twisted itself into a seething knot. "Know, then, that we hate thee, for all men are a reminder of our greatest folly. For all that your miserable race has stolen from us, yea even the earth, every loss only rubs salt in the deep wound of our regret, for it was we who sowed the seed that hath grown into such as thee.

"When the world was younger, and Valusia was but a nest, the earth was ruled by others who raised from the slime all that walks or crawls or flies or swims to serve them as slaves, or as meat. Time had passed them by, but the science they left behind taught us to rule somewhat as they did, for a time. But in the passage of millions of years, we grew as degenerate, as decadent as they. We thought to raise up slaves of our own, the better to devote ourselves to the pure pursuit of knowledge. To this end, we did infect the first of your loathsome ancestors with a virus so terrible that only a few of our number ever knew it existed.

"It was a draught of pure thought, and changed your kind from lowly scavenging primates into something truly blasphemous, for nature never intended that your kind would be more than chattering monkeys. It changed you into men."

The haruspex touched Avasquiddoc's brow, and the great laboratory vanished.

He loped across a meadow surrounded by towering cycads. Great lizards wheeled in the amber sky on membranous wings, and a shadowy figure beckoned from the sable shadows of a liana-draped mangrove tree.

In his bestial reverie, he could form no thoughts, only the reflex of instinct and the onrushing panorama of infinite sensation, an ever-present joy in all things, a momentary hesitation at the presence of the strange figure, overcome almost instantly by the swelling hunger in its belly, redoubled at the sight of the ripe fruit in the figure's outstretched talons.

Heedless of Avasquiddoc's trepidation, the proto-human skulked up to the figure and snatched away the fruit from its scaled claw and devoured it on the run.

His blood went cold, but his brain burned with fever. He ran away, but he could not outrun the growing shadow of fear that rose up like smoke from the pyre in his slope-browed skull. The shadows became fearsome shapes in his mind; more terrible still, they became thoughts.

Realizing he was only one fleeting specimen of a race that was itself a short-lived offshoot of ignominious ancestry, the warm-blooded scavengers who picked the bones of the dinosaurs. Knowing, too, that one day he would die, as would his children and theirs, that one day, his entire race would be doomed, and the world would go on…

Avasquiddoc opened his eyes, and tears rolled down his sallow, sunken cheeks. The true nature of the vision was impossible to divine, for while serpentfolk are the authors of all deceit as well as the other sciences, to the apprentice, it had the veracity of a memory, albeit an ancestral one conjured out of his blood.

All the dreams of knowledge and power, all the achievements and disasters, all the wars and arts and religion of humankind, proceeded from that fateful serpent's jape, when a stupid primate came loping out of the jungle for a piece of poisoned fruit.

"Humans grew wise, but would not be tamed. Because you had not won your wits by the rites of selection and mutation, you were cravenly bloody-minded, with a genius for slaughter that beggared even our most prescient warriors. We were helpless before the plague we'd sown in your despicable race, so when you began to use our own arts against us, we were demoralized, and sought only the peace of oblivion.

"Most of our kind perished from sheer apathy, but in places such as this, we carried on the struggle to resurrect that which had perished, to reclaim that which was stolen, and take back that which was rashly given."

"Knowledge saves none," the blind mage admonished, "for the pursuit of knowledge itself destroys, as it will one day destroy your race." Its horny talons brushed the eternally self-devouring sigil of the Ouroboros painted in blood at its breast. Avasquiddoc thrilled for a moment to an echoing vibration of that flickering dream of his animal ancestors, who thought only of survival, and wanted for nothing.

"O Masters," Avasquiddoc pleaded, "I would gladly work toward such an end, for the honor of learning at your side the lost arts of glorious, once-and-future Valusia." In his mind, a bubble of memory surfaced and popped and disclosed some Cerngothic spell which might yet extricate him from this predicament, for it had been vouchsafed him by the Key and the Keeper of the Gate, who recognized no boundary to Its transdimensional peregrinations.

If only he had time to perform the ritual gestures to define the gate, if only he had learned Squarvash-Yun's spells properly, instead of by the awful method he'd learned from ghoul-parchments unearthed from the necropolis of Ultima Thule. "I would undo all the ghastly injustices which my kind has perpetrated upon yours, and reset the cosmic balance in your favor."

The serpent magi took this into consideration for several minutes, then finally, the haruspex spoke. "I think, pitiful rodent, that we could make you one of us…"

Even as Avasquiddoc made the White Sign and delineated a door, a serpent mage in a hooded cloak stepped forth and flung a blinding black powder into his face. He inhaled to scream, and then vanished.

~*~

When the constabulary of Commoriom finally felt emboldened by the prolonged silence within Varka Zhom's shell-tower to investigate, they found much to drive all but the boldest out into the woods to collect kindling to burn the place down.

The heartiest of the watchmen discovered the master seated beside the gaping door to his inner sanctum in a posture of catatonic rigor, his baleful gaze fixed upon a point somewhere beyond infinity. Though he breathed yet, and his heart beat, he was left for dead where he sat, with a blackened bowl upon his lap that proved to be the putrefied, oddly elongated skull of a Cerngothic sorcerer. The crown of the skull had been expertly sawed off, then reattached by iron clamps, the eyesockets and nasal cavity stuffed up with corpse-tallow. The interior of the skull had been scraped to an immaculate polish, and in Varka Zhom's petrified hand, there rested a spoon.

They could not know that the apprentice Avasquiddoc had used ghoulish sorcery to absorb the mind and memories of his erstwhile master as he devoured the contents of his skull. In this wise had he learned almost all that the miserly Squarvash-Yun knew, though he had not yet emptied the skull of its grisly victuals when he was swallowed up by the Ouroboros Demesne.

Upon awakening to find Avasquiddoc gone and the circle disturbed, Varka Zhom had leapt at the chance to search his closet. The head he recognized as an artifact of ghoul magic, and he proceeded to bolt down what remained of the overripe memories of Squarvash-Yun. Only a few morsels had remained, but Varka Zhom greedily ate them, and marveled at the upwelling of knowledge that whelmed his senses.

New languages, lore and spells sprang whole into his brain, recreating as his own memory the last crumbs of Squarvash-Yun's centuried life. At the climax of it, however, he discovered too late why Avasquiddoc hadn't finished his ritual meal; for Squarvash-Yun's last thoughts stole into Varka Zhom's brain and became his own.

I am murdered… by Avasquiddoc, he thought another man's final thoughts. I am… dead. Not having any familiarity with ghoul sorcery, the beleaguered constables were unable to disabuse him of his fateful mistake, and couldn't be bothered to try.

Upstairs, they found a prodigy of a serpent writhing among the debris of Varka Zhom's ransacked sanctum. The serpent's frantic perambulations made it most difficult for them to catch, particularly when the constables who seized it realized that it was not a proper snake at all, and that it spoke—or rather, babbled.

The wriggling captive bore a disquieting likeness to the vanished apprentice, though from the neck down, it possessed the scaled black body of a water-viper.

It cried out incessantly amid its thrashings, though its diminished lungs scarcely gave it the voice to make itself heard, let alone to tell all the dreadful secrets it had learned, or to voice a warning.

Whatever they heard, the older and wiser of the two constables saw fit to silence it with the most readily available restraint. He took the creature's tail and stuffed it into its mouth until it choked to death.

# Daughter of the Elk Goddess

## By John R. Fultz

In the valleys of southern Mhu Thulan the poppies bloomed wild and crimson. Above the hollows glided silvery fogs, bloated apparitions carrying the breath of winter. White mists haunted the sapphire lakes, whispering a promise of icy doom.

An advancing glacier had devoured the northern precincts of the Hyperborean continent, swallowing its cities one by one for centuries. Grinding walls of ice and freezing vapors had moved southward from frozen Polarion, entombing the jeweled ziggurats of Cerngoth, the marble wharves of Leqquan, and the onyx temples of Oggon-Zhai. Of all the cities north of the Eiglophian Mountains only Iqqua remained beyond the reach of the inexorable glacier. Surrounded by fertile vales alive with icy freshets and glassy meres, humble Iqqua remained a prosperous center of trade and culture, even as its winters grew colder each year, and the ice crawled inevitably toward its walls of polished basalt.

Outside the ramparts of Iqqua the scattered settlements of tribal chiefs watched over the wild lands in the name of Illubrius Vaal, the ninety-eighth king of the last northern city. Vaal was both the King of Iqqua and the High Chieftain of the Iqquan tribes. Each tribal chieftain brought to Vaal a yearly tribute, most often the pale hides of giant land-sloths hunted on the fields atop the glacier, the tawny furs of saber-toothed tigers, or the ivory tusks of the wooly mammoths that were the favored game of Iqquan hunters. The tribes who traded pelts, produce, and game in the city were generally poor folk with little else to bestow upon their king, and certainly nothing in the way of jewels, gold, or other precious materials. Yet King Vaal, already possessed of a legendary hoard, gladly accepted such earthly tributes.

On a bright spring day when the prophecy of eternal winter seemed far from the walls of Iqqua (though it was ever close at hand), a procession of soldiery from the black-walled city emerged from its iron gates. The caravan travelled due west toward a certain village known for the valor of its hunters and the loyalty of its chieftain. Among the forty tall warriors in copper chain mail and horned helmets came a band of twelve well-muscled slaves bearing two fanciful litters on their shoulders.

Six slaves carried each of these palanquins, and the foremost of the two flew the crimson flag of Uzuldaroum from its tiny turret. The second litter was like a miniscule house of white and purple silks, which sat lightly upon the shoulders of its bearers—as if it rode empty, or at least contained a personage of no great bulk. The simple, white-and-green flag of Iqqua rose from its peaked roof. At the head of the soldiers stalked their captain, a scarlet cloak billowing from the shoulders of his black iron breastplate. A great scimitar lay across his back, and his iron helm bore a lizardine crest with a pair of sparkling rubies to mark his rank.

In the nearby village of Uhng the tribal folk were mending ropes, smoking hocks of bear-meat, and crafting arrows for an impending hunt. The tribe's most respected hunter dwelled in a modest hut set apart from the rest. His name was Atanequ, and today he spent the morning carving the second of two great mammoth tusks won during his last expedition. The first tusk he had carved into the likeness of his dead wife, Shwangi. This idol he had placed inside his empty hut as a tribute and reminder of his lost love.

The couple had been childless when the White Plague blew into the village on the night wind. The shaman of the tribe had worked his magic over Shwangi, sacrificed goats and a strong-legged ox to battle the spell of the plague, but in the end it was of no account. The frost gathered on Shwangi's limbs, even as she sat shivering before Atanequ's hearth-fire. Her breath had become cold blasts of crystalline frost. The chieftain could do nothing as he watched the sparkling rime spread across the limbs and body of his beloved one, just as the great glacier (which his tribe called Atuhlo the Ice Demon) was slowly spreading itself across Mhu Thulan. Eventually the white frost filled Shwangi's open eyes, and she died a frozen effigy of her living self, along with six others who had caught the White Plague.

The villagers had burned all seven victims in a communal pyre fourteen days ago. Atanequ could still smell the ashes of his wife on

66

the wind. It was a reek that would linger forevermore in his wide nostrils. When he slept at night he saw Shwangi's dark, slim eyes looking at him free of frost, and he held her warm and living in his arms once again. Yet always he woke to the smell of her ashes on the wind, and even in the hides and walls of his domicile.

Now that Atanequ had carved Shwangi's likeness in opalescent ivory and placed it at the center of his small house, it gave him some measure of comfort. But still he missed the girl who had stolen his heart and died before she could birth even a single child. Any woman of the tribe would be glad to take Atanequ as her husband, but the chieftain had chosen none of them yet. The wound in his heart was still too raw. So he carved ivory and kept his thoughts to himself.

The green-yellow hills cast long shadows across the village in the light of a golden afternoon. Somewhere beyond those hills the Ice Demon glacier stood blue and defiant in the naked sunlight. Atanequ was finishing the detail work on his latest creation when the procession from Iqqua topped a nearby ridge. The children of the huts ran and bellowed for their mothers. The chieftain had crafted a great war-club from the second mammoth tusk. He had also inscribed a litany of runes and sigils about the head of the ivory mace. For any other man such a heavy weapon would be useless, but the stature and strength of Atanequ was legendary among the Iqquan tribes. In his hands the tusk would be a bone-breaker, a stone-smasher, a thundering death-bolt for any man or beast that opposed him.

When the procession from Iqqua entered the village, men spoke with the lizard-helmed captain, then directed him toward the hut of Atanequ. As the chieftain sat carving the last sigils into his ivory mace the captain approached with his helm in the crook of an arm. The captain's hair was as black as the folk of the village, his skin the same dusky shade, yet his oiled beard and the golden rings on his fingers spoke of city customs and wealth. He introduced himself as the Lord Oolzar Dalimgru, Captain of Iqqua's 13th Legion. The captain already knew Atanequ—his fame as a hunter of beasts and climber of mountains was the talk of every tavern in Iqqua—and his name was a benediction on the lips of every villager who visited the city.

"It is said that Atanequ the Great Hunter once crossed the Eiglophian range in winter by virtue of a hidden pass," said Captain Oolzar, "and that he has faced the cannibal Voormis who stalk the highlands. Men say that he alone has slain a hundred Voormis and hunted them in the depths of their haunted catacombs. Are you the same Atanequ who performed these deeds?"

Atanequ continued his ivory carving and nodded his shaggy head.

"In the name of King Vaal I seek your aid," said the captain. He waved a hand toward the two curtained litters and the soldiers awaiting him at the village edge. "A high priest of the elk-goddess Yhoundeh, blessed be her name, came to Iqqua by ship twenty days past. A vision has led him to discover in our humble city the holy Daughter of Yhoundeh, a maiden of unsurpassed beauty and purity. This priest, who stands close in the confidence of the King of Uzuldaroum, claims to have found this holy virgin in the personage of Quarha, daughter of his majesty Vaal. In order to seal the fragile peace between our cities, the king has agreed to give his only daughter to Yhoundeh as requested. She must be taken to the Great Temple in Uzuldaroum, there to honor the goddess that is her new mother, and she must arrive before the Festival of Springtime. Yet the sea has grown wild and dangerous as the Season of Storms falls upon us. Therefore we have no choice but to escort the high priest and the Daughter of Yhoundeh across the Eiglophian Mountains and the southern wilderness to gain the capitol in time. In order to do this, we require a guide. King Vaal has instructed me to call upon your honor, Atanequ. I ask you to guide us across the black mountains. For this deed your tribe will be rewarded with fame, wealth, and precious stones. The king has also instructed me to take your head if you should refuse. What is your answer, Great Hunter?"

Atanequ sat his curved mace on its head and stood up to face the Captain of Iqqua. The hunter's head and shoulders towered above the armored Oolzar, but there was no trace of fear in the captain's eyes. His scimitar would meet the hunter's mace if it must, and one of the two men would lie dead in moments, if the chieftain refused the king's command.

Atanequ's dark eyes scanned the purple horizon. He sniffed the winds that blew from the region of the deadly mountains. Oolzar awaited his answer with steady breaths and a cool hand.

After a moment Atanequ picked up his ivory mace and slung it across his shoulder.

"The snows fall early in the high pass," he said. His voice was deep as an icy canyon, frosted with the bitterness of his recent loss. "The sooner we depart, the better our chances."

With that simple agreement the pact was made. Atanequ set off in the company of the Iqquan soldiers and their two litter-borne passengers, one a high priest of Uzuldaroum, the other a daughter of both a goddess and a king. Atanequ held no belief in the gods of the cities. His people worshipped nameless gods that were forces of nature: fire, wind, rain, and frost. The spirit-animals of the wild tundra and deep forests were also their deities. Yet he understood the worship of Yhoundeh the Elk Goddess and the importance of honoring the religion of Uzuldaroum, even in a land as far removed from the capitol as humble Iqqua. Whatever men believed, they made real by their beliefs. So if the kings of the two cities believed that the journey of this princess to some southern temple would unite their lands in a lasting peace, then such belief was true enough.

The procession travelled south across hill and valley, fording shallow rivers and scattering herds of yellow bison in their wake. For several days Atanequ led them toward the highlands where the great, dark peaks of the Eiglophian commanded the sky with ice-clad crowns. He saw little of the two who rode in the litters, but he caught glimpses of the priest and the princess at night when the caravan gathered around a raging fire to keep warm. The priest was an old man in gaudy robes alive with dangling gemstones and hoops of platinum. His bald head was topped by an elaborate headdress that seemed too complex and heavy for his skinny neck to bear. Yet he wore it proudly as he squinted into the dancing flames and chewed on the dried blubber that was a northern soldiers' traveling fare.

The first two times Atanequ saw the princess she was little more than a slight figure wrapped in snow-white robes and a cloak made from the hide of a snow tiger. Yet the third time he saw her was by an accident of fate. He stumbled across her path between the crude tents that formed the nightly encampment. He had slept alone each night, removed from the laughter and ribald humor of the marchers, as well as the stern gaze of Oolzar. Yet tonight the full moon had pulled him from sleep and sent him walking beneath the stars. He smelled rain on the wind, and was glad to be far from the smell of his dead wife's ashes for the first time.

He stopped suddenly as he recognized the cloaked princess standing nearby, her gaze on the sparkling carpet of stars above the black immensity of the mountain range. The moonlight fell upon her face, and he saw then that the daughter of King Vaal, the daughter of the southern goddess, might have been any woman of his own tribe. Her hair was black and without curls, her cheekbones were sharp, and her eyes slim and dark as midnight. Her skin was the same lovely brown shade of all Iqquan girls. The same russet hue as poor, lost Shwangi.

Atanequ stood silent before the girl, a great black cave-bear looming above a small white lynx. The wind caught her unbraided hair and tossed it about her shoulders, and her head turned to regard Atanequ. In the instant that her eyes met his own, Atanequ knew that he loved her. This was not a conscious thought in his head, for his people had no conception of infatuation or lust. These things were of one substance, a single state of mind that transcended body and soul, and that state was what other men call "love," but which the tribe of Atanequ called *i'imbru*. It was simply the condition of being attached to someone other than one's self, both physically and spiritually. One did not seek such a condition; it fell upon men and women like a sudden rain.

Atanequ was caught in the glow of *i'imbru* as a stray leaf is caught by a blast of flame (or frost). It was the same spell that had fallen on him when he first saw Shwangi, the magic that gave him no choice but to proclaim her his wife. Yet now the *i'imbru* was a completely different sensation as well, for this was not a tribal woman who stood before him. This was Quarha, Daughter of Yhoundeh the Elk Goddess, Daughter of King Vaal, the virtuous Princess of Iqqua.

Yet, too, she was only a simple girl.

A thin, tall figure emerged from the shadows. The aged priest with his ridiculous headdress. His keen eyes roamed over the giant frame of Atanequ, then turned to Quarha with suspicion. "Come, Princess," he said. "Return to your litter and take your rest while you can. The hour is late and you'll catch a night vapor."

Atanequ paced about the camp like a dazed hound until sunrise.

Two more days of hill travel brought the procession to the mouth of the upward winding pass. The glossy black slopes of twin mountains rose on either side, sheer facades slick as onyx and bright with sunlight. Small plateaus of scrub and stunted trees dotted the heights, but the highlands were mostly barren. Tiny black lizards crawled between the rocks. Chill winds fell from the upper peaks where the snows never melted and the ice dripped eternally, sending rivulets of freshwater down into ravines and jagged chimneys of rock.

Here the litters were abandoned, for the way must be climbed more than walked. Priest and princess joined the marching slaves and soldiers, although the slaves took turns carrying Princess Quarha on their brutish shoulders, her slim legs wrapped about their sturdy necks. Atanequ longed to carry her thusly, but he knew better than to ask it. He was an unwashed tribesman, unworthy of even speaking to the princess, let alone touching her. So he climbed the snowy stair of the pass ahead of the procession and showed them the way with painstaking grace.

The following day the caravan crossed the middle length of the pass where the snows were knee-deep between steep drifts. After midday dark clouds surrounded the peaks and cast the marchers into gloom. The fierce wind blew curtains of snow into their faces. Night rose up early from the dark gorges, and the stars were lost behind a blanket of stormclouds.

The caravan paused in the pregnant gloom. Atanequ grew wary, for this was the prime hunting weather of the savage Voormis. Soon a cacophony of inhuman howls filled the pass. There was no mistaking these bloodcurdling shrieks as the wails of honest wolves. The Voormis had crept down from their cave aeries and found the caravan.

Twenty soldiers unsheathed scimitars while the other twenty knocked arrows in their longbows. The warriors formed a ring about the princess, the slaves, and the shivering priest.

"They will come soon!" Atanequ shouted through the wind. "They are all about us."

The first of the shaggy beasts rose from a drift of snow, waving clawed arms and gnashing its teeth like a jungle ape giving challenge.

*This pass is ours*, said the guttural howling. *As are your flesh and bones.*

Atanequ sent a feathered shaft flying from his great bow. It took the creature in its breast and sent it toppling into the drifts. As if waiting for this signal the barking and roaring Voormis rose up on every side and rushed the ring of soldiers. They loped on all fours like pale, grotesque hounds the size of men. The archers let their arrows fly, and Atanequ felled three more beast-men before the creatures pounced on the outward line of defenders. They tore open the throats of men, sending gouts of crimson across the snow.

Atanequ cast his bow aside and took up his great ivory mace. He waded into the thick of the Voormis, crushing skulls and breast-bones, sweeping the creatures from his path. They squealed like speared boars as the heavy tusk pulped their brains and splintered their spines. At the center of the defending circle, the princess stood arm-in-arm with the frightened priest. She did not scream as many other women would have done.

Atanequ fought like a devil. He felled Voormi after Voormi, ignoring the rents their grasping claws made in his flesh. They tore through the boiled hides that encased his skin, but they never lived long enough to sink their claws deep. More of the shaggy ones descended on the pass, and the slaves gathered about the princess waving spears given them by the soldiers. They would be Quarha's last defense if the warriors failed to repel the beast-men.

The men of Iqqua died swiftly, the claws of the Voormis too quick for their blades, too strong against their shields. Captain Oolzar managed to slay a heap of the hairy cannibals, yet none of his troops were his equal at combat. Brave men perished in red agony as their leader fought on.

As Atanequ smashed the skull of a raging Voormi into red mist, he heard the princess screaming at last. This distraction turned his head long enough for a bloated Voormi to slam itself into him. Its claws dug deep into his arms as it tumbled with him across the snows. It breathed a hellish stink into his face as the earth fell away beneath them.

Locked in a death-grip with the snarling creature, Atanequ toppled over the edge of a deep fissure. How far the fall must be he could not know, yet he strove to strangle the life from the stinking Voormi even while they twisted and fell. The white earth rushed upward to greet him. The wind rushed from his lungs as darkness stole away his senses.

~*~

He woke gasping in the darkness of true night, smothered by snow. His flailing arms discovered the dead body of the Voormi next to him, its bull neck broken. Atanequ dug himself from the deep snow that had swallowed him. He realized dimly that the snow drift had saved his life, for the fall had been great. His bones ached and his flesh was bruised, but he was whole. The stormclouds had parted and moonlight found its way into the wide crevice. Ice-slick walls of rock rose about him.

Taking from his belt a pair of long iron knives, he used them as spikes to climb the icy wall. After hours of painful work he topped the lip of the fissure and saw the bloodstained snows and the mutilated remains that filled the pass. All of the soldiers and their captain were dead, and the valiant slaves as well. Many were missing arms and legs, grisly trophies taken by the Voormis to be eaten raw in their cavernous lairs. The bellies of men were gnawed open, the bones of rib cages glinting obscenely in the moonlight. The Voormis had feasted before departing. Many of their own shaggy corpses lay among the dead, yet not nearly enough.

A man who had never before witnessed the slaughter-work of the Voormis would have sickened at the sight of the massacre, but Atanequ steeled himself to the carnage and searched for the body of the princess. He found no trace of her but a white cloak spotted with blood. Though he could not tell if it were her own blood or that of her defenders. A slight groaning drew his attention, and he found the priest lying beneath the gnawed body of a slave. The old man had lost his headdress, and his fine robes were torn and soiled. Claws had raked his face and chest. His wounds were deep and bloody, but he had refused to die.

"Great Hunter," called the priest. "Help me…"

Atanequ rolled the carcass away and helped him to stand. The priest fondled an elk-shaped amulet about his neck and mumbled a prayer to Yhoundeh. Fresh blood spilled from his wounds across his spoiled vestments.

"She is gone," said the priest. "They have taken her." Atanequ wrapped crude bandages about the man's cheek and chest. The old one was made of sterner stuff than he had guessed. Perhaps the codger had once been a warrior before turning to religious duty. The muscles of his wiry arms were lean and hard. He took up a broken spear and leaned on it as staff. His eyes met those of Atanequ, and there were indefinable emotions brimming there. "They have taken the Daughter of Yhoundeh."

"Alive?" asked the hunter. "Are you certain?"

The priest nodded.

Atanequ's eyes scanned the battleground again for any sign of Quarha's corpse, which he desperately did not want to see. Yet if the beasts had taken her alive, it could only be for one purpose. The Voormis had a single nefarious reason for abducting human women.

They did not breed with them, being more likely to devour them. Abducting a woman both whole and unharmed meant nothing less than a sacrifice for their subterranean god. They would give her to the Toad God of Black N'Kai, who slumbered in the deep world beneath the mountains, waking once every generation to devour living tributes.

The *i'imbru* blazed like a hot fire in the heart of Atanequ.

"I must find her," he told the priest. "Before they give her to Tsathoggua."

In ancient times all of Hyperborea worshipped the heinous Toad God. Humanity had turned away from Tsathoggua only when the Ice Demon sent his glacier to devour the continent. According to beliefs spread by the priests of Uzuldaroum and adopted by Iqqua, only the power of Yhoundeh prevented the world from falling to the Ice Demon's spell. Yet one day, when men at last had lost their faith in the Elk Goddess, the ice would find its way further south. Iqqua would be the first city to fall beneath the Ice Demon, followed by Uzuldaroum, and the last remnants of humankind.

Atanequ followed the tracks and spoor of the Voormis across the pass and up the frozen slopes. The priest refused to stay behind. Ignoring the pain of his terrible wounds, he climbed behind Atanequ. The hunter thought the old man might be insane, but perhaps they both were mad. Perhaps the priest, too, felt the pull of *i'imbru* connecting him to Quarha.

The trail was easy to follow since the Voormis were filthy and unconcerned with stealth. Fresh-gnawed bones and foul-smelling offal marked their path. As a grey sun rose to replace the dying moon, the searchers found the mouth of a cave warren where the fecal stench of the Voormis was palpable. Atanequ unstrapped the ivory mace from his back and gave the priest one of his long knives. They plunged into the cavern without a word between them.

How long they searched through the labyrinth of descending and twisting tunnels Atanequ could not say. It could have been hours or days. They fought roaming packs of Voormis, which the hunter beat to pulp with his mace. They skirted sunken chambers where chittering female Voormis gathered to birth and feed their hairy offspring. Bits of tangled fabric from the princess' robe led them closer to where she must be taken for sacrifice. Somewhere in the heart of the hollow mountain was a temple dedicated to the Toad God, and to that temple the hunter's path must go.

Twice the two explorers faced massive onrushes of Voormis that threatened to overwhelm them by sheer numbers. Yet the bleeding priest fought like a madman with knife and broken spear, while the swift mace of Atanequ splattered brains and bones across the tunnel walls. Eventually the Voormis learned to flee Atanequ's blood-soaked visage and the red shadow at his back muttering prayers to an unknown deity.

At last the searchers came upon a broad cavern of massive stalagmites where the great stone idol of Tsathoggua squatted above a bowl-shaped altar filled with black pitch. Volcanic flames leaped from black fissures to light the cavern-temple. The hollow chanting of the Voormis had drawn them to this place, and the shaggy cannibals danced about the temple, caught in the throes of their strange and ineffable rites.

A black, oily substance dripped from the fanged maw of the toad-idol directly into the altar bowl, as if the Toad God were drooling a dark spittle in anticipation of his offering. On a crude block of stone before the idol and its drool-cup altar lay the unconscious body of Quarha, stripped of her royal garments and pale from the frigid air of the caverns. The marks of misuse lay upon her body in the form of bruises and scratches, but she seemed alive. Atanequ surmised her calm state to be the result of a drugged slumber. No doubt the Voormis would awaken her at the climax of the ceremony, so their god could enjoy his prey alive and wriggling.

The hunter fell upon the dancing Voormis like a whirlwind, spinning ivory death. Clouds of blood-mist erupted in his wake, and the priest scrambled behind him slicing the throats of entranced Voormis with dagger and spear. The shaggy ones were so engrossed in their ceremony that they did not resist Atanequ's advance toward the altar.

A dozen pulped Voormis marked the hunter's wake as he stood before the slab of granite where the princess lay helpless. Atanequ took up her slight body and placed it across his left shoulder, wielding his tusk-mace now with one arm. Yet no Voormis raced forward to challenge him. The beast-men writhed on the floor like a clutch of serpents, foaming at the mouth and spewing guttural invectives. Their chanting had become a chorus of groaning, grunting obscenities.

As the hunter turned from the altar stone with his precious burden, the black substance in the bowl leapt upward like a pillar of smoke. It swirled and extended oily tendrils, while two coal-bright eyes kindled at the tip of its serpentine head. It towered over the altar bowl like a great, black python of darkness, and the old priest regarded it with utter horror.

"Do not look upon it!" the priest told Atanequ. "The Spawn of the Toad has crawled out of its belly. Take the Daughter of Yhoundeh from this place, Great Hunter. Take her to Uzuldaroum. She must arrive in time for the Festival of Springtime. Go now!"

The black presence writhed and bubbled as Atanequ raced toward the cavern's exit with Quarha on his shoulder. The priest remained behind, placing himself between the horror and the hunter. He sang an ancient song, his fingers painting a pattern of sorcery in the smoky air.

When Atanequ reached the threshold of the exit tunnel, he turned back to see a glowing, five-pointed star with a blazing eye at its center. The serpentine entity seemed transfixed by the priest's glowing sigil, its tentacles waving wildly about the old man yet unable to touch him. The monstrosity grasped at the senseless Voormis instead, crushing them to death in its viscous coils.

Whatever ancient spell the priest had used to fend off the Spawn of Tsathoggua, it did not affect the rousing Voormis in the same manner. The shaggy ones staggered to their feet and rushed toward the priest, tearing at him with claw and fang, rending his flesh as the glowing symbol flickered. Atanequ heard the old man's death cries ringing through the tunnels as he ran toward the distant surface with Quarha in his arms.

~*~

One month later the Great Temple of Yhoundeh welcomed its newest holy daughter with cascades of white flowers and bands of singing maidens. Before the antlered statue of the great Elk Goddess herself, Atanequ was praised for guiding the princess through the icy mountains and the wild jungles beyond. When the highest of the high priests heard the tale of the hunter's exploits and the daring rescue of Quarha from the subhuman worshippers of Tsathoggua, he assigned a place of honor to Atanequ during the opening rites of the festival.

Atanequ and Quarha had grown very close during their month of travel through the jungles south of the Eiglophian range. The *i'imbru* that possessed Atanequ became known to the princess. Yet she had refused to give Atanequ the gift of her love, for her body and her virtue were both promised to the Great Temple of Yhoundeh. Atanequ had come to understand this, although his *i'imbru* was in no way lessened by her adherence to religious propriety. Perhaps he would linger in Uzuldaroum awhile, and the princess' heart would eventually soften toward him. It was the hunter's first time in the great city, and the splendor of its silver towers, lush gardens, and broad arenas fascinated him.

On the morning when the Festival of Springtime began, Atanequ stood among the honored guests of the temple and watched Quarha walk toward the eight-sided altar at the foot of the giant Elk Goddess, who was sculpted of purest white marble. The Daughter of Yhoundeh stood proudly upon the raised octagon, in sight of a thousand priests, acolytes, nobles, and even the King and Queen of Uzuldaroum. Quarha basked in the glow of their admiration as she raised the long, curved dagger in her fists and directed its point toward her beating heart.

The day grew silent but for the warbling of temple birds in the trees, and Quarha sang the holy words she had been taught by the highest of high priests. Atanequ looked about him with some consternation. He had never witness this rite and did not know what to expect, but he did not like the position of the dagger in Quarha's gentle hands. All the observers about him were calm, yet he seethed privately inside the silk raiment the temple had afforded him.

When Quarha's song was finished, she drove the blade deep into her heart with a single practiced thrust. She made not a sound, yet it was Atanequ who cried out as if his own flesh had been pierced. Quarha's lifeless body tumbled across the altar-stone, spilling crimson as the citizens of Uzuldaroum applauded her noble and selfless sacrifice.

Now the bounty of spring was assured, and the threat of eternal winter staved off for another year by the grace of the Elk Goddess, and the blood sacrifice of her holy daughter.

Atanequ shouted his lone protest and ran across the temple yard toward the altar. Priests and noblemen fled from his path as he leaped into the waters of the sacred wading pool and splashed his way toward the body of Quarha. At last he knew what it meant to be chosen as the Daughter of Yhoundeh, but he could never love that harsh goddess.

"*The Ice Demon take you all!*" he wailed as he wept.

Before his strong arms could sweep the dead girl into his embrace, a volley of arrows from the temple guards caught him in the chest. Seven blessed shafts pierced the Great Hunter's body and sent him reeling across the eight-sided stone, where he lay next to Yhoundeh's brave daughter.

# The Darkness Below

## By Brian M. Sammons

Borsk's sod-walled, thatched-roofed tavern sat next to an eastward jutting spur of the road between the once mighty capital of Commoriom and the new seat of power, Uzuldaroum. The sagging structure had been raised by his father's father when orichalcum merchants still regularly came to the mines in the foothills of the Eiglophian Mountains. There slaves had once dared the darkness that slept beneath the nearby ebon peaks to wrench riches from the earth for their avaricious masters. The orichalcum mongers would then haul their golden-coppery plunder by the wagonload back to Uzuldaroum, and in their comings and goings they would stop at the earthen tavern for food, a dry bed, some mead, and willing women.

Then, one night decades past, the long-slumbering dark beneath the mountains awoke. Perhaps it was the greedy miners scratching in the earth that roused it. Perhaps it was just its time to awaken and remind men why they feared the dark. Whatever the cause, the darkness flooded into the mines, engulfing them completely. Before the next cock's crow the Three Pits, as the trio of ancient mines were commonly known, were abandoned amidst screams, blood, and prayers for protection from the consuming darkness. Over one hundred and fifty slaves never left the Pits that night, not to mention a number of proper men from wealthy families.

The priests of Yhoundeh were summoned and arrived three days later. They blessed the mines, burnt incense, read incantations from an ancient scroll, and made blood sacrifices. Their servants collapsed the entrances to the Three Pits and the priests declared that the foothills were now sacred to the elk-goddess. Any trespass upon them was punishable by death. Faced with two ways to die, either by Yhoundeh's ever-vigilant inquisitors or the horrors that lurked below, the miners never returned to the Pits.

When the mines died, so too did the most of the trade on the eastern road, which turned the once busy tavern Borsk would inherit into a leaking, slouching hovel of mud and straw that no one bothered to visit. The beds moldered unoccupied, the mead became increasingly watered down, and the coin-hungry night ladies left for more prosperous places to spread their legs.

So when, many years later, eight rough men came to Borsk's door, demanding to be served food and drink, the tavern keeper did his best to accommodate them within his meager means. He did so not only out of greed for the pazoors in their purses, but out of fear of the sharpend bronze that hung from their belts. Each man wore the boiled mastodon-hide armor of Uzuldaroum's slave infantry and carried well-worn weapons. They had the look of seasoned reavers to them, and surely not a band to be trifled with. Still, despite his fear, Borsk could not help listening in on the drunken ramblings that grew in volume as they drained the tavern's last mead barrel.

"You sure all that orichalcum is just lying there; ready to be harvested like ripe fruit? We don't have the skill or the time to cut it from the stone. If the followers of the she-elk discover us…" The smallest of the slave soldiers let his question hang in the air until a one-eyed, scar-faced brute put down his cup to answer.

"I told you, my father's father was in the Pits when the slithering shadows rose up out of the deeper dark. He and his fellows escaped with their lives, but left everything behind to do so. That includes the orichalcum they had mined for the night. It was still in the carts, waiting to be hauled up when they ran away. It is still down there now. No one ever went back after the elk priests condemned the place."

"And what of Yhoundeh's inquisitors?" Another of the eight said.

"Have you seen any yet? Just as the darkness has no doubt returned to slumber over the many years, so too have the followers of the she-elk become soft in their duties. After generations of finding no one treading their cursed hills, they now stay in their keep, only venturing out for supplies."

"You had better be right about both the inquisitors and the sleeping dark," A mountain of a man from the ice-bound wastes of northern Polarion said. "Should we encounter either, I will make sure you pay for convincing us to risk our necks thrice over for orichalcum dreams that are naught but smoke." He had the coldest eyes and largest axe out of the warriors and spoke to them with authority. So absolute was his command, that none spoke further of their plans, and soon the runaway slaves were singing drinking songs, cursing, laughing, and at last snoring as drink claimed them.

In the morning the rough men left the tavern, grumbling about thick heads and sour stomachs. Moments later Borsk left, himself. Whereas he had seen the slaves continue west towards the Eiglophian Mountains, Borsk ran north towards the stone and timber temple-keep of Yhoundeh. It was just before midday when he found himself before the fearsome horned captain of the inquisitors.

"You have something for me?" The highborn holy warrior asked. He sat on his massive white auroch, gleaming in the high sun as its rays reflected off his bronze breastplate and elk-antlered helm.

"Men, eight of them of them. Escaped slaves, heading towards the Three Pits." Borsk said.

"How do you know this?"

"They were in my tavern last night, boasting of their plans to plunder the mines."

"Why risk their possible wrath by telling me? I've never known you to be especially brave or pious, barkeep. In fact I've always thought you to be a worm."

"Your words wound me, sir," Borsk said. "I pray to the elk-goddess every night. Also the darkness from the depths has slept for three generations. Should these slaves enter the mines, they might stir it up again." He grinned through his brown teeth, squinted against the glare coming off the bronzed warrior, and added, "And perhaps there might be a small reward for such information? For helping to keep the sacred hills free from trespass?"

The captain laughed. "I thought as much. Fear not, brave barkeep. Should your information bear fruit, you shall be rewarded. Yhoundeh is generous to her faithful."

The holy warrior rode off towards the east with twelve of his best men following close behind. Borsk returned to his sagging tavern where later that night he had his own dreams of newfound riches, although his were all about pazoors with the symbol of the elk pressed into them.

~*~

Two days later Borsk was walking through a damp morning fog, hauling two full buckets from the nearest stream on a yoke across his shoulders. Heading back to his tavern, in the feeble gray light he spied a large antler-crowned figure waiting for him along the trail. The shadow signaled to him in recognition.

Borsk smiled and picked up his pace; counting the coins he would soon have even before they crossed his palm. But after just a few hasty steps, he faltered. Something was off about this, but it took Borsk some time to for his greed-muddled mind to put the pieces together.

The man in front of him wasn't mounted and Borsk could not recall ever seeing the captain of Yhoundeh's inquisitors without his pale auroch underneath him. Then there was the silhouette, it was all wrong. The man in front of Borsk was both much taller and heavier by far than the inquisitor. And then there was the large double bit axe that rested against the man's leg…

"Oh no," Borsk whispered as he shrugged off the yoke and water buckets. He turned to flee but gasped at the sharpened bronze just inches from his face. The well-notched sword belonged to one of the slave soldiers from the other night, and even though the dark-haired southerner from Tscho Volpanomi had one arm in a crude sling, he still looked twice the killer Borsk could ever hope to be.

The trembling barkeep began to babble for mercy when the one-armed thug kicked him square between the legs. Borsk sucked in air, hit the moist earth, and buried his face in a cool patch of moss. He laid there, tears running from his eyes, breath catching in this throat, hands on his aching manhood, and waited for the sword to fall and finish him.

The blade never descended. Instead a kick to the gut flipped him over on his back like a turtle on its shell. When Borsk finally opened his pain-clenched eyes, he saw the large leader of the slave soldiers smiling down at him. The man's bushy beard was streaked with dried blood and upon his head was the bronze elk-antlered helm of the inquisitor captain, now with a fist-sized dent to one side of it.

"Just the piece of filth we've been looking for," the Polarian said.

Protests, pleas, and prayers sprang to Borsk's lips, but the brute silenced him with a wave of his hand.

"Keep your lies between your teeth. We know it was you that sicced Yhoundeh's hounds on us. We got that from the man who wore this," the mighty warrior tapped the helmet on his head, "after we killed his men and put the fire to him."

"I am so sorry, I didn't-" Borsk began, but a giant, muddy boot to his stomach drove the wind out of him.

"Silence, dog. I know why you did it. You were greedy, not to mention foolish to cross me, but then you are also lucky. Normally I would kill you for what you did. You got all my sword-brothers killed but Troamar here. You also nearly wrecked the sole reason I risked my life leaving Uzuldaroum's damned army and came all the way to this foul place. But like I said, you are lucky because I am also greedy and I can use you now."

"What?"

"Troamar broke his arm in that battle you put us in, and while I am strong, I am not strong enough to carry all the orichalcum out of the mines that would make this trek worth all the trouble. So you will go with us to the Three Pits to help us haul out the orichalcum. If you do your job well and do nothing else stupid like trying to run away before I say you are done, then I might just let you live. Oh, I will take your left hand off at the wrist to teach you a lesson, but I will leave you with your miserable life."

The bloody-bearded man leaned over and spoke through gritted, yellow teeth. "But piss on my good nature again, and you will die screaming more than the she-elk's champion did. And that man took half the night to die. Understand?"

Borsk surely did. While he grew up with tales of the nightmarish Three Pits plaguing his childhood dreams, the Polarian barbarian that towered over him was a much a monster as anything from the dark. Had he not killed the inquisitor captain and a dozen of his best men? What could Borsk do in the face of such a real and frighteningly close threat but say yes? So he agreed and the giant hauled him to his feet, spun him around to face east, and give him a shove to get him going.

The trek was both long and hard. The land was not only hilly but heavily wooded with yuka and pine. It soon became clear that the slaves were avoiding the easier travel the road offered for fear that more followers of Yhoundeh would be out looking for their missing brethren. For two nights the trio slept rough in the wilderness without even a simple blanket to put down on the cold, damp earth. To add to the misery, the large Polarian, who Borsk learned was called Kjeljuk, would allow no fire lest vengeful eyes spy it and come searching. While the runaway soldiers seemed used to such hardships, Borsk suffered greatly, but he was wise enough to do so in silence. As for food, Kjeljuk begrudgingly shared some of their tough, dried and heavily salted army rations with the barkeep as they had no time to harvest the bounty of the forest or the many nearby streams.

By mid-morn of the third day the three men stood at last at the feet of the darkly looming Eiglophian Mountains. Before them was the crumbled and moss-covered entrance to one of the long-shunned orichalcum mines. A silence as still as the grave hung heavy in the air and none of the men, not even mighty Kjeljuk, seemed eager to break it for fear of what they might summon.

Troamar was the first to speak and it was only his all-consuming greed that overcame his good sense.

"That be silver, no?" The warrior asked, and then raced forward towards the caved-in mouth of the mine.

Before the pile of rubble there were etchings in the stone that shone with a silvery glint. It was an unbroken semi-circle around the mine entrance, and along the line were arcane silvered symbols that gleamed despite the sun being behind dark rain clouds.

"Markings of sorcery." Kjeljuk said with both fear and respect in his voice.

"The priests of Yhoundeh did that, or so my father told me when I was young." Borsk said. "He said the touch of those symbols would be an anathema to the Shadows Below and that they would dare not cross them for fear of being consumed by holy fire."

"What about us? They burn us too?" The one-armed savage from volcanic Tscho Vulpanomi asked.

"Only one way to find out." Kjeljuk said.

He then grabbed hold of the pleading Borsk and tossed him to land on the silver symbols with a heavy thud. The barkeep's posterior sent bolts of pain to his brain, but no more than any hard fall onto unyielding earth would produce. No mystical holy fire sprang forth to consume the trespasser, much to his relief.

"So we can take this silver, then?" Troamar asked as he pulled a copper dagger from his belt. His eyes all but twinkling as he went towards the silvered half-circle.

"No," Kjeljuk quickly ordered, which caused Troamar to stop dead in his tracks. "Just because we can touch these symbols does not mean I am willing to mar them. No telling what magic you might release. Leave them be. Besides, we are here for the orichalcum and there is plenty of that to be had in the mine. All we have to do is get to it."

Kjeljuk dropped a large, hide-wrapped bundle he had been carrying for the past three days and pulled off his mastodon-leather cuirass, with Troamar quickly following suit. He then untied the bundle, which revealed a pair of pickaxes and shovels. He grabbed a pick in each of his mighty hands and tossed one at Borsk, who yelped, flinched, and failed to catch it.

The two slave-soldiers laughed before Kjeljuk turned to his smaller sword-brother and said, "Troamar, take to the woods and make your traps."

The dark-haired thug nodded and then ran back the way the trio had come to vanish amidst the trees. Borsk picked up the fallen pickax as Kjeljuk walked past him towards the collapsed mine and began to assault the cave-in with a series of thunderous blows.

Borsk walked up behind the mighty Polarian, the heavy pickax feeling good in his hands, his eyes locked on the warrior's bare back. But before courage could send his arms into motion, Kjeljuk spoke without bothering to turn to look at the barkeep.

"I know what is in your mind; we are alone at last and you finally have something deadly in your hands, but you will find it easier to burry that pickaxe into these stones than into my hide. Or need I remind you of the inquisitor captain?"

"N-n-no, nothing like that at all, I swear it. I was just looking for a place to start digging." Borsk stammered.

Kjeljuk grunted and the tavern owner could all but hear the smile in the bestial sound. "Next to me, there is no use trying to remove the entire collapse. We just need to clear a path big enough to squeeze through. There's plenty of earth to move and time is not our ally."

"Then why not have Troamar aid us? Even with one arm he could help." Borsk said as he stepped up and swung his pick at the cave-in.

"He will, but we must be sure that the hounds of Yhoundeh you put on our trail do not catch us unawares. Troamar was the scout in our troop. He has eyes like a hawk, the ears of a fox, and can run the woods like a deer. He can also make all manner of deadly traps with just a knife, some wood, and twine. Should the inquisitors come our way, they will meet a nasty surprise before they get too close."

"The inquisitors know you were making for the Three Pits -"

"Thanks to you." Kjeljuk interrupted.

Borsk carried on quickly, "They are sure to come here eventually."

"Yes, but that will take time. When their riders don't return after a few days, they will send out more, who will spot the carrion-birds where the inquisitors and my brothers fell in battle. If we are lucky then they will think each side killed the other to a man. But luck has been pissing on me lately, so they will probably keep looking for us. Troops will have to muster and then ride back here and then they might make for the Three Pits. I am betting our lives that we can get through this collapse and retrieve the orichalcum before that happens, so less talk and more digging, if you know what is good for you."

And so the trio dug. It was backbreaking work, something Borsk was not accustomed to, yet he tried his best to hide the fact from the others. The three divided the task by having two men dig while a third rested, this way the excavation never slowed. It was approaching twilight of the next day when Troamar and Borsk finally broke through the wall of rubble to see the darkness beyond.

Kjeljuk was roused from slumber by his excited one-armed companion, and the three men cleared the remaining loose stones and dirt until they made a gap wide enough even for their broad-shouldered leader to squeeze through. Then all three stopped, and while huffing and puffing from their labors, they stared into the benighted mineshaft.

"Borsk, you said you have lived out here all your life. What have you heard about the darkness that killed so many?" Kjeljuk asked, and Borsk realized that it was the first time he had called him by name. It was also the first time the mighty warrior had ever shown concern for what might be waiting for them in the long sealed tunnels.

"No one knows for sure. It happened too fast, and those that got a good look never came out," Borsk said in whispered reverence, just in case the darkness was listening. "A slave overseer some nights after the slaughter was deep in his cups at my grandfather's tavern. In between bouts of tears he told my grandfather that it was like the shadows themselves rose up to attack. That's all he saw, the black of night itself tearing into and ripping apart the diggers under his command. Later when the priests of Yhoundeh came, they told everyone that what befell the mines was a curse of the Sleeper of N'kai."

"Tsathoggua." Troamar whispered, which caused Kjeljuk to cuff the man upside his head. Such names were not meant to be spoken aloud, especially when close to an opening to the stygian depths.

Borsk continued, "They said their prayers and rituals had returned the darkness to slumber with their foul lord. That should the darkness awaken again and try to leave the tunnels, they set silver sigils at the mouth of each mine to keep it from escaping."

Kjeljuk walked back to their camp and donned his thick hide armor and picked up a torch Troamar had made out of a sturdy yuka branch and pine resin. He used a bit of flint to light it, and then hefted his huge battle-axe.

"We didn't come all this way, lose our brothers, and move half the damn mountainside just to be scared off by the dark."

Troamar nodded and as he got into his own battle gear, Kjeljuk walked up to Borsk, pulled a long-bladed bronze dagger from his belt, and pressed it into the tavern keeper's hand.

"Grab a torch, we'll need the light. You won't be able to swing a pickaxe one-handed, so use this if any shadow creeps too close."

Borsk went to get a torch, keeping his questions to himself, like how a dagger would do him any good against living darkness.

Once armed with fire and bronze, the three entered the mine. The air was thick with damp and the smell of the rotting timber and raw earth was pervasive. None of the three wanted to be the first to break the oppressive silence so they moved without speaking, following a well-worn trail made by heavily laden mine carts. There were also several thick chains trailing into the darkness on the ground. Presumably each was tied to a cart and at one time had been attached to a winch outside of the mine, of which the looters had seen no-sign.

Inside the mouth of the tunnel there was no evidence of any violence. Tools were stacked neatly in corners next to moldering support beams, and a small mushroom-spotted table held four oil lamps. Whatever fuel they had once held had dried to sludge over the decades.

Eighty paces further into the long-undisturbed darkness, the men saw mining tools scattered about where they had been hastily dropped. There were also dark stains in splatters and streaks on the walls and floor that even Borsk could identify as blood spilt years ago.

"There." Troamar whispered, breaking the silence at last as he pointed to a nearby cart.

Approaching and using torches to burn away the darkness and

cobwebs that shrouded the cart, they saw that it was half filled with chunks of stone that had golden-copper glint of orichalcum running through them.

"The stories be true." Troamar cracked a yellow grin across his filthy face.

"Looks to be more stone than orichalcum in there," Borsk said.

"Quiet, orichalcum is orichalcum." Troamar said, his grin now a scowl.

"Quiet, both of you," Kjeljuk said, keeping his voice low. "Let us follow those chains and hope the other carts bear more treasure."

"Shouldn't we pull this one out first?" Borsk asked while his eyes returned to the crimson stains on the walls.

"Then come all this way in again for more? No, we keep going, find all that we can, and then we pull the best carts up. Now come on, this place is not getting any more pleasant." Kjeljuk led the way deeper into the earth. Troamar followed with a bit more spring in his step than before; obviously his fears were overshadowed by thoughts of riches. Borsk, not wanting to be left in the dark alone, had no choice but to follow.

Down, down, down the three went, passing more red stains without comment, stopping only to inspect other carts as they came to them. Some of the small wagons were empty, but most were filled to varying heights with orichalcum and stone. The best chunks, those that glinted the brightest with orichalcum's golden-copper color, Kjeljuk gathered. He placed them in the hide bundle that once held the digging tools that he had slung over one of his broad shoulders.

Troamar was remarking for the fourth time that they were going to be rich while Kjeljuk kept a watchful eye on the shadows all around them, lest one begin to slither and shift with no aid from their sputtering torches. That's when Borsk had a realization.

"Where are all the bones?"

"What?" Troamar asked through his grin.

"We've found blood, but no bones. If well over a hundred men died down here, what happened to their bodies?"

"Rats must have taken the bones," Kjeljuk said.

"What? That's --" Borsk began, but shut his mouth with a click of his teeth when he saw Kjeljuk's eyes blazing at him.

"I said it was rats. If it was anything else, what good does it do to think about it?"

"So now can we start back to the surface?" Borsk asked. "Our torches are burning low, and we've found much orichalcum in these carts."

"Besides what I have picked up, we have found only scraps. The remains of already bled-dry orichalcum veins. Mine tunnels grow to reach new, richer veins and so the best pieces, the ones that will be more orichalcum and less useless stone, will be deeper down." Kjeljuk pointed to the five remaining chains that went deeper into the mine. "We follow those and we will find what we came for. Most of these carts here are not worth the effort of pulling up."

Troamar readily agreed, and since Borsk didn't get a vote, the matter was settled.

Deeper they delved, and the mineshaft grew warmer with each step, while an oppressive fungal stench overpowered all other odors. That warmth quickly became a stifling heat that had each man sweating and wishing they'd had the foresight to bring water.

And then there were the sounds.

There were whispers in the deeper dark. Not words, not voices, just faint rustlings, creeping, secretive noises, and they came from all around them.

"Are you hearing this?" Borsk whined.

Kjeljuk shushed him. His head cocked to one side like a wolf's, straining to listen to the muttering dark, as if trying to make sense of the whispers.

"Another cart," Troamar said, and went to investigate it.

Thankfully, the next few things, as terrible as they were, happened very fast.

"We need to leave." Kjeljuk said, perhaps hearing something in the faint sounds he didn't like.

Troamar ignored him and reached the mine cart. Inside he did not find stone and orichalcum, but the dull ivory of bones. The cart was filled with them, more than what half a dozen men could account for. Then from the gaps between ribs, femurs, skulls, and vertebrae, a darkness slithered forth. It coalesced and rose out of the cart to confront the intruder.

The thing from the cart was like the moonless night given form. It was an absolute blackness that flowed like water, yet it mocked the pull of gravity and rose up like an ebony serpent. It was obviously alive and could sense the one-armed man in front of it though it had no eyes, ears, or any other features. Many thin tendrils budded out of its fluid mass and elongated to a length longer than Kjeljuk was tall. They whipped around, swooshing and cracking through the hot, still air.

Kjeljuk dropped his torch, his bundle of orichalcum, and pulled his great axe from his back.

Borsk was motionless, a scream caught in his throat, his eyes wide with shock.

Troamar took a step back from the horror in the cart and let loose a womanly scream.

The darkness reached for Troamar with a number of its tendrils and the southern savage swung his torch to keep the beast at bay. Several black coils shot forth and pierced the soldier's body like spears. When they burst out of his back, they slithered towards each other, merged together, and made a lattice running through Troamar that he had no chance of escaping.

Kjeljuk swung his mighty axe and bellowed in rage. The heavy, notched blade cleaved through the writhing shadow as if it was water. One part of the darkness fell back into the cart while the other fell with Troamar to topple onto the tunnel floor.

Borsk saw more shadows slither into the flickering torchlight, moving out of the darkness all around them and flowing towards the pair of warriors. He wanted to shout a warning, but only a pitiful squeak escaped his trembling lips. He felt his bladder let go and he took several steps backwards until he hit the tunnel wall behind him.

Kjeljuk grabbed his sword-brother's arm and started to drag him back but the black horror in the cart was quicker. It surged out and reunited itself with the part of its formless body that still ran through the bleeding, weeping warrior.

"Kjeljuk, behind you!" Borsk screamed, finding his voice at last as another shadow rose up behind the giant man to more than equal his height.

Kjeljuk dropped Troamar's arm, grabbed his axe with both hands, turned and swung the weapon in a sweeping arc. Once again he cleaved a shadow in twain.

And once again it did little good, as both parts of the ebony nightmare quickly flowed back together.

Borsk watched through wide eyes as Troamar was dragged away into the darkness by the obsidian coil. The man was no longer screaming, as gouts of living, writhing blackness emerged out of his mouth and nose in place of breath.

Kjeljuk took only a moment to look around before reaching down to pick up the dropped bundle of orichalcum. He then spun on his heel, ran to Borsk, grabbed the smaller man by the shoulder, turned him round to face back the way they came, and shoved him forward with a mighty bellow of, "Run, fool!"

The giant's command got through to Borsk's fear-addled mind and the barkeep ran faster than he had ever run before. Kjeljuk stayed close on his heels, as Borsk held their only remaining torch, and kept telling him to go, go, go.

While neither man dared glance behind them, they both heard the strange whispering sounds following them as they ran up mineshaft. Borsk kept his eyes cast down at the cart chains on the ground, focusing on them, using them not only as a guide, but something to fixate on to block out the horrors that pursued him.

Just follow the chains, follow the chains, follow the chains, he said to himself.

The two ran in silence, their pounding feet, huffing breath, and the sinister whispers the only sounds. The chase continued for an unknown time and while the lungs of each man burned and their legs grew heavy, neither slowed a step.

"I... I Heard them..." Kjeljuk said, after a stretch of time and in between panting breaths.

"What?" Borsk grunted. In doing so, he lifted his eyes from the chains on the ground and saw that the mouth of the mine fast approaching. The dull gray daylight beyond had never looked so glorious.

"I heard them whisper... they were..." The northern giant huffed out. As if giving voice to the nightmare that had befallen them would somehow have it make more sense.

Borsk didn't want to know what the cursed shadows had been whispering. They were within fifty paces of freedom and putting this horror behind them. All Borsk wanted to do was to go home, drink plenty of his watered-down ale, and forget about the damn Pits forever.

But Kjeljuk continued.

"They said His name. Over... and over again... they were whispering of the Sleeper of --"

Kjeljuk was interrupted when one of the slithering shadows wrapped itself around his leg. The large man tripped and hit the ground hard enough to cause his jaws to clack together with his tongue between them. An inch of the warrior's tongue was bit off, so when brave Kjeljuk tried to scream, only gurgles escaped his red lips.

Borsk heard the big man fall behind him and the gargled pleas that followed, but he didn't stop. He didn't slow down. He didn't even spare a backward glance. He was less than thirty strides from the mouth of the tunnel, and that was all he cared about.

The barkeep burst out of the mine with a triumphant smile on his face. He made sure that he crossed the line of silver carved into the ground before allowing himself to collapse in an exhausted heap. There the man stayed, lying prostrate on the naked earth, his hot cheek pressed against the cool ground, arms and legs stretched out motionless. He gulped in air to soothe his burning lungs as tears made trails across his filthy face. Only now that he was out of the Pit, now that he was safe, did the whole measure of the terror he had experienced come crashing down upon him. So for a long stretch of time Borsk could only tremble and cry in the dirt.

When the tears finally stopped and the fire in his lungs was quenched, Borsk stood and looked back at the yawning mouth of the tunnel behind him. The fear he had felt just moments before was now replaced by guilt. Sure, Kjeljuk and Troamar had taken him to this hellish place against his will. Yes, they were both no doubt killers of many men. But the Polarian barbarian did save his life when he peeled Borsk's paralyzed body off the tunnel wall and got him running for the exit. He didn't have to do that, or so Borsk thought, and the small man was at a loss to understand why the warrior would do such a thing.

*He needed your torch to light the way*, a part of Borsk's mind reasoned. *He couldn't carry it, his axe, and his bundle of orichalcum all at once.*

*No*, a louder voice in Borsk's head chastised him. *Kjeljuk saved your miserable life and you left him behind without a thought.*

"What could I do?" he cried aloud. The cold hillside gave no answer, but the shriveled suvana pit that was his conscience did.

*You must see, at least, if he is dead. You owe him that much for saving your hide. If anyone could fight free of that darkness, it would be Kjeljuk.*

"No, no, no," Borsk whispered to himself, at the same time picking up his dropped torch and slowly approached the mine. He hesitated before stepping over the silver barrier the priests of Yhoundeh had carved generations ago into the hilltop and peered into the darkened mineshaft.

"Kjeljuk? Kjeljuk you there? Do you yet live?"

There was no answer.

"Kjeljuk, please answer. I am… I am sorry. I was afraid and…"

Borsk silenced himself when he saw movement in the shadows of the mine. He took a step backwards, ready to turn and run, when he recognized the hulking silhouette.

"Kjeljuk!" Borsk cried, and forgetting himself, he stepped into the mine. When the flickering light of his yuka torch fell upon the slowly approaching soldier, Borsk let out a gasp. Kjeljuk's face was covered in grime, his bushy beard completely matted with blood. The once fearsome giant walked unsteadily, one hand on a wall for support, eyes glazed and unfocused, feet dragging. But still, the amazing northerner had somehow fought his way free of the shadows that had pulled him down.

Suddenly remembering the black horrors, Borsk waved his torch about to cast the light in all corners and crevices around him in case an ebony nightmare was creeping towards him. He saw nothing. He strained his ears for the soft whispers of the things, but only heard Kjeljuk's shuffling approach.

"How?" Borsk asked, when he was within arm's reach. "What happened back there?"

Kjeljuk stopped for a moment, his head lolling on his neck to look down at the little man while his eyes rolled in their sockets. The giant did not reply, probably could not speak for all the blood on his lips, but he did stretch back an arm and point behind him. Then Kjeljuk continued his slow, uneven gait out of the mine.

Borsk silently watched the man pass, then turned and peered into the deeper darkness.

*What was he pointing at?* "Who cares, time to leave this place for good," He said to himself, but Borsk's restless mind continued, *Wait, listen; no whispers. And look; no slithering shadows. The darkness has returned below.*

Then his torchlight reflected back on something golden and coppery spilled from a rough-hide bundle.

"Kjeljuk," Borsk called out. "Your orichalcum, you left it behind."

The large Polarian did not answer, slow or even turn around. Kjeljuk just kept slowly plodding forward, out of the mine.

*Quickly, go and retrieve the orichalcum. The Darkness has gone back down to the lightless hell that spawned it. You are safe and those few rocks alone are worth a fortune.*

"Damn it all." The little man said, but he cautiously moved forward, deeper into the mine.

He did not have to go far.

In the middle of the mineshaft, his torch-light reflected not only off the spilt orichalcum, but from a wet, misshapen, and still steaming mound next to it. Borsk had hunted his share of deer, so he recognized a gut-pile when he saw one; he could make out lungs, liver, heart, and seemingly endless coils of dripping intestines. There were also bits that no one saw in a pile after a hunt: bones. Dozens of dull white shards poked out of the red mess here and there. Most of the bones were fragments but some were intact. He could identify a curved rib and the knobby end of a thighbone.

"Yhoundeh protect me," Borsk prayed for the first time since his early childhood. He had no idea what the gruesome sight before him meant, but he knew he did not want to be near it. He turned and ran back out of the mine, scurrying from the mouth of the Pit and into the fading gloom of twilight outside. There he spied Kjeljuk on his knees, head bowed, the barbarian's long hair hanging over his blood-covered face. The warrior looked too exhausted to continue on.

Borsk knelt next to the Polarian and then straining, he hauled the silent soldier to his feet.

"Let us leave this cursed place." The barkeep said, dragging Kjeljuk several paces forward. The pair stepped over the silver barrier carved into the ground and that's when a new horror was born.

Kjeljuk began to convulse, arms flailing, and one mighty limb struck Borsk on the face, sending him sprawling. Upon landing, Borsk's hand went up to find his nose bleeding, but his eyes were held fast on the jittering barbarian. Then came a horrible ripping sound and in a blink Kjeljuk fell backwards at the waist, bending in a way impossible to man. The front of the warrior opened up like a worn coat and out spilled several globs of writhing darkness.

The living shadows hit the ground and elongated into ropy tendrils as Kjeljuk toppled from his feet. The ebony creatures slithered forth at incredible speed, leaving glistening trails behind them in the fading light of approaching night. Within the span of three of Borsk's terrified heartbeats, the dark things were gone.

As for Kjeljuk, what was left of him lay crumpled and deflated like an empty wineskin. The red pool that formed around the flattened corpse had nothing to do with grapes.

"Wine..." Borsk tittered as the horrible truth of what he had witness became clear to him. The dark, formless monsters from below had indeed been clever. They had known that they could not cross the silver line carved in the earth by the priests of Yhoundeh, not without the proper disguise. Once on the other side of the barrier, they discarded the remains of the man and now, after untold years...

The darkness below was free.

# The Conquest of Rhizopium

## By Dieter Meier

Before the pungent coronal oil of his anointing had even dried, Zyzotha the Fourth of Commoriom did begin to hatch schemes to consolidate and expand his mighty empire. In the fullness of time, all of Mhu Thulan had fallen beneath the Commorion banner—all save one lesser treasure, which had resisted and bedeviled his avaricious ancestors. Rhizopium, the secluded city of the tree stones, lay but three days' ride from the capital, though the empire extended beyond the reach of daylight to the west. For a score of red lustrums, Commoriom had thrown its armies at the defiant city, yet still it stood, implacable as death itself.

Until one day, when a sorcerer of Tscho Volpanomi, vulpine of aspect and cloaked in glossy ebon-green diatryma feathers, came to court and issued such a claim as made Emperor Zyzotha's royal blood sing with dreams of epochal bloodshed.

"With a bit of knowledge I have," proclaimed Uvumbra Ovis, "I might achieve for you in a day that which has been denied all your ancestors."

Zyzotha took care not to hear the magician's proposal in open court, but ordered his vizier to lead the beetle-browed ancient to his private chambers, for the worldly people of Commoriom had always mistrusted sorcery in those crude, bloody days of the empire's first age, and the intrusion of dark arts into the imperial city's martial affairs was unthinkable.

The emperor was loath even to entertain thoughts of magical subterfuge, for legend told that the crown of Commoriom would never rest on the head of a coward; but would fly from his shameful head to seek the strong brow of the one destined to lead the empire to greater conquests. And even if the legend proved false, the crime would be swiftly and mercilessly avenged by his younger brother, Uzotha, the jealous general of Commoriom's armies.

If Zyzotha had set more stock in his brother's military prowess, or if he did not so brazenly desire to add the neighboring city-state to his empire, he would have prudently rendered his decision with a headsman's sword.

But the sorcerer was most eelishly persuasive, and repute of his thaumaturgical prowess had already reached the court.

Some twelve lustrums past, the barbaric mountain nomads of Polarion raided their lowland neighbors' lands at harvest and escaped into the mist-bound northern mountains, where they wintered in a high, secluded valley impassable most of the year. Hunting sorties lost their way in the fog, only to be ambushed and driven into bottomless chasms. Uvumbra Ovis's solution demanded enormous sacrifice, but it was unsettlingly elegant.

From a perch atop the summit of Mount Ghorthigromm, he invoked and betrayed two conflicting schools of elementals, and let the feud run its course. The rampaging primal forces transmuted the valley's protective cloak of mist into a shroud of solid stone. The thunderclap of the petrified clouds falling to earth was heard and felt on the shores of benighted Lemuria and savage Atlantis, and added an hour to each calendar round thereafter. Of the ferocious Polarian raiders and the secluded valley they called home, no sign was ever discovered.

In more civilized and pragmatic lands, such feats of sorcery would have earned the mage incalcuable fame and fortune, and a lifelong sinecure from a grateful ruler. But in the vulgar adolescence of Commoriom, to call upon dark forces was the most craven and blasphemous strategy imaginable. While no earthly solution could pry the intractable Rhizopians out of their vaunted aerie, yet some more subtle enchantment would be needed, to bring them to heel.

The scholarly city of Rhizopium perched atop a forest of sheer, towering pillars of basalt connected by tunnels, spiral ramps and suspended bridges, so that a single shepherd-monk could easily hold it against an army. Though they spurned warfare and cared only for the contemplation of the heavens and the tending of their drowsy ceratopsid flocks, the defiant citizens of Rhizopium had reluctantly mastered only such knowledge of warfare as would hold their neighbors at bay.

For a considerable fee in orichalcum ore and first pick of the loot from the famed libraries of the city, Uvumbra Ovis proposed to do away with every last citizen of Rhizopium, leaving the gates open for the conquering armies of Commoriom to march in and raise the imperial banner.

Such a prospect was naturally quite tantalizing to Emperor Zyzotha, but fraught with peril. His people were ever a superstitious and fearful lot, and would take the sudden vanishing of their hated neighbors as an ill omen.

To lay blame for the sudden vacancy upon plague or the monks' own sorcery would unman even his most battle-mad berserkers, the brute-men raised as beasts in his stables and fed on the flesh of the subject races of the empire. None would dare take possession of the land, and the phantom of the empty city would vex him until death and blot his legend forever.

Uvumbra Ovis silkily polished away every fault that the Emperor noted in his plan, until it shone like a perfect, star-born opal in Zyzotha's diademed head, shining its seductive, crepuscular light into his dreams and making a pale shade of his mundane imperial duties.

At last, he agreed that this was his greatest idea, yet.

That very night, Uvumbra Ovis received a wagonload of orichalcum ore from the Emperor's mines in the south—prized because they were hundreds of leagues beneath the sea—and yielded up by such of his subjects as dwelled upon the ocean floor.

The sorcerer vanished from the capital the next morning, despite a host of spies and a retinue of elite men-at-arms encircling his apartments. The Emperor set loose his guards to search the city and sent winged messengers to the far corners of the empire, but to no avail. Uvumbra Ovis had vanished, and with him, a preposterous fortune and the Emperor's pride. He could not rest until the charlatan was returned in red-hot chains to lay his scurrilous head upon the imperial chopping block.

He had nearly dictated an order of execution when he discovered the note which Uvumbra Ovis had left for him. And after having a scribe read it to him and then killing him, Zyzotha declared war upon the city of Rhizopium for the crime of abduction of Commoriom's beloved and invaluable chief counselor.

Bravely did the kingdom rally to the cause of war, and all the more courageously for all that Uvumbra Ovis was universally despised and feared throughout the kingdom. Then a messenger returned from Rhizopium, claimed that he'd found the impregnable gates of Rhizopium standing open, and the spiral-streets deserted.

The shock of suddenly receiving one's fondest wish is often the unmaking of a man, but Emperor Zyzotha presently recovered his wits and charged into his imagined destiny at the head of a full legion of infantry and mastodons and cavalry mounted on shrieking diatrymas to engage the alien threat on Commoriom's border. In his war chariot drawn by a snarling sabertooth, Zyzotha dashed impatiently ahead of the creeping column, which flowed like wax in the sullen tropic sun of Mhu Thulan's squandered youth.

Stuffed into the unforgiving bronze ceremonial armor of his forefathers—titans on the field, but pygmies, one and all, next to their heir—the Emperor could not hold back his scorn at their desultory progress. Almost as if they knew their prize lay unprotected and, thus, no test of their battle-prowess, they lagged on the road and sulked at his whip. He rode down a flock of refugees fleeing the doom of Rhizopium to raise their spirits, and was rewarded with an impromptu song in his honor, which he did not enjoy.

At the sight of the empty ramparts of Rhizopium, his army levied a dutiful cheer and raced to storm the battlements, but finding the entire city empty, they began to mutter about sorcery, and to burn the pitiful loot they'd pillaged. Well prepared for the unease of their easy victory, Zyzotha plied his army with kegs of cycad wine and wagonloads of dancing girls from the territories, and set his elite brigades of artisans to work redecorating the conquered city with statues of its liberator.

The uneventful occupation soon grew tiresome. Uvumbra Ovis covertly spread blessings and charms against disease and curses, but still the soldiers speculated about what malign force the unholy monks of Rhizopium must have conjured up, only to be devoured by it, and even the sergeants' fanged whips were not enough to quell whisperings of mutiny.

Emperor Zyzotha well understood the warrior spirit of his men. They would face any enemy of flesh and bone, but the specter of the unseen chilled their bloodlust, and left them as toothless as herd beasts before the fall of night.

The Emperor took Uvumbra Ovis to his tent and made him another offer. Long and lustily did they bargain into the purpling of dusk, but the wily wizard knew he had the Emperor at a disadvantage, and shrewdly pressed it.

In the bowels of the night, the tiny alpine city's walls were shaken by a barrage of bestial hooting and bombarded with volleys of noxious excrement. The addled imperial army rallied and took to the walls, spears and axes a-quiver with rekindled battle-joy.

The simian challenges and jeering canine half-speech of the sub-human Voormis horde proved a tonic for the soldiers' uneasy nerves, and they ripped into them with lusty war-songs and razor-bladed iron.

The brutish invaders managed to wound several careless soldiers, and even killed a captain, knocking the plumed imbecile from the ramparts when he had his back to the enemy to lecture an oafish pikeman. But the loathsome beast-men were routed all too easily, and word began to seep back to the Emperor in Rhizopium's council hall—the backward shepherds had not even advanced enough to crown a king—that the Voormis leapt onto their spears like tame beasts to the slaughter, as if they were under an enchantment, or a geas.

If Uvumbra Ovis expected to be showered with gratitude for his sorcerous ruse, he was soon rudely disabused of any such illusions. In Commoriom of that age, the hunting of Voormis in the wilds was a sport for unblooded initiates, while the thinning of their numbers in the city's sewers fell to seedy untouchables, usually cashiered soldiers. Such disgraceful foes were an insult to the perfumed nobles who led the cavalry.

But the sorcerer was far too consumed by his own studies, to worry over Zyzotha's scolding. With possession of Rhizopium's libraries, surely, he could have conversed with the gods, but for reasons known only to himself, he instead retired to a crooked tower, as remote as possible from Zyzotha's court, to peruse his new scrolls and observe the inscrutable stars.

Eventually, Emperor Zyzotha grew weary of ruling a city inhabited only by his own statues, and the army was sent forth to Commoriom's conquered neighbors, armed with lists of tradesmen and citizens in arrears on taxes. A merry chase was led, but soon the victorious army returned with a new citizenry for Rhizopium. A magistrate and an executioner were chosen, and itinerant priests were assigned to convert the strange local shrines to the fat, happy godlings of Commoriom.

With order, peace and martial parades restored to Rhizopium, Zyzotha would fain have taken his army back to the capital, if only the new citizens of Rhizopium did not prove nearly as superstitious as the soldiers. Deserters were hanged by their feet at the gates for the raptors to feast upon, but the soldiers' full attention still had to be turned upon the new Rhizopians, for fear they would leave with the next sunset, rather than sleep in the eerie, empty city.

The first colonists were hardly galvanized by pioneer spirit, and no surprise; the subject cities had tithed only their most expendable citizens, padded with any unwary country folk the cavalry caught on the road. There were precious few criminals left after the first few weeks, for the headsman's two-handed sword was ever hungry to cut off injustice, but none could be counted upon to occupy the city any longer than they were forced. Thus, the soldiers had to stay and keep the peace.

~*~

The peace lasted for two unbearable days.

Emperor Zyzotha went again to see Uvumbra Ovis in his tower—more a supplicant now, than a ruler, before the vulpine sorcerer. He went away looking more regal than he came, however, and smiling.

That very night, a cadre of armored warriors appeared in the very heart of the city, and slaughtered a score of infantry and their sergeants, and uncounted scores of hapless citizens with such fury that the scattered victims did not notice their assailants had charged out of the city's museum, or that their fearsome copper and onyx armor was encrusted with nitre and verdigris.

After the panic inspired by the initial ambush, the shambling warriors proved a less than formidable foe; their brittle obsidian-bladed axes splintered against sturdy bronze shields, while the ghastly liches themselves were brought down by blood-mad soldiers with axes and nets, who found that their enemies seemed imbued with an awful, alien vitality that rendered them nigh-invincible until they were totally dismembered. This service the soldiers were only too happy to render, for the invasion had aroused hysterical cries of blasphemy and sacrilege.

The invaders' weapons and armor were relics from Commoriom's own first forges, and many of the indomitable fighters were the mummified ancestors of their own victims.

The outraged soldiers soon decided that the Rhizopians had not all died, and that some treacherous magus still haunted the city. Having lured the Commorian army into a trap, he would conjure demons to whittle away their forces. Perhaps, the drunken chorus mused over guttering campfires, the enemy was hiding within their ranks, stabbing them in the back…

Emperor Zyzotha observed the decline in morale with a bewildering blend of pique and admiration. So heedless of their own safety were his dogs of war, that a host of apparitions that would have driven lesser men shrieking from the city, had only served as petty distractions from the gloomy war-lust that haunted them. Zyzotha initiated another campaign of harlots and cycad wine. And before they could return to brooding, calamity struck again.

From every gutter and sewer-sluice in the columnar city of Rhizopium, there emerged a noisome fetor, as if the bowels of the earth itself had split asunder, and its infernal waste oozing out onto its moonlit skin in an unspeakable reversal of the natural order. The noxious miasma had all but incapacitated every adopted civilian of Rhizopium, leaving them helpless before the authors of the unbearable stench, when they finally burst forth into the twisting staircase streets of the beleaguered city.

A gluttonous flood of bubbling black protoplasm erupted from the sewers of Rhizopium in implacable waves, sweeping the streets clean of human flotsam with a rapacious hunger that betrayed an awful sentience about the flailing fuliginous breakers and bludgeoning tentacles, for the catastrophic flood was not any mere deluge of terrestrial effluvium, but a massed horde of Tsathoggua's abominable spawn, endowed with monstrous sentience and a will to purge the city of its despised, two-legged occupiers.

Swords, clubs and arrows alike could get no purchase upon the squamous, rubbery hides of the lapping, formless atrocities, while battering pseudopods smashed all but the stoutest defenses into kindling. Their insidious, fluid forms could penetrate any opening larger than a keyhole, and so sought out and devoured all but the most vigorously protected human prey.

Only when an enterprising captain of the guards thought to douse the anthropophagous black wave with the city's stores of lamp oil and palm wine and set them alight, was the awful invasion turned back. Engulfed by licking tongues of blue-white fire, the waves subsided and dispersed into squirming rivers of sizzling, shrieking amoebae, streaming over the city's bridges and igniting them as well, severing the city's outer districts from the central court of the Emperor.

A ragged but lusty cheer shuddered the tree-stones of Rhizopium, tempered by the bleak realization that the city was all but empty of women, and completely bereft of wine.

Morning broke upon Rhizopium with disquieting silence. Those few survivors who could walk had all flown in the night, leaving half the army skulking in the shadowy arcades of Rhizopium, with no enemy to curse save their emperor. The situation had become untenable.

Uvumbra Ovis approached the Emperor with yet another proposal, but he was intercepted by the bold captain whose quick wit had saved the city from the spawn of Tsathoggua. He ordered Uvumbra Ovis placed under arrest and confined to his tower. A canny ensign in the Emperor's court had tumbled to the wizard's suspicious behavior, and accused him of treason by sorcery.

Infuriated by the usurpation of his powers, Emperor Zyzotha ordered Uvumbra Ovis released, and in turn arrested the captain, whose popularity had begun to gnaw at Zyzotha's hereditary mantle of command. When dissent over the order began to percolate up even to the Emperor's ears, he had the rest of his officers taken, as well.

Uvumbra Ovis, as always, had a solution.

The problem all along had not lain with the occupation or the Emperor's plans, but with his men, and not in their hearts or hands, which were unswerving in their loyalty, but in their heads. Therefore, Uvumbra Ovis, proposed an elegant response.

Chop off the problems.

One by one, the shackled officers were driven to the chopping block, and the weary executioner dutifully lopped off their treasonous heads. And one by one, the headless cadavers rose up and drew their swords to follow their emperor to victory.

~*~

At last, peace and order reigned in Rhizopium. The few citizens unable to flee hid in bricked-up boltholes night and day from the patrols of headless corpses puppeteered by an exhausted Uvumbra Ovis.

But Emperor Zyzotha gnawed at his own nerves, for the fear of remaining in thrice-damned Rhizopium was only checked by the unbearable shame of abandoning it. His warrior spirit demanded a clean outcome, to prove his mettle once and for all before his openly mocking army, before he could retire in honor to the capital.

So pervasive was his terror of failing the crown of Commoriom was Zyzotha, that he bound the golden, corundum-studded diadem to his careworn head, lest the myth come true, and the crown fly away of its own accord, to seek a more fitting monarch.

If the Emperor felt ill-served by fate—reduced to presiding over a derelict ghost-city and commanding a demoralized army of the living dead—his ire was as a child's pique, next to the bilious gall nursed by his collaborator in the flawed occupation.

Chief among the wizard's grievances was the mounting difficulty of finding enemies for the army to slay. The Voormis had come in response to a night of grunting, animal-like incantations at a tunnel off the city's sewer system. In truth, the "spell" was little more than earthly cursing in the Voormis tongue, which is uncannily suited to carry through miles of subterranean passages.

The resurrected warriors were even easier, as necromancy was Uvumbra Ovis's prime sphere of expertise. The arousal of the spawn of Tsathoggua had, likewise, been a simple ruse, brought about by casting the city's idols of the repulsive bat-toad god into the sewer-sluices. But the resulting invasion had been quite out of his control, and he had nearly perished, himself, in the offing.

To summon elementals or other wild supernatural entities, as he had so famously and recklessly done in the past, would betray his own lack of mastery, and surely would destroy, if not himself, then the emperor and his dwindling army.

Worst of all, Uvumbra Ovis had simmered in secret throughout the occupation of Rhizopium over an injustice which he had heretofore shared with no one; for the wealth he had squeezed from the Emperor was trash to him without the other half of his reward, and he had been quite unable to take possession of the treasures of Rhizopium's libraries.

The secrets he burned to possess—the summoning of demons and spirits of the outer sphere, even the invocations of the Outer Gods—were all inside the library of the monk-magi. Why did he not use them?

Having polished off the last dregs of the imperial stores of cycad wine, the Emperor had Uvumbra Ovis hauled to the central arcade by his own headless henchmen, and brought before the chopping block, which stood before the doors of the library.

Zyzotha flew into a rage at the collapse of his city, at the web of deceit which the sorcerer had spun around him with his treacherous magic. In a fit of vainglorious wrath, he commanded Uvumbra Ovis to produce the monster which had brought the doom to Rhizopium, that he might slay it, and have done with this charade.

Uvumbra Ovis rose from the chopping block with a sardonic grin, but made no move to cast any spells of invocation. Instead, he merely shuffled to the doors of the library of Rhizopium, and unlocked them.

Emperor Zyzotha uttered a blood-chilling oath and charged at Uvumbra Ovis with an ivory-tipped javelin, but he never reached his target.

The sorcerer threw wide the heavy, malachite-scaled doors of the great library, but he did not flee inside, as Zyzotha expected. Uvumbra Ovis retreated and lay flat across the hexagonal paving stones of the arcade just as the emperor hurled his javelin.

No matter how the aging Uvumbra Ovis might have twisted to evade the emperor's javelin, the keen-eyed Zyzotha could have taken his life with a single throw. He could have, and would have, if the javelin were not arrested in midair, as if it had struck something invisible, yet horribly tangible.

By the frantic flailing in space of the transfixed javelin, it came clear that the unseen interloper was only mildly irritated by the blow, for it was plucked out and shattered, and the shards flung back at Zyzotha.

Any common mortal man might have withered before such an abominable prodigy, but Emperor Zyzotha of Commoriom was not ruled by the superstitions that plagued his lesser cousins and countrymen. He had never seen any foe that could withstand the force of a single blow of his adamant javelin, but he had planned for such a dark day, and stood ready and eager with a response.

He had another javelin.

Before he could fling it, the invisible abomination had engulfed the emperor and begun to bloom into the visible spectrum as it glutted itself upon his imperial body and blood, digesting all but the vaunted imperial crown. Still, the ghastly star-born vampire only seemed to glimmer in and out of sight as Zyzotha's vital essence pulsed through its alien architecture.

So massive had the amorphous bloodsucker become, so hideously bloated upon the liquid life of an entire city, that even the celebrated violet hue of the royal ichor and the indigestible crown racing through its unfathomable cavities could paint only the barest, mercurial outline of the repellent form of the slavering cosmic lamprey for Uvumbra Ovis's awestruck eyes; but he saw it all too clearly, for just a moment, as it fed upon him.

All those nights he'd spent in deep meditation and casting spells, had not been in the service of Zyzotha's lust for a bigger conquest for his idiotic army. He had come to the emperor with the plan for Rhizopium—the mad, foolish plan—convinced of its perfection, despite his gnawing uncertainty over the spell, itself.

The triangular tablets of the serpentfolk were so treacherously inscribed, as if the ophidian magi knew that their successors would be the hated warmblooded Hyperboreans, and made of all their lore a deadly trap.

For how else to explain the uncanny ease with which the cosmic abortion materialized and descended upon the defenseless city as its due offering… while the prescribed method to dispel the monstrosity, and indeed all his geases and glamours, had done nothing to unseat the engorged parasite of the outer spheres, which had not returned from whence it came, but retired to digest the inhabitants of Rhizopium and hibernate—lightly, as it turned—in the scroll-stacks of the great library.

Thus it transpired that the closely guarded arcane knowledge for which Uvumbra Ovis had sold the lives of a city, an army, an Emperor, and himself, lay open to the elements, for the next passerby to inspect at his leisure. And in spite of the isolation of Rhizopium and its recent ill repute, another traveler came to the empty city, by and by…

~*~

As General of the Imperial Army, Zyzotha's younger brother was perpetually kept on the frontier of the tropical super-continent, pushing the empire of Commoriom out into backwaters and jungle hinterlands where the subjects could scarcely be told apart from the animals they ate, and that ate them.

To survive his brother's ambitions, General Uzotha had to be as fierce, as clever and as arrogant as the Emperor, but also far more ruthless. He believed in the legend of the crown of Commoriom as a standard that he must defend against a world seething with usurpers and enemies. The other standard, cherished in the dark of his heart, was the knowledge that his brother was weaker and less crafty than he, and the faith that the legend would come true.

He had left the frontier as soon as he heard of his brother's victory at Rhizopium, that old thorn in the side of generations of monarchs ever since Commoriom was but a rude settlement. When he heard that the occupation had turned into a parade of catastrophes, he forced his men and beasts to run at full charge. The trail he followed from the upper steppes of Gondwanaland was littered with the bodies of the unfit.

And it must have been destiny that he arrived just when he did, and no later, for he dismounted before the tree-stones of Rhizopium just in time to witness the fulfillment of the legend of the crown of Commoriom as prophecy, and to step into the role of savior.

For what was it, if not destiny, that showed him the crown of the Emperor of Commoriom, stripped from its unworthy pretender and seemingly floating in thin air tinged with a strange red halo, racing towards him, exactly as in so many of his dreams?

# Zolamin and the Mad God

## By Lisa Morton

As Zolamin drove the wagon bearing the stolen god out of the jungle and onto the main road heading west, she heard the first cries of pursuit behind her.

She'd hoped for a wider lead; the theft had been accomplished quickly and quietly. She'd dragged the carcasses of the four guards and one priest she'd slain into the thick growth near the temple, had maneuvered the god's heavy box onto a pallet, and loaded it up onto the wagon before the sun had risen. As she'd whipped the reins and urged her team of feathered gastorns through the jungle, she'd dared to hope for an easy escape.

But now, a glance back showed at least a dozen mounted Dulambri warriors giving chase, their spears held overhead as they rode one-handed on their dinictis, fierce predators they'd somehow subjugated. The Dulambri's oversized cats were faster than Zolamin's powerful, flightless birds and they had the additional advantage of not pulling a wagon laden with a god. Zolamin knew they'd be on her in minutes, so she considered her options.

The best seemed to be to slit her own throat and avoid the days of torture the Dulambri would inflict for the sacrilege she'd committed.

She thought back to everything she knew about the Dulambri, hoping to find some tribal flaw she could exploit, even the smallest advantage – and she felt a tingle at the base of her skull, a prickling like a blade being drawn lightly over skin. She wondered briefly if she'd been hit by something the Dulambri had tossed or shot, and then –

The road before her fell away, replaced by visions that her mind could never have conjured:

*A clan of squat, furred Voormis divide over the worship of their gods, and the followers of Y'n-Tharqqua attack their brethren who worship Tsathoggua / they heft primitive clubs, bare their gore-stained teeth, and shriek the name of their god as they attack / the worshipers of Y'n-Tharqqua rip still-beating hearts from the chests of their enemies offering them to the sarcophagus that holds their unreasoning god / the victors build a temple to their god / artisans line the temple walls with intricate, obscene carvings / on a sacred day the priests conduct an orgy before the altar, a tangle of writhing limbs and orgasmic groans / the generation that springs from the ecstatic couplings are different, evolved, hated by their now-distant relations, and Voormis attack not-Voormis / unseen in his sarcophagus, Y'n-Tharqqua screeches as blood spilled in battle within his temple seeps in beneath the sarcophagus lid –*

Focus returned, and Zolamin found she was still on the wagon, her wrists bleeding where she'd wrapped the reins around them, the driver's bench rumbling beneath her as the gastorns pounded down the road. The sun was high overhead now, and a glance back revealed no sign of pursuit. Ahead of her, jungle gave way to veldt; she'd escaped, although she knew the Dulambri would be coming again soon enough.

She stopped the cart to check on the box; it was the size and shape of a child's casket, cast in some sort of metal that thrummed to the touch. The box was still safe and intact, secured in the cart's bed by the ropes she'd tied, undamaged by the violent flight…but she viewed it with fresh unease. The priest Nin Zaggadolh, the one who had hired her, had warned her about the mad god's visions, but she hadn't quite believed him; nor had she believed that this box – barely large enough to hold the body of a toddler – cradled a god. Now she knew the truth: That a mad deity named Y'n-Tharqqua slept in the box, his dreams sometimes escaping and afflicting any human unlucky enough to be nearby (the effect was permanent on males). She heard a shriek in the distance and looked up to see one Dulambri staggering down the road behind her; she drew her sword, but the screaming man fell to his knees while he was still a hundred meters away. Not yet dead, he crawled off the road into the thick brush lining it, his cries evidence of Y'n-Tharqqua's ability to inspire madness. She knew the rest were farther behind, sanity lost forever.

She thought herself lucky that the Dulambri warrior caste did not accept women.

~*~

Her gastorns managed to keep up a steady pace until nearly sunset. They'd left the jungle behind, and now headed southwest over the open country that separated the lush, primeval landscape of the jungle and eastern Hyperborea from the plains near Tscho Vulpanomi. She'd have two days' ride before she'd reach the city-state of Dhaq Maqqun, home of the Maqqi clan that had hired her to retrieve their god. Then she could receive her final payment, and consider this damnable job done.

Hard to believe that she'd first met the priest Nin Zaggadolh only a week ago, in a crowded, raucous tavern called The Broken Blade at the treacherous north end of the Hyperborean capital city, Uzuldaroum. Zolamin kept a room above the tavern; the owner, Amarkosa, was a former comrade-in-arms who'd turned to bartending after he'd lost one leg in a battle – a battle that Zolamin had pulled him from – and he remained the only man alive whom she truly trusted. He acted as landlord, agent, banker and advisor for her, and she paid him well in return.

Six nights ago she'd returned from a job protecting a shipment of jewels bound to a wealthy moneylender named Avoosl Wuthoqquan, and had just beaten a barbarian from the frozen wastes of Polarion at a dice game. The barbarian, a handsome brute who'd drunk even more than Zolamin, snagged her wrist as she left the table with her winnings. "You can best me at dice, girl, but let's see how well you do in my bed."

She'd grinned, but Amarkosa had shouted from the bar, "You, sir, would be well advised to release her arm while you've still got one of your own." The spectators had all guffawed, but the barbarian had flushed and yanked Zolamin close. "I think I can handle this –"

When she broke the bottle of ale over his head, he was only stunned – but when he found the jagged bottleneck pressed to his throat, he'd sobered up quickly. "You can leave like a good boy," Zolamin told him, "or you can leave like a dead man. Your choice."

He released her, snarled once, and left.

"Good boy," Zolamin muttered to his departing back, and those close enough to hear laughed in drunken appreciation.

Only then did Zolamin notice the man in yellow robes and strange tattoos marking his shaven pate. He locked eyes and approached her, bowing. When he spoke, his accent was not one Zolamin knew. "A thousand pardons, lady, but this humble supplicant begs a moment with you."

She glanced at Amarkosa, who shrugged. "One moment," she said, before asking him if they could use the private room curtained off at the rear of the building.

Once there, she'd listened as the priest, who called himself Nin Zaggadolh, related his story, in that guttural accent.

He came from a place called Dhaq Maqqun, across the great central plains, in the shadows of Tscho Vulpanomi. His people had been at war for decades with a rival clan, the Dulambri, who claimed to share blood with the Voormis, the half-human savages who had once roamed Hyperborea before civilization had begun to claim the continent. The Maqqi and the Dulambri both worshipped the same god, Y'n-Tharqqua.

"I know that name," Zolamin said, searching back through half-forgotten conversations, overheard snippets. "They call him the Mad God."

Nin Zaggadolh smiled wryly. "Do not the actions of all gods seem mad?"

Zolamin, who bowed to no god but money, had to agree.

The priest told her that his clan had lived with the god for decades, until the Dulambri had staged a surprise attack one night and, in the midst of chaos, had taken Y'n-Tharqqua. Maqqi efforts to reclaim the divine prize had so far been unsuccessful, and had resulted only in the deaths of many young warriors.

"The Dulambri are skilled fighters, then?"

Nin Zaggadolh shifted in his rough wooden chair, uncomfortable. "No, they're primitive and lack leadership. But…"

She had to prompt him to continue. "Yes?"

"Y'n-Tharqqua is powerful. He sleeps, but occasionally rouses… and those times can be dangerous for any who are not trained in serving him. These moments are no more than a sigh for Y'n-Tharqqua, but they provoke madness in men. We priests spend years training in mental disciplines to resist these…disruptions, but ordinary men – like our warriors – have no such defenses. We tried to instruct our brave soldiers before we sent them off, but they were unable to develop the necessary protections in so short a time. They all succumbed."

"So," Zolamin paused, thinking, before continuing, "you want to hire me to recover something that will, in all likelihood, drive me mad?"

"Note, please," Nin Zaggadolh said, holding up a finger for emphasis, "that I referred to our men. Women are less vulnerable to Y'n-Tharqqua's delirium."

"'Less vulnerable'?"

The priest nodded. "The god's visions target men's most worldly ambitions. Women possess different ambitions, and so will experience some of Y'n-Tharqqua's effect, but it will be more akin to…a dream that one awakens from, remembering."

Zolamin almost dismissed the priest right then. She knew that she'd never shared her male companions' dreams of glory and vast wealth – she wanted only to retire alive someday, and not to a palace – and so perhaps she would be protected from Y'n-Tharqqua, but she disliked the idea of stealing a deranged being that could force its way into any head. It seemed like a violation, and one that she, as a non-believer, had spent her life avoiding. She wanted no part of it now.

Nin Zaggadolh must have sensed her irritation. "We know of your reputation, and are prepared to offer you two thousand djals to start with, plus an additional two thousand if Y'n-Tharqqua is returned safely to us."

Zolamin blinked once, in shock. *Two thousand djals?* She'd just been paid fifty djals for a month of risking her life to guard a rich man's treasures. Surely rescuing a stolen god was no less offensive.

"Do you have the money with you?"

Nin Zaggadolh nodded and reached inside his robes, producing a large leather bag. He untied the bag from around his neck and set it before her. Zolamin emptied it out and found twenty hundred-djal pieces within. She examined them briefly to be sure they weren't counterfeit. When she was convinced, she returned the money to the bag.

"We leave in the morning," the priest said.

"Of course," Zolamin answered, as she slipped the bag's long tie around her own neck.

~*~

As dusk fell across the Hyperborean plains, Zolamin sought a safe place to pass the night. Amarkosa had told her that the Dulambri possessed extraordinary night vision as a result of their Voormis blood, and that her best strategy would be to hide from sundown to sunrise. She passed a narrow gully hidden by a rock outcropping; it was just wide enough for the cart, and she should be invisible with a minimum of camouflage. She released the gastorns to graze, ate a small meal of salt pork and bread, and spread her furs out on the ground near the wagon. She knew it would be safer to sleep in the wagon, but she preferred putting distance between her and the thing in the box that dreamed.

The stars faded in overhead, the temperature began its nocturnal plunge, and Zolamin pulled her furs tighter...but sleep refused her invitation.

She lay staring up at the ribbon of night sky framed by the sides of the gully, and she thought about what had brought her here, even before she'd made the deal with Nin Zaggadolh.

She remembered her mother, forced into a life of prostitution after her parents had traded her at the age of ten for a pair of oxen. Zolamin's mother had borne her while still a teen; her father could have been any of dozens of men. Determined that her daughter would not follow in her footsteps, mother had done her best to disguise the child's gender and raised her as a boy; little Zolamin had learned how to brawl and curse better than any other child before she'd begun to bleed each month. When her mother died at the age of twenty-nine, the bordello madame had given Zolamin a choice: She could leave, or she could take over for her dead mother. Zolamin had chosen exile, but soon found her fighting skills served her well; a few years spent scuffling on the streets of Uzuldaroum prepared her for life in the local warlord's army. She quickly rose through the ranks despite her sex, but left when she realized she could make more as a private mercenary for hire. Money mattered a great deal to Zolamin, because while she may not have possessed her male friends' vast ambitions, she still kept her own goal: She wanted to buy the brothel that had employed her mother and where she'd grown up. She'd buy the brothel, release all of the whores with enough money to live comfortably for the rest of their lives, and turn the two-story building with many bedrooms into a school for girls who had no interest in becoming wives or mothers.

Or prostitutes.

She'd always assumed that she'd be working for decades to save the amount of money she needed; she'd pictured herself taking on the new life when she was gray-haired and scarred from too many battles. But with 4,000 djals, she could quit soldiering now and settle down. No more risking herself every day for wealthy men who cared more about jewels and mad gods than mere warrior women.

Lulled by her simple dream of leaving war behind, she finally drifted into sleep.

~*~

The attack came several hours before dawn.

The high-pitched cries of the gastorns brought Zolamin abruptly awake. She instinctively reached for her sword and had just unsheathed it when the first Dulambri hurtled towards her.

She made out only a dark shape blocking out the stars above, but it was enough – her sword arm swung up, and she felt hot blood rain down. She rolled aside, swinging the sword, and something parted beneath it. Satisfied that the first attacker was dead, she crouched with her back against a rock and waited for the rest.

Amarkosa had been right about the Dulambri's night vision – the first attacker had lunged directly at her in the dark, while she'd relied on guesswork as much as input from her senses. She could only hope now that chance still favored her, even as her ears strained for sound, nostrils flared to catch an approaching scent.

The next two Dulambri made no attempt to disguise their attack – they screeched in the night as they leapt into the ravine before her. Zolamin caught the glint of moonlight on raised spearheads, then she threw herself to the left. Something sharp pierced her right calf, but the sudden solar flare of pain didn't slow her down – she threw her sword arm out in a wide arc, and her blade met with a descending spear shaft. She heard the shrieks of more Dulambri; she had no idea how many now filled the gully around her, but it didn't matter – it wouldn't take many of them to kill her. She would die here, in a crevice in the earth, the mad god reclaimed by the Dulambri while her body was left to feed scavengers and windstorms.

She stabbed blindly in the darkness, determined to at least put up some sort of fight even as she knew she had seconds of life left.

Whether it was the sound of clashing metal or the smell of blood that stirred Y'n-Tharqqua, she didn't know, but...

*She stood tall, victorious, still clutching a dripping blade, above a field littered with Dulambri bodies / she rode back to Uzuldaroum on a saddle ornamented with gold and emeralds / the barbarian from the frozen north stood before her, stripped, bound, erect, and she took him on a bed covered with the finest imported silk / she sat on a throne carved with skulls and monstrosities, as all of Hyperborea bowed beneath her –*

Zolamin jerked out of the vision, panting, heart pounding, trying to orient herself to the concepts of here and now. Now: Late morning, with the sun high, the ground beneath her already warm to the touch. Here: The bottom of a plains gully –

– and a man with a shaven head standing over her, dagger uplifted, ready to plunge it into her heart.

She acted instinctively, simultaneously rolling to one side and lashing out with a leg. She connected with his ankle and sent him sprawling. In that time her hand found her own sword and she rolled, coming to her feet. Her opponent stood as well, took one look at her, and fled. She started after him – and stumbled over a dead body. It was only then, as she struggled to her feet, that she saw the dead Dulambri. There were at least a dozen; two were still alive but whimpering, minds gone. One was beheaded, and she thought she'd done that; the rest seemed to have slain each other. A survivor crouched in the shadows of the gully, gnawing on one of his fellow's arms, and Zolamin took grim pleasure in ending his macabre feast along with his life.

She heard the sound of wagon wheels and gastorns' claws overhead just then, and stood stunned for several seconds, trying to understand what had happened: The man who'd nearly stabbed her must have moved the cart out of the gully before she'd regained consciousness. Now he drove it, urging the great birds on, the sounds already dulling with distance.

"Gods, NO!" Zolamin sheathed her sword, ignored the pain of a wound in her leg, and looked for the way up out of the ravine. Her mind was sluggish, still wrapped in Y'n-Tharqqua's visions of conquest and triumph. She pushed aside thoughts of armies bowing before her, of gleaming palaces and muscled slaves, and clawed her way up a narrow cleft. Some of the Dulambri dinictis stood about, restless at the scent of spilled blood; the heavily-muscled predators unnerved her, with their gleaming tusks and yellow eyes, but she had no choice.

She approached the nearest, warily, ready to defend herself if it turned on her…but it remained still as she mounted. It felt odd beneath her, not like the slender, tufted sides of a gastorn, but it responded to her kicks and sped off, following the trail of dust kicked up by the wagon.

Zolamin tried to think about the man she now pursued – *not Dulambri, too tall and hairless, familiar* – but her own thoughts flew from her more quickly than her steed's swift paws. Logic and comprehension were buried beneath wants and ambitions which she'd never had before. Desire – for money, for power, for sex, for worship – flooded her head. She had forgotten why she chased the man who'd stolen the wagon, but she relished the anticipation of what she'd do to him when –

It hit her, abruptly, a single coherent thought slicing through the vortex in her skull: These notions were mad, *she* was mad, just like all the Dulambri she'd left behind. Y'n-Tharqqua had invaded her mind and replaced her own ordered thoughts with lunatic fantasies. The priest Nin Zaggadolh had lied to her when he'd said women…what exactly was it he'd said again? She tried to remember…tried to recall the priest, and –

Of course. Nin Zaggadolh…that was why the man she was riding after seemed familiar. He had the same shaven head and sunflower-tinted robes that Nin Zaggadolh had worn. He was younger than the other man, but there was no question that he belonged to the same priesthood. But what was he doing out here? Why had he tried to kill her, then stolen the god Nin Zaggadolh had hired her to return?

Sanity returned as Zolamin saw the truth: She'd been defrauded as surely as any city dweller with a backache hopefully passing djals to the traveling salesman perched on the backboard of a gaily-painted wagon. Nin Zaggadolh had never meant to finish his payment to her; the promise of an additional two thousand djals was as illusory as one of Y'n-Tharqqua's visions. She hoped the money he'd already paid her was still safe with Amarkosa back in Uzuldaroum, and that the treacherous priest hadn't slipped into her friend's sleeping chambers and slit his throat in the night.

Fury over the possibility of injury to her friend – already mutilated by his time at war – drove Zolamin, and she spurred the dinicti. It responded with a burst of speed, and within seconds she was nearly abreast of the slower wagon. She drew a throwing knife from her boot, took aim, and the blade buried itself up to the hilt in the driver's back.

He clutched at the dagger, releasing the reins, and the gastorns began to slow. After a few seconds he tilted forward and fell. Zolamin saw the wagon bounce as the rear wheels rolled over him.

It was another five minutes before the birds came to a halt, and Zolamin was able to climb aboard the wagon. She quickly set the brake and checked the god's box, which was undisturbed. Then she rode the dinicti back to check on the priest.

He was dead, his blood leeching into the tan dust of the plain, his limbs crushed into new shapes. Zolamin searched him, her fingers reddened in the process, but found nothing.

There was no question, though: He was one of Nin Zaggadolh's men. Aside from the robe, his single undamaged hand had fingers too soft for a warrior, and he had withstood Y'n-Tharqqua's mental assault while she'd dreamed in the bottom of a gully. He was more muscular than the older man, but that made sense: Nin Zaggadolh wouldn't have sent a weakling out to take his hired mercenary's life.

Zolamin rode back to the cart and considered her options. She saw no other signs of pursuit from either Dulambri or Maqqi, so she thought she was momentarily safe. At least long enough to think:

She could return the god to the priest and threaten his life unless he paid her…but she'd be threatening him on his home ground, where he'd be surrounded by acolytes and guards. She dismissed that option.

She immediately ruled out returning Y'n-Tharqqua to the Dulambri.

She could simply ride away, leaving the box and its abominable contents here, to sink slowly beneath the plains dust. But then she saw herself in a year, ten years, twenty, thinking about travelers being driven mad in this area, dying after they'd wandered the plains for weeks lost to everything but spurious visions of glory. Perhaps Y'n-Tharqqua would even dream of her, and the mad ones would die cursing her name.

No, if she was going to spend the rest of her life imagining horrors committed in the name of Y'n-Tharqqua, she would find some pleasure. Money could buy her not just comfort, but more ways to salve her conscience. She imagined outfitting Uzuldaroum's liberated whores with not simply a converted brothel, but mansions and fineries. She no longer cared if these ambitions were her own; all that mattered was fulfilling them.

Surely a god would bring a fine price. She imagined someone like the ruthless and malicious moneylender Avoosl Wuthoqquan – for only a man like that would be able to afford to purchase his own god – being offered a deity that could induce mass insanity.

It wasn't enough.

Zolamin, furious with the desires raging in her, leapt into the back of the cart and stared at the god's box as if she could demand an answer from it. Driven by that thought, she untied the ropes holding the box. The lid was secured with a single simple metal clasp, held shut by a polished bone, which she withdrew. She threw back the lid and sunlight hit the interior of the box for the first time. When Zolamin saw what lay within, she gaped; then, as comprehension hit, she laughed.

Ten minutes later, when her hysteria had passed, she closed the box again and hitched the dinictis to the sides of the cart, then took up the reins. She'd need to sell the cart and the animals to realize her plans.

She turned the cart north, smiling as she drove.

~*~

It'd been ten years since she'd last visited the Sleeping Devil Inn, but the place hadn't changed.

It stood alone in the vast Hyperborean plains, at a nexus where three roads converged and the Eiglophian Mountains drowsed far to the east. Built of thick clay walls and looking more like a fortress than an inn, the Sleeping Devil had gained its name by enduring centuries of dust storms like a drunk napping through a bar brawl. The inn's cooks and bartenders were unremarkable (although their snake stew had earned them some renown, if not exactly for the taste), but the next nearest stop was a two-day ride, and so the Sleeping Devil was constantly busy.

Its clientele were what Zolamin was interested in, though. The outpost inn drew warriors, assassins, thieves, the occasional nervous merchant on his way to somewhere else, and youths who'd come here looking to make money. Doing what didn't much matter.

The place would serve her purposes well.

First she sold the cart and the animals. If her plan succeeded, she'd be able to buy far better soon enough; if it didn't, she'd be dead.

Next, she used the money to rent a room on the second floor of the Sleeping Devil and to buy two messengers. She offered a few djals up front and more when they returned with proof that they'd delivered. She knew timing the messengers was the most critical part of the plan.

She sent her messengers two days apart. Both returned on schedule. She paid them their remaining wages, and then waited.

It wasn't hard to spot the first contingent of Maqqi. They'd tried to disguise themselves as merchants and bodyguards, nearly two-dozen of them, wearing dirt-colored robes with hoods, but the timing of their arrival and the way they carried themselves – like priests, not men of business or security – was immediately transparent. As they entered, shaking off road dust and peering around, the heads of the Sleeping Devil's usual guests turned, weighing their worth. Zolamin hoped no one else would rob the Maqqi before her plan could unfold.

Seated behind a support pillar in the shadows of the second level, she looked down on the ground floor bar as they presented a heavy trunk to the innkeeper, who inspected it, then made a pre-arranged gesture.

The trunk held the money her messenger had demanded.

She moved to her room, which faced out onto the empty plain that stretched across Hyperborea. Perching in the window with a flask, she waited.

Several hours later, a lookout rode in from the east, leapt from his mount, and rushed into the inn.

After a few minutes, the disguised Maqqi appeared in front of the Sleeping Devil, led by the young messenger to where Y'n-Tharqqua's box waited, unguarded and alone, in the sandy waste. His task finished, the young messenger fled.

The lead Maqqi stopped, made a sacred sign, and threw back his hood. It was Nin Zaggadolh, as she'd hoped…because she desired more than just money. She also wanted vengeance.

The priest knelt before the box and tenderly opened it.

His scream of outrage was audible even over the noise of the inn below her.

She grinned and glanced at the wrapped bundle on the floor behind her – at the dusty blankets that held Y'n-Tharqqua.

The Maqqi turned back to the inn, drawing swords, and for a second Zolamin felt a stab of anxiety. If she'd timed this wrong, if her lookout had made a mistake…

The priests had almost reached the inn when the sound of thunderous paws rumbled across the plains. They stopped, peering to the east, at the approaching dust clouds that hid the riders.

Then, as they neared the inn, the twenty Dulambri warriors riding in on dinicti were revealed.

The Maqqi panicked. Some tried to rush into the inn, only to find the heavy doors already bolted. Left with no escape, they turned to face the enraged Dulambri.

The fight was bloody and fast. Twenty minutes later, only Nin Zaggadolh still stood, facing the last two Dulambri. The priest's left arm was already gone, and he staggered from blood loss and shock but fought on against the smaller Dulambri.

Zolamin was done waiting. She paid the Sleeping Devil's inn-keeper; her fee included a better cart and faster steeds, and a round of drinks that she hoped would slow any of the thieves who would surely pursue her. She unbolted the door and stepped outside, sword already drawn. She paused only long enough to slay the last two Dulambri, leaving Nin Zaggadolh to watch as she collected the money both parties had brought to redeem Y'n-Tharqqua.

"Whore…" It was all Nin Zaggadolh said before he died.

She had no time to spare for the dead priest, especially now that she had his god, his money, and his life. She whipped her gastorns; she hoped to make Uzuldaroum in two days, where she would sell Y'n-Tharqqua to Avoosl Wuthoqquan.

And then, once she'd claimed that final payment, she would kill Y'n-Tharqqua. Because what she'd seen in the box – what now rode with her to Hyperborea's capitol – was no god. When she'd looked inside the box, she'd expected perhaps a roiling cloud, a blinding light, something so alien it defied understanding…but she found instead something that might once have been human. It was no larger than a child, but pruned and bleached by the centuries; its hairless skin was grey, the eyes closed but fluttering beneath translucent, blue-veined skin.

The force of the visions staggered her:

*Y'n-Tharqqua is a thing of only a few millenia, unique and curious / he lives apart, watching, knowing he can never be part of the world but nonetheless fascinated by it / he watches the others evolve, fight, and slaughter / he falls victim to their avaricious thoughts, losing his own / Y'n-Tharqqua retreats into the solace of sleep, and his disturbed dreams repay the favor to those who drove him mad.*

The dreams ended. Zolamin blinked, to clear her vision. She still stood poised above Y'n-Tharqqua, whom she now knew was no god, but something that could be slain. She laughed.

Now she headed to Uzuldaroum, where she would live the last of Y'n-Tharqqua's dreams before ending the monster. She gave no thought to the forty dead men she'd left at the Sleeping Dragon Inn; she knew the Dulambri and Maqqi clans would recover, and would find something else to worship soon enough. Some part of her screamed in protest, told her to stop and kill the thing in the box, to give the money away and leave Hyperborea forever, to spend her life trying to forget Y'n-Tharqqua's cursed visions…but that part was buried beneath the weight of djals.

Instead, she gripped the reins tighter and thought about what name Hyperborea's grateful whores would call her.

# Having Set Out to Be Vanquished

## By Garrett Cook

**T**he toad," said the elder, "has eaten."

"Then he can eat again," said the young man, defiant. "I will be sacrificed. You will not stop me."

The elder shook his head.

"If we feed him again, then he will expect two next month. I cannot allow you to do that. Die fighting the Voormis, if you want a noble death."

A woman had taken her leave of the young man, and she had taken his senses with her, as women often do when they take their leave. He had come to the elder to tell him that he wished to give himself to Tsathoggua, the toad that was death. He could see no semblance of a future, no purpose for him as a craftsman, as a soldier, as a priest or as a man. And there were few in the village who would dispute this.

"I would die before I killed a single Voormis and men would die protecting me from harm. I want to be of help, and I could be of help by sating the hunger of the gods."

The elder sighed. The youth before him was obstinate, indeed unskilled with a sword, and showed no knack for any trade. And there was no persuading him otherwise, so all he could do was send the dead boy on a fool's errand during which he would, of course, be killed.

"Atlach-Nacha," the elder mumbled.

"Hmm?" the young man's ears perked up.

"Atlach-Nacha. You can give yourself to the spider."

The young man's sunken heart bobbed to the surface again.

"Is the spider a terrible, ferocious god?"

"Yes," said the elder, "one of the worst. Its hunger is nearly insatiable."

"Then I shall go forth and I shall feed it."

The elder embraced the poor suicidal youth.

"May your journey be safe as it can be."

He set out with the elder's blessing, dubious though it was, weaving, ducking and hiding, struggling to stay warm in the wide white wastes. Though he shivered, though he suffered, he was intent. He had surrendered the prospect of living well, so was unshakeable, imperturbable in his desperate drive to die well. In town, they would remember his name forever and they would speak of him forever as a noble, upstanding man who had chosen to die as best he could. The thought kept him warm and kept his eyes sharp for foraging and hunting.

Indeed, foolishness, death wish and lack of skill could not contend with his determination. He came at last to the cavern where he would find the spider. It shimmered with promise and its wide open maw brought to mind the hunger of the gods, a hunger he would sate to become a redeemer of men and a hero in the eyes of the villagers. He was afraid, in part, to die, but more ecstatic by far. He had meditated and dreamt of nothing; but, his journey blessed by promise of spiderteeth and eternal digestion and the time when he would no longer have to live with the burden of being the man he was becoming.

He entered the cavern, frightened of what was inside it, but with a heart that was joyful, perversely joyful to know that this had to be the place. Walking through, he found lizards of a million colors, birds of brightness, birds of strangeness, plants hanging upside down from the roof above him quietly humming songs, sawtoothed gnomic fiends who leapt from the dark to frighten him, then returned to the shadows, the unfathomable shadows they came from. He wandered a great while and in his wanderings, he felt he could find most anything here except the spider, except the promise of dying well.

He spent what felt like days in the cavern, days during which his zeal even for dying began to wane. There was no end of wonder and confusion to be had among the shapes and concepts around him, among the dreams and the phantasms, but there was not the thing he wanted. He realized that he had come to the wrong cavern. He had heard stories of this place and they brought little consolation. The cavern was connected to the spider's lair, but the caves did not meet for a great long way and he was sure to perish in here among the archetypes before he could reach the spider.

The girl frightened him at first. He was sure that she would peel away her face and reveal something foul beneath it. She was not a day over thirteen, dusky skinned, hair thick darkness, opaque shadows. Her dress was white as she was dark, her feet bare. She held a candle and the fiends that would frighten backed away from her.

"You are tired and hungry," she said.

"Are you him?" he asked her, not quite lucid.

"You are tired and hungry," she said, cutting through the night with her little candle, "rest and eat."

"I will not rest until I find him. I need the spider."

"Rest and eat," she replied.

And he felt the urge to rest and eat. He hated her for the urge to rest and eat. She made him feel less than a man, tinier and slighter than her, and though her candle was substantial, she was tiny and slight indeed. He followed her for not very long. Her home was close, or it wasn't and she moved quickly. It couldn't matter less which was which. The cabin was full of light and the smells of better food than he deserved. This wasn't the way to death but he did not turn away.

"You're welcome here," she said, "my mother and sister are always expecting. Rest and eat."

He came in and there was food upon the table. A girl was seated there, his age, not young as the dusky girl. Her hair was blood. Her face flushed. Her eyes green as green could be, greener than a man who dwelt on the tundras had ever seen, greener than the Earth had given up yet. Her dress was white and plain as the dusky girl's. Her smile was sad but inviting. It seemed likely to taste bloody as her hair, sweet as the hut smelled. He hated her because she distracted from the task at hand. The hut and the food and the rest distracted from the task at hand, the task of dying well.

"Will you sit?" she asked. And he would sit. He took a seat at the table beside her and the dusky girl sat down beside him. A white haired woman, old as any he had seen, was at a hearth nearby. She was stirring a cauldron as it cooked.

"Company. We've been expecting company," said the white haired woman.

She ladled the contents of the cauldron into three bowls.

"Don't look into the bowl," she said, "just eat. Can you do that?"

"Yes," he said. She served him a bowl. She did the same for the other women and sat down with a bowl of her own.

He tasted the soup. The broth was filled with chunks of meat that he did not recognize, but the taste danced upon his tongue, alternating between a great many flavors, but never did they clash. His stomach filled with joy. His body filled with joy and he thought of the only joy he'd known on his journey.

"I am looking for the spider Atlach-Nacha," he said between bites.

"Odd thing to search for," said the young woman with red hair.

"If he wants it," said the white haired woman, "he will find it."

"I want nothing more," he said boldly, "I have come to die in its jaws."

"Then you'll find it," said the dusky girl, placing a hand on his shoulder, "you seem like the type."

When he was done eating, the white-haired woman led him to a comfortable bed. He lay down on it with no reservations, no protest that his journey was slowed down. He dreamed of the spider's jaws again, accomplishing his quest, growing so big in the spider's stomach that it never needed to eat again. He sighed and moaned in his sleep until he was roused, suddenly, violently.

A young woman, naked and golden-haired, was lying on top of him. Her skin was wet and joyful, the weight against him felt nice. He tried to remember the woman who had once lain on top of him and what color her hair was, but it faded from his memory. The spider in his dreams and in his heart had eaten the girl that drove him to find it. Had she golden hair like this woman? Were her nipples and lips rose pink like these?

She brushed his lips gently with hers. It was not a kiss but an inquiry. His breathing grew heavy in reply to it, his manhood, numbed from cold and numbed from self hate, rose in reply. He did not know this woman but he knew her. And as she answered his body by sliding him inside her, he knew her better. She was smooth and life was easy and they moved together forceful but calm, whims uncontested, wants the same. Life grew quiet as he respired excess thoughts.

And as the scent of a man pleased and a woman pleased perfumed the night, he drifted to sleep again. He did not dream of jaws. So calm and clear and still was he that he dreamed of nothing at all. There was nothing he could have dreamed of.

When he awakened, a girl of around twelve, pale, covered in freckles, hair blazing orange, was seated on his chest, a mischievous smile on her face. He felt as if he had met her someplace before, but it could not be. He looked to his side, confused.

"My sister," the orange-haired girl declared, "has gone out to gather flowers."

"I don't know what..."

"Come to breakfast," said the orange haired girl.

She crawled off his chest and went to the kitchen so that he could dress. He did so hastily, remembering that he needed to resume his search for the spider. The village was depending upon his being devoured. There was no telling what consequences invoking the god's wrath would visit upon them. At least this is what he told himself. He was calm and satisfied and refreshed, and thus he had to return in his mind to his quest and the import of his life, which could be measured only in the gnashings of primordial teeth. He went to the kitchen to find a dark-skinned woman, face ancient and craggy, hair wispy and grey, at the cauldron.

"My daughter has gone to gather flowers," said the old woman, "we will eat when she returns."

"I thank you for your hospitality," he said, "but I will have to take my leave. I am seeking the spider Atlach-Nacha. I am to be sacrificed, so I will need to move fast, lest the spider be displeased and visit pain upon my village."

The orange-haired girl giggled.

"Sacrificed. You must be very proud."

"You may leave," said the old woman, "if you wish."

"Thank you," he said, "for understanding. It is most important that I find the spider."

Though he said this, he took a seat instead of heading out the door. It would be unwise of him to embark on this journey with anything but a sharp mind and a full stomach. Even though he was seeking death, he was moving with purpose, and to move with purpose takes strength, insight and energy. There was also a part of him that had a sneaking suspicion that these three women knew something of Atlach-Nacha and if he stayed here to eat, he would be able to find something out, perhaps even the location of the monster's lair.

The blonde girl soon returned, in her arms a bundle of flowers of all imaginable colors, which she solemnly handed to the old woman. The old woman kissed the blonde girl on her forehead and tossed the bundle of flowers into the cauldron, filling the kitchen with a sweetness that made the young man's stomach growl, but made his heart feel very light indeed.

The blonde girl embraced him, kissing his lips.

"I am grateful that you decided to stay and eat," she told him, "the spider is fierce."

"What do you know of him?"

"He sits," she said, "between here and the world of dreams. Do you ever dream?"

"Only of the spider," he said.

Her eyes moistened with tears.

"That's terrible."

"We should talk of other things," said the old woman and the young man was quick to comply. They conversed, laughed, ate and drank through the day. They got up and danced, all four of them, to a music of no discernible origin. The name of the spider was not spoken. The jaws of the spider were not contemplated. The young man felt as if the world was oddly fresh and beautiful and though he was still in a cavern, vast. They were together until nightfall, full and content.

"It is late again," said the old woman, "you should stay in this place."

He did not protest or bring up his quest or the jeopardy his village would be in if he were to accept their hospitality another night. He stayed up with them until the time came where he was weary to tuck himself into the comfortable guest bed and turn in. And when he did, he was at ease, not anguished not tossing, fright far away from him. He dreamt of nothing and was not jarred by the hand on his face that awakened.

The young woman's skin was a healthy brown, her hair black as black could be, her waist slender, her legs long and powerful, her buttocks round and firm, her breasts heavy with dark nipples, her mouth small and thin. Her brown eyes were calm, but passionate and expectant. She was lying beside him, quiet, naked and ready for his touch. He traced her body with his hand, letting out a sigh that grew tall and vast in the quiet of the hut at night. He let his lips follow where his hands had traced, then continued downward feeling the bristles of dark pubic hair against his face, smelling her excitement and at last planting his lips on her, thrusting his tongue into her and drinking deep of her until the quiet vanished, replaced by pleas for pleasure. Pleas that he answered joyfully until once again sleep claimed victory over him.

No noise til morning when he was roused by a willowy whiteness, young, platinum, around the same age as the dark haired girl he first met and the redhaired girl who had roused him the previous day. The women of the house seemed to grow young and old as he slept, one a child, one a crone and one a woman his age. Such things made sense in the cavern. The blonde was a joyful and quiet child, rousing him with only a soft touch on the cheek and a whisper of "breakfast is ready". And from the smell of roasted meat, he could tell it was.

Though the old woman cooking was ancient, her red hair had only faded slightly into a pinkish color. She spooned him some soup quietly, a sharp, vulpine smile upon her face.

"I trust you had a pleasant sleep," she said.

The dark haired girl, already up and seated at the table looked nonplussed.

"Mother!"

The blonde tried politely to hold back laughter.

"We're all women in this house. We all know what goes on in it."

The young man could not help but blush.

"It… it was a nice night."

The old redhaired woman laughed heartily.

"I'm certain it was. Eat up. Tell us about love."

"Love?"

"Yes," said the blonde, "I would like to hear you speak about love."

The young man had not thought to speak about love before. It had only brought him pain; it had led him, in fact, to his quest to be eaten, and to this cavern. He spoke of his love and of the man she had chosen instead and of the betrayal and the disappointment and of the loss and the unworthiness. He did not speak of the spider but of what had brought him to the spider. The spider was far from his mind. He spoke then of the night he had with the blonde and then with the dark-haired girl and of the satisfaction he had felt staying in this place.

The red-haired old woman planted a kiss upon his forehead.

"And you are welcome here as long as you would stay."

"I do not know," he said, "how long I will stay."

"As long as you will, you will find what you desire."

And there was no more talk of staying or going from there. He enjoyed the company of the women; they were full of stories and songs, as one could truly only expect from residents of the cavern. They had chores to do about the cottage that made him feel useful and the dark-haired girl made him feel quite comfortable as he sat and rested his head in her lap. He spoke and laughed and sighed with contentment and the sighing became yawning and night came round again. Though he had only stayed there three days, he treasured the days and nights in this place equally and felt a certain amount of both excitement and regret as he turned in.

Kissed out of slumber, the red-haired woman he saw on his first day at the cottage lay beside him. She clutched his hand tightly and smiled at him, warm as the phoenix plume of her hair, cool and soft as her snowy skin. The kisses they shared were long but gentle then grew in ferocity sharing blood drawn from bitten tongues. The fervor between them grew, taking from the place where they lay into itself, timeless, above and beneath judgment. They loved and played fought at once until nothing was left in them and they needed to rest.

He stayed there through cycles of lovers, sisters and mothers, nights without judgment, days without consequence. He stayed there and forgot sacrifice and the name and the face of the one that had driven him to this place and the end of his life. He stayed and he became joyful, eager for the evening and eager for the morrow. He grew to love the three equally, for their words and their cooking, and their company and their sharp insights and their loving touch. If forced to choose, his heart would shatter but he would never be forced to choose by them. This place was not for that.

But as a man who set out to be vanquished, there came a day when he dreamt once more of the spider and its jaws and the salvation of his village and the purgation of all that he had brought with him, things he had thought were purged among the women. He awakened and there was no bed and there was no house and he was alone once more among the gibberings of the archetypes and the objects without meaning and the objects too full of meaning to comprehend them.

He tried to call out the names of the women and beg for them to come back to him and beg for him to take him back to the place that he had left, a place he knew in his heart was out there somewhere. Heart heavy, he set out, not knowing if he would find the spider or if he would once again see joy and hope and potential. He wandered intent but aimless, full of fear, knowing that he would find whatever he desired.

# The Lost Archetype
## By Brian Stableford

Under normal circumstances, Durul Nariban would never have gone into the cave, because going into caves in the remoter slopes of Eiglophian Mountains was, in general, a very unwise thing for a human being to do. Even if one did not believe—as he did not—in four out of five of the monsters described in fireside tales, including most of the bastard spawn of the allegedly-beleaguered toad-god Tsathoggua, there was no doubt at all that Voormis still existed in the black peaks, and were extremely ill-disposed to humans, not least because persecution by human hunters had driven them to live in caves. Circumstances, however, alter cases, and when a man is being pursued by a dozen-strong gang of heresy-hunters avid for their ration of sacrificial blood, led by a crazed and vengeful priest like Yziug Imnuv, there are times when a sufficiently unobtrusive cave seems attractive, because, rather than in spite of its darkness and narrowness.

The narrowness, in particular, seemed attractive. Durul Nariban had never seen a Voormi in the flesh, but they were reputed to be large, and he was glad to suggest to himself that any gap through which he, a thinner than average specimen of paltry humankind, could only squeeze with difficulty, was unlikely to seem hospitable to a furry giant.

The last thing he was expecting to encounter in such a place was a snake, but when he felt something glide smoothly over his shoulder, around his neck, and then down his arm, it merely seemed that his run of bad luck was continuing to exercise its obstinacy.

Ever-resourceful, Durul Nariban immediately conceived the bold plan of grasping one end of the snake—preferably not the end with fangs, although that would be a matter of chance—pulling it clear of his body and cracking it like a whip, thus, perhaps, dislocating its spine. In the darkness, however—for the dawn light was only just beginning to filter into the narrow cave-mouth, and his eyes had not yet adapted to the gloom—he could not see the slithering creature at all, and his ardently groping hands not only failed to find an end, fanged or otherwise, but failed to grip the creature at all, even as it curled swiftly around his midriff and formed itself into a kind of makeshift belt, wound three times around his waist.

Although he could feel the pressure of a strange surface against his own, which certainly gave the impression of a cylindrical entity at least as long as he was tall and slightly thicker than his thumb, when he tried to grasp it and pull it off he could not do it. His fingers simply could not get a grip, as if the surface were somehow immune to friction, perhaps even devoid of true substance. Nor, when he had recovered from his panic sufficiently to reflect, did the soft surface seem scaly upon the flesh of his belly, as a snake's would have done, but more akin to the texture of some luxurious and precious fabric. It was certainly not hempen, but the idea that the entity was not, after all, a creature of flesh and blood caused him to relabel it mentally as a rope.

The idea of a rope was far less intimidating than that of a snake, and he wanted to gather whatever crumbs of self-confidence he could, for the ongoing ordeal.

When he had made that mental adjustment, he felt the odd sensation that the entity was somehow satisfied: that it was content, for the time being, with the substitute identity in question…at least until it could find a real one.

His hands, having given up trying to grip the remarkable entity, reached out to either side to support him against the walls of the cave, lest he fall over under the pressure of his exhaustion, but the harsh stone walls were far too cold for comfort, and there was, after all, no reason at all why he should stand up, given that his legs were aching horribly. Durul Nariban therefore let himself ease down into a sitting position, put his elbows on his knees and his head in his hands and cursed his fate.

"Even if you were a real belt," he said bitterly, you'd be no use to me." It was, alas, true. He had been in bed when Yziug Imnuv had led his acolytes to seize him, trying to take him by surprise in the small hours, and he had been forced to flee in his nightshirt, only having only time to put on his clogs before leaping through his window and sprinting away.

His nightshirt had been comfortably warm in his bed, beneath his rug, but it was no longer warm now that he was half way up the mountain, having run for more than three hours. He had gone up the slope because he thought that his pursuers might lose their enthusiasm more easily if forced to go uphill, but he had obviously underestimated Yziug Imnuv's bloodlust and his authority over his followers. The advantage of his youth had only enabled him to gain a hundred paces in the space of those three hours, and he had to suppose that the hunters would find the cave eventually, now that daylight had come.

"I'll just have a rest," he said to himself, "and then I'll continue up the mountain. I'll shake them eventually, even if I have to go all the way to the peak." He spoke aloud, albeit in a whisper, because there was some slight comfort in hearing the sound of his voice.

The voice that replied to him made no sound at all—and could not, therefore, really be a voice, as such—but he understood it nevertheless, and understood, too, that he was "hearing" in his guts rather than his ears.

"Best go down, not up," said the unvoice. "Go up, and you'll probably run into the Voormis—and that will work out just as badly for you, as for me."

It was no time for debating the limits of the possible, so Durul Nariban simply accepted the fact that the temporary rope had spoken to him. He focused on the essential point.

"Voormis?" he queried, in a tone a little too shrill to qualify as a whisper.

"Six of them," the unvoice confirmed. "Led by the last of the Voormi sorcerers, at the extreme edge of desperation. They went up to the peak to conduct their rite, and then headed down again, when I gave them the slip."

Had it been a mere matter of arithmetic, the number of Durul Nariban's pursuers would have outmatched the one quoted by the temporary rope, but one of the furry monsters had to be reckoned equivalent to at least two humans, and he guessed that even a crazed priest of Yhoundeh possessed by evil intentions and bloodlust was probably not as dangerous as the last of the Voormi sorcerers at the extreme edge of desperation.

Durul Nariban did not waste time contemplating the eccentric symmetry of the fact that while the heresy-hunters had been pursuing him up the mountain, the Voormi had apparently been pursuing something or other down the mountain, and that both quarries had taken desperate refuge in the same cave. Ever the optimist, he wondered, instead, what might happen if the Voormis who were coming down should happen to run into the humans who were coming up, while he and the temporary rope were able to hide out on the sidelines. His ready imagination showed him a satisfying shower of severed heads, torn limbs and glorious fountains of blood.

Perhaps, after all, he thought, things were not as bad as they seemed.

"And what would you do then?" asked the unvoice, whose possessor was manifestly not given to reckless optimism.

It was a good question. Durul Nariban had a sneaking suspicion that he would not simply be able to go home. Although, technically speaking, he had been declared outcast and fair game for murder on the grounds that he was a secret worshiper of the forbidden god Tsathoggua, everyone in the village knew that the real reason was that he had seduced the youngest wife of the headman, Kokol Ammunix— or Kokol the Mighty, as he liked to call himself—who also happened to be the elder brother of Yziug Imnuv, high priest of Yhoundeh, the unforbidden goddess. Everyone in the village probably sympathized with him, if only secretly, because they were just as sensitive as he was to the horrid unfairness of Kokol Ammunix having six very attractive wives that he had no hope of satisfying, while there were good men and true who would never get the chance to try. That did not mean, however, that anyone would even be tempted to try and defend him against the supposedly-legitimate wrath of Kokol the Mighty, who would not be the village headman had he not had more than a little entitlement to his soubriquet.

"There's a lot more to Hyperborea than your village," the unvoice pointed out. "You'll have to go back down the mountain eventually, if you are able to give your pursuers the slip. Perhaps it's time to broaden your horizons."

"And you want me to take you with me," Durul Nariban deduced. "That's why you've wrapped yourself round my waist, pretending to be a coil of rope. I suppose I ought to be glad that you didn't continue pretending to be a snake."

"I'm not pretending," the temporary rope replied, "and I didn't have a choice. That's not how it works."

"How does it work?" asked Durul Nariban, unable to resist the pressure of curiosity even in the darkest of circumstances—although the sun was a little higher now, and his eyes had adapted to the gloom well enough to show him the surfaces of the surrounding walls, so the circumstances were not quite as dark, at least in literal terms, as they had been. On the other hand, the space in which he found himself was exceedingly confined—there was no convenient tunnel leading deep into the heart of the mountain, into which he might go in the hope of finding another exit—so it was not entirely clear that the metaphorical darkness of circumstance had been alleviated at all.

"It's an essentially mysterious process," said the unvoice, providing an answer of sorts to his question. "The sorcerer didn't understand it either. Not too bright, the Voormis, especially when it comes to philosophical matters."

"Bits of rope aren't exactly renowned for their intelligence," Durul Nariban pointed out.

The rope seemed to tighten momentarily about his midriff, but if the action was intended as a threat it probably didn't work as intended. The rope's strange lack of substance caused it to seem as if it were sinking into his flesh rather than squeezing it, almost as if it were trying to fuse its mysterious unsubstance with his own all-too-substantial and bitterly complaining flesh, but not quite succeeding. "It obviously doesn't work that way either," Durul Nariban observed. "Why are the Voormis chasing you?"

"They want me to become a monster capable of exterminating humankind."

"But you can't?" said Durul Nariban, hopefully.

"I probably could," the unvoice replied, "but I can't do it just by wishing, any more than they can. Nor do I believe there's magic enough even in the Book of Eibon to force or control the process. On the other hand, I'd never have believed that a hairy sorcerer, even on the edge of desperation, could conjure a nascent archetype out of the mists of being, so I could be wrong."

A dozen questions immediately sprang to Durul Nariban's mind, but he shoved them all aside when a shadow suddenly fell across the faintly-lit floor of the cave. Someone or something was approaching the entrance, still hidden as yet by the jagged lip of the opening.

Durul Nariban looked around desperately, hoping for some hidden corner where he might remain unnoticed by poorly-adapted eyes, but there was none. Whoever or whatever was about to stick a head into the gap to investigate the contents of the cave might not see him immediately, but would do so a matter of seconds.

The one thing that gave Durul Nariban hope was that as the shadow became more distinct, it also became obviously human. He did not hesitate, knowing that the advantage given to him by the gloom would be very brief, and that he had to make the most of the element of surprise. He gathered the remnants of his strength, mercifully reinforced by his brief rest, and hurled himself out of the cave-mouth, head down, already knowing approximately where he would have to aim if he were to ram his head full tilt into the searcher's belly.

Partly by luck and partly by judgment, he hit the target dead on. The man, who was armed with a spear—not the most convenient of weapons, in the circumstances—folded up with an agonized "Oof!" and fell backwards, badly winded. That prevented him from issuing an immediate call for help: a considerable advantage to Durul Nariban, as Yziug Imnuv's men had obviously split up in order to search the area after losing track of him, and there was no one else nearby.

Durul Nariban was distressed to see that the mountain slope was very uneven, full of gullies and asperities, which would make running downhill a more perilous exercise than running uphill had been, even by starlight, but he soothed himself with the thought that it would make things just as difficult for Yziug Imnuv's men, all of whom were momentarily out of sight, hidden by those same asperities and gullies.

His eyes immediately picked out a relatively smooth path, whose one disadvantage was that it was itself a ridge snaking down the mountain-side, on which he would be very easily visible to anyone on either side, whether upslope or down. The fact that one searcher had reached the altitude of the cave, however, suggested that the others would not be far away, and that there was a real possibility that none of the heresy-hunters would be in a position to climb the ridge ahead of him in order to intercept him. There was, in any case, no time for hesitation.

Rapidly, he clambered up on to the ridge, measured his stride, and set off along it.

Immediately, he was seen, but only from above, not below. The voice of Yziug Imnuv himself, marked by its towering rage, called attention to his presence and the direction of his flight, and the heresy hunters—who were spread out in the gullies to the left of the ridge—instantly set out to regroup and give chase. Fortunately, Durul Nariban had at least thirty paces head-start on the foremost of them, and they could not, as yet, move as rapidly as him. They did not even try to climb up on the ridge, but were content to run parallel to it, being unable to see, as he could, that the going would much more difficult for them than him.

For a moment, he was quite exultant—until he glanced at the right-hand side of the ridge, and saw the Voormis.

His first impulse was to curse his luck, realizing that if the furry ape-men had only come down the slope a little was further around the mountain they might indeed have run into the humans coming up, and his lovely dream of soaring body-parts and jetting blood might actually have come to pass—but his diehard optimism told him that all was not yet lost for that particular dream, even though the ridge was now between the humans and the Voormis and neither party could presently see the other.

On the other hand, he was obliged to take note of the fact that, whether or not they were able to see and recognize the rope wound around his waist, the Voormis were now giving chase, and were highly unlikely to treat him any more gently than the villagers, if they caught him.

He had, at any rate, no alternative but to run, as fast and as far as he could. That is what he did, hurtling down the mountain on what seemed, at times, uncomfortably like the top of a fence or the edge of a jutting sword-blade.

The simplicity of the action gave him a little time to think again, and he recalled once having heard a story—obviously false, since it was one of those stories that, if true, could never have been told, because its protagonist ended up dead—about a certain Ralibar Vooz, who had allegedly visited the cavern where the strangely insubstantial archetypes of Earthly species lived a curious semi-existence. Clearly, Durul Nariban thought, surprised at the keenness of his own logic, that peculiar underworld must also contain the "raw" archetypal un-substance of creatures yet to emerge on the surface of the Earth: new creatures, new monsters.

Evidently, the last of the Voormi sorcerers, faced with the prob-able imminent extinction of his race, had made a desperate attempt to turn the tide of destiny by somehow conjuring up a quotient of that raw archetypal unsubstance—a nascent archetype—in the hope of forging some kind of hideous predator or parasitic plague capable of driving humankind to extinction, instead. Alas for the Voormis, and perhaps for the nascent archetype too, that wasn't the way things worked. The nascent archetype could not be forced to take a particular misty shape, nor could it make a final choice for itself, although it evidently had some capacity for reflexive provisional materialization, having gone astray in the material world.

"Have I got that right?" he asked the rope around his waist, certain that, even though he had not voiced his thoughts, his passenger would know exactly where his conjectures had led him.

"We would be more accurate," was the reply that formed behind his navel. Presumably, the rope was crediting itself with having inspired his insight—and who was he to argue, given that it had never entered his head before to employ a phrase like reflexive provisional materialization?

"So what do you expect to happen to you if, by some miracle, I can get you out of this?" asked Durul Nariban.

"I wish I knew," was the reply. "Does a tadpole know how to become a toad, or a nymph a dragonfly? The one thing I do know is that I'm not immortal—no nascent archetype has any god-given right to assume form and give birth to substance. I can be destroyed by brutal means. And once again, it's we who'll be doing the getting me out of this, if it turns out to be possible. Do you really believe that you're as sure-footed as this, without the kind of help that I can give you?"

Like all natural optimists, Durul Nariban was not starved of self-regard, and really had believed, up to that point, that the magnificent grace and speed of his flight along the narrow, steep and often treacherous ridge of rock had been due to his natural agility and athleticism, but once the doubt had been planted in his mind he had to concede that the temporary rope might not be wrong. He really was doing amazingly well, leaving Yziug Imnuv's men further behind with ever soaring stride he took, and the Voormis too.

Indeed, in spite of the fact that the Voormis were mountain-dwellers, he seemed to be leaving them even further behind than the villagers, perhaps because their giant size required stouter legs, which were undoubtedly sturdy but not exactly nimble.

Durul Nariban would, of course, have preferred the humans and the Voormis been able to keep pace with one another, thus facilitating a collision of agendas when the ridge finally petered out and allowed the two sets of pursuers to perceive one another, but he tried to be philosophical about it.

In fact, when the ridge did peter out, the two groups of pursuers would probably still have been unable to see one another, even at relatively close range, because it did not disappear until it had plunged into the conifer forest below the tree-line. There, the going became much easier, because the forest floor was strewn with a centuries-old layer of dead pine-needles and there was little or no undergrowth. Nor was it any easier for either party of pursuers to see their quarry than it was for them to see one another. Durul Nariban still had to keep moving, though; no hiding place he could possibly find could be reckoned safe, especially in broad daylight. If he paused, he would be lost.

Unfortunately, whatever help the temporary rope could offer him in terms of agility, it could do nothing for his weary muscles and overtaxed lungs. Now that the slope was less steep he could no longer summon up the illusion that he was half-flying, and he was very conscious indeed of his own seemingly leaden weight and the ebbing of his strength.

Now, he felt that he was staggering rather than running, and knew that he could not possibly be gaining ground any longer, even if many of his human pursuers must be just as tired as he was. It required all his reserves of optimism even to tell himself that at least Yziug Imnuv, who was possessed of a fine priestly pot-belly, could not possibly be getting any closer, and that perhaps his pursuers would be so strung out by now that their chances of falling upon him as a mob were distinctly limited.

"You have to keep going," the unvoice urged him, with an edge of desperation in its atonality.

"What happened to *we*?" Durul Nariban gasped. "How about turning yourself into something that could carry me for a while?"

"It doesn't work like that," the temporary rope reminded him, bleakly.

"Mysterious processes," said Durul Nariban, sadly. "As mysterious, I suppose, as the ways of the human heart."

"It wasn't your heart that got you into this mess," the unvoice told him, cynically. Evidently, it felt that there was nothing very mysterious about the ways of human lust, and their ability to override common sense and rational calculation.

"I'm just a poor material print stamped from the archetypal mold," Durul Nariban assured his passenger, even though he no longer had enough breath to make any actual sound as he formed the words. "Blame the archetype, not the victim." It occurred to him that the word *mold* had more than one meaning, but the pun did not amuse him. Puns never did. Nor did much else. Human life, as Hyperborea waited patiently and gloomily for the long-prophesied ice to devour and doom it, did not seem to be a laughing matter.

"You have to keep going," the unvoice insisted, evidently aware of the fact that he would soon be incapable of taking another step.

The forest was becoming mixed now, birches mingling with the pines, and even the occasional secular oak. The ground was leveling out. Soon, the cultivated fields forming a band around the mountain side, nourished by its various springs, would come into view...if he could keep going that far. There was at least a possibility that he might be able to find temporary shelter and food in some woodcutter's cottage or farmer's barn, where the news that he had been declared outcast might not have reached, as yet.

The rope was right. He had to keep going.

Summoning up his last reserves of strength, screwing up his eyes with the effort, he rounded a thicket and staggered into a clearing—and was met by a fist in the face that laid him out flat.

He had not been knocked unconscious, but that hardly mattered. The simple fact was that he was utterly incapable of getting up again. He was finished—and it really would not have mattered overmuch how many faces he could see peering down at him, although he could not help his heart sinking even further when the silhouetted head of the man who had punched him was joined by three others, and then by the shaggy head of Kokol the Mighty himself.

Kokol Ammunix certainly had a mighty voice, and proved it by roaring—partly in triumph, but mainly to inform any and all other searchers that the runaway had been found and caught.

Obviously, when daylight had come, Kokol Ammunix had summoned the entire village to join the hunt for the alleged heretic, and, while Durul Nariban had been running down the mountain ahead of Yziug Imnuv's acolytes, a much larger company of searchers had been painstakingly making their way up it, strung out in a line in imitation of the mesh of a inexorable net.

140

"Shall we take him back to the village?" someone asked,

"No," said Kokol the Mighty. "We'll kill him here."

"Shall I cut his throat?" asked another villager, eager to please.

"No," said Kokol the Mighty. "I want to watch the great lover dance. We'll hang him from yonder tree with that rope around his waist and watch him choke."

Still helpless, Durul Nariban felt obliging hands fumbling at his waist. For a moment or two he thought that the fingers would be unable to grip the nascent archetype, as his had been, so that their inability to detach it would at least offer one last petty frustration to his would-be murderers, but the entity seemed to have acquired more semblance of substance while in contact with his flesh, and the members of the murderous mob were able to uncoil it as if it really had been a mere length of rope.

"Thanks a lot," was the last thing Durul Nariban said into it before losing contact altogether. There was no time for a reply.

The villagers seemed slightly surprised, because he had spoken aloud and they assumed that the words were addressed to them, but none of them said: "You're welcome."

Eager hands immediately set about fashioning the rope into a noose. It made not the slightest attempt to resist or to lash out on behalf of its former protector.

Ingrate, thought Durul Nariban, silently.

Left to his own resources, and on the edge of desperation, Durul Nariban made an effort to sit up, but Kokol Ammunix planted a heavy boot on his chest and forced him to remain supine.

"Not yet, my frisky friend," the headman growled. "We'll wait for a few more souls to gather, in order that you'll have a proper audience for our dance. Don't worry; I won't wait for the entire village to gather—but Yziuf Imnuv really ought to be here, to send you to the afterlife with Yhoundeh's curse upon your head, as befits a filthy worshiper of Tsathoggua."

"And I'll depart visiting Tsathoggua's curse upon every witness to my passing," Durul Nariban articulated, hoarsely, although he knew that the gesture of defiance was pointless. Anyone idiot enough to believe that Tsathoggua's curse had any power to injure him was also probably idiot enough to believe that Yhoundeh's blessing had the power to protect him.

While the rope that was intended to hang him was secured to the branch of an oak, and Kokol the Mighty selected two other strong men to help him lift his victim up to place the noose around his head, Durul Nariban observed from the corners of his eyes that approximately thirty villages had now gathered in the clearing, including two women and half a dozen children. That was considerably less than half the community's total population, but enough to spread a tale far and wide in no time at all.

Then Yziuf Imnuv arrived, accompanied by three of the men who had followed him in the initial chase, and Durul Nariban knew that his time had come.

He felt strangely naked without the rope around his waist, and strangely alone. He wished that he had at least been able to put his trousers on. There was something essentially undignified about being hanged in a nightshirt.

Kokol Ammunix was not a man for undue ceremony, and certainly not a man to make speeches. Durul Nariban felt himself picked up and hoisted upwards. One villager climbed on to another's shoulders in order to place the noose around his neck. All in all, it was an absurdly awkward process, carried out in a stupidly ungainly manner, but it did the job. Durul Nariban was released, left to dangle on the end of the rope with a three-foot margin between his heels and the comfortable ground.

But he did not choke, and he did not dance. The noose—not such an ingrate after all, and perhaps a clever tactician—refused to tighten. Instead, the nascent archetype contrived, this time, actually to reach inside his flesh, seeming to fuse with his muscle and his bone, thus able to sustain him without constricting his windpipe.

Not knowing what else to do—and well aware that it could only be a temporary reprieve, while the villagers had so many knives, sickles and sword with which to hack him to pieces—Durul Nariban began to do as he had threatened, and improvised a curse in the name of the forbidden toad-god Tsathoggua.

Although he had no experience at all in such matters, being entirely innocent of the heresy charge leveled against him, it had the sound of a fine and hideous curse, perhaps because he was not improvising it unaided. The fact that he was hanging there, neither choking nor dancing, probably added an edge of plausibility to it that it would not otherwise have had. At any rate, the watching crowd not only failed to run forward to hack him to pieces with their miscellaneous blades, but actually recoiled in superstitious dread.

When he had finished the curse, Durul Nariban improvised a smile. It was certainly not a smile of triumph, because he was convinced that he only had a few seconds to live, nor was it a smile of amusement, because he really could not find much in the situation to amuse him, but it was a smile nevertheless, and the assembled villagers—who must now have numbered forty—all saw it, and sensed that there must be some malicious meaning in it.

Whether he was mighty in imagination or not, Kokol Ammunix was not a man to be intimidated by so slender a foe, even in bizarre circumstances, and he raised his own blade—a brightly polished sword—in order to take the lead, as was only his right, in the orgy of vengeance. As he took one step forward, however, to make up the ground that his involuntary recoil had conceded, the rope slowly drew Durul Nariban upwards toward the sustaining branch, still without exerting any fatal pressure on his throat.

Again Kokol Ammunix hesitated—but the idea that his prey might be lifted far enough to grasp the branch with his hands and swing himself out of reach into the crown of the tree cut the hesitation short. Roaring with wrath, he leapt forward, clearly intending to cut the dangling Durul Nariban in half, if he had strength enough.

Then the Voormis arrived—all six of them, including a sorcerer at the extreme of desperation.

The rational thing for the humans and Voormis to do would have been to join forces in order to secure their common prey, divide it up and go their separate ways, but that was not the way things worked in Hyperborea. Instinct trumped rationality, and the Voormis attacked the humans, probably without even being consciously aware that they were blocking the path to the nascent archetype.

Now the blades came into action—all except one of them directed at the furry attackers. The one exception was Kokol Ammunix's blade, which still directed the headman's ire against the seducer of his sixth and youngest wife, of whose lack of satisfaction he was all too well aware. Had he had time to take another step forward, the blow might well have been fatal, but the arrival of the Voormis had prompted him to strike too soon. Durul Nariban was able to reach up and grasp the branch, and swing his lower body out of the sword's reach, with an acrobatic twist as graceful as it was effective. Then Durul Nariban was able to swing forwards again, pendulum fashion, and kick Kokol Ammunix in the face as the big man's momentum carried him forward. He delivered the kick with all the power he could muster.

Under other circumstances, the kick would not have damaged anyone overmuch, but in the midst of a brawl with six frenzied Voormis, it certainly did the headman no favors.

Durul Nariban swung himself up onto the branch, and then sat on it to watch the carnage. In a way, it was disappointing; there were not nearly as many severed heads and limbs flying through the air as he had earlier imagined, and the blood-flow was more a matter of trickles than fountains, but, all things considered, he could not complain overmuch about the final body-count.

When it was over, all six Voormis lay dead, not exactly hacked to pieces, but very extensively stabbed, and seventeen villagers lay dead with them, many of them mangled is a satisfactorily hideous manner, including Kokol Ammunix and Yziuf Imnuv.

"Now that," said Durul Nariban, as he unwound the helpful rope from around his shoulders and draped it over the branch of the tree, "is what I call a good curse. Anyone else want to try his luck against the power of Tsathoggua?"

Unsurprisingly, no one did. There is nothing like a massacre, especially one involving monsters and a dead high priest, to summon up belief in the efficacy of curses where none existed before. When Durul Nariban let himself down from the branch and dropped to the ground, the surviving villagers literally cowered before him.

The village clearly needed a new headman, but the issue was not put to a democratic vote; there were no challengers when Durul Nariban asserted his right to the title by conquest. Only he knew that, strictly speaking, he had not really earned it. He maintained that position for many years, in spite of the difficulty of keeping all six of his wives satisfied, thanks to the awe inspired by the legend that grew up around him as the tale of his exploit grew in the repeated telling.

Durul Nariban's only regret, after that marvelous day, was that he had not wound the rope around his waist before dropping from the tree, and that when he looked up at the place where he had draped it, it was no longer there.

Privately, he always assumed that, in saving him from the fatal dance, it had somehow found its true vocation, and had undergone a metamorphosis that had taken it back to its own half-world, as the misty archetype of a new species of snake, or a new kind of flower—

but he never risked telling anyone else about that, lest it cheapen his personal mystique. He died without ever having confessed the secret of his adventure to anyone.

Remarkably, however, in the way that stories seem to have of taking on a life of their own, independent of any individual teller, let alone any witness to the relevant events, those who told his tale after his death soon begin to allege that he had met a nascent archetype in a cave on the mountain, and that his indomitable heroism had found a mysterious way to inform the lucky archetype of its destiny, not as the mold of any mere substantial species but as the archetype of an idea: the idea of black comedy.

We storytellers are, of course, secretly and cynically bound to believe that the final rhetorical twist in question is as nonsensical as the rest of the tale—but even we must concede that if there really had been any such archetype lurking in the otherworldly caves beneath the mountains of Hyperborea, as the continent waited for the all-consuming ice, it would probably have been one of the busiest of all, and perhaps also one of the proudest.

# One Last Task for Athammaus

## By Ran Cartwright

The shadows were long and growing longer with each night. The night, darker than before, smothered the glow of braziers and oil lamps that lined the alleys and byways of Uzuldaroum near the home of the aged former Headsman, Athammaus.

The whispers had been faint and distant for some time. Now they were near. And they spoke in a strange tongue to Athammaus.

Only at night.

Only in the dark.

Athammaus merely nodded and smiled. A faint chuckle now and again escaped his lips. Not that he knew what the words were or what they meant.

They were a foreign tongue from long ago. There was a faint remembrance. Perhaps they were a mix of tongues, languages.

Human and some blasphemous abomination. With hissing overtones.

Still, the old man nodded and smiled. *Bah! Too much foum-wine!*

Then the night came when Athammaus had a thought.

A strange thought. Something that he hadn't thought of for a long longtime.

Commoriom.

The ancient capital.

*By the Great Gods of Hyperborea…!*

He shuddered, sat back in his wingback chair, lit his pipe, and stared into the orange fire that danced in his fireplace.

*Commoriom.*

Why after all this time should he think of such a place?

He hadn't thought of the former capital since the night he spoke of its collapse and abandonment to the scribe who had recorded his story. That had been nearly eight lustrums ago. Seven lustrums after everyone had fled the city.

Long deserted. Now crumbling ruins. Overgrown with strange vegetation pushing up between blocks of granite and cobblestone, vines shrouding the once glorious marble architecture.

*The public square, no one has been there since...*

Athammaus sighed. The thought faded.

The whispers had returned.

And the dark, a sorcerous darkness that blotted out oil lamps and stars.

A shadow passed by his window, crossed the wall of his study, a strange shadow that seemed human, but misshapen; a black phantom.

The old man tapped his pipe out in an ashtray and rose from the chair. The whispers spoke. One last task needed to be done, they said.

The former Headsman of Commoriom nodded and smiled.

"Yes, yes, one last task," he muttered to no one but himself. "One last task."

Though he knew not what that task was.

The strange black phantom rolled slow along the wall to a door, reached out a blackened hand, and guided Athammaus from his home.

That one last task would take him back to Commoriom.

~*~

It was a single day's journey from Uzuldaroum to the ruins of Commoriom. But for an old man of Athammaus' age, it could take two or more days.

He had left Uzuldaroum in the middle of the night. Guided by the strange black phantom, he took to the old road. The unused road where none dared to tread after dark. Even highway robbers refused to venture onto the old road.

There were stories of terrible death and madness. Of people found nailed to trees, or hung by their feet from twisted branches, eyes plucked out or gutted with innards hanging like vines. Some had simply disappeared, the beginnings of wild tales and legends told around campfires.

Athammaus had no fear of such things. Such tales and legends.

The black phantom guided him. It was there, ever present, gliding through the night, whispering to him, soothing, soft, sustaining.

*One last task*, it said. Strange hissing words that Athammaus heard in his thoughts. *One last task.*

The old man continued on. Voices whispered, taunted.

Shapes moved in the night. More than the black phantom that guided his steps. Many more as he ventured close to gaze upon them.

Bodies he saw under the light of a full moon that fought its way through the ever thickening canopy of vegetation and trees. The moonlight illuminated a mist that clung to the ground and the ghostly shapes of bodies, headless bodies.

Few at first, then more, hundreds more. Thousands more.

All of them headless corpses aimlessly wandering about in the dark, looking for their heads.

Athammaus stopped, watched, and wondered.

Faint traces of recognition, dim and distant in the tattered rags they wore. They were criminals, all of them. Sentenced to death by decree of King Loquamethros, beheading their punishment to be carried out by the Headsman.

Commoriom's Headsman. Athammaus.

Voices began to intrude upon his thoughts, not the same whispering that had guided him, but the voices of the dead. The disembodied voices of those terrible apparitions that now wandered aimlessly before him, searching for their heads.

"You killed me, Athammaus," said a retched voice. "You took my head."

"It was my job...I..."

"You killed me too, Athammaus," interrupted another, "my crime didn't warrant such punishment."

"And me!" cried a fourth, "You killed..."

"Me..."

"Me, Athammaus...me!"

"And me!"

There was a brief moment of silence, then...

"We died, Athammaus, we all...died!"

"I did my job for King Loquamethros!" Athammaus cried angrily. Gaining resolute strength, he added, "You died, all of you died for your crimes! You deserved to die! You are naught but phantoms! Be gone from me! Now! Go!"

And they were gone.

So sudden.

Apparitions vanished in the night. All but the strange black phantom.

The former Headsman turned narrowed eyes of contempt to his phantom guide. "And you!" he shouted, "be gone with the others! Go!"

The black phantom faded and was gone as sudden as the apparitions had departed.

The old man stared a brief moment and then continued on the rest of the night, his journey uninterrupted by ghosts, the dead, the black phantom, or highway bandits that would never ply their trade along the old disused road.

Then just before dawn, just before Athammaus need turn his course to the north through the towering ancient jungle vegetation that crowded the old road to Commoriom, he laid himself down for rest.

And dreamed a strange and terrible nightmare.

~*~

*A hush had settled over the public square in Commoriom. Townsfolk had gathered; they were expectant, yet fearful. There was to be an execution. No trial, no tribunal, no setting of a future execution date. The execution was to be immediate. The victim was the deposed King Loquamethros. The new king seated in the King's Box on the edge of the square was Knygathin Zhaum. The horrible hybrid beast from the Eiglophian Mountains slowly rose to his feet; his yellow and black mottled skin rippled like a thick viscous fluid. Upon his head he wore the Royal Crown of Hyperborea.*

*King Zhaum pointed a black pulpy finger.*

*The Headsman understood.*

*Hands bound behind, the former king was forced down upon the eighon-wood execution block.*

*"Athammaus! Athammaus!" the former king cried.*

*Athammaus raised the great curved blade of his executioner's ax and let it fall with unconscious added thrust.*

*A clean cut severed King Loquamethros' head. The head pitched forward as the body lay across the block.*

*"Athammaus!" the severed head continued to plead.*

*"Take it away!" King Zhaum commanded from the King's Box at the side of the square.*

*Athammaus turned to the King's Box. The king was gone; a black phantom stood in Zhaum's place. And a low guttural laugh, slow and taunting, echoed across the public square.*

It was the last Athammaus remembered before he awakened on a new afternoon along the old road to Commoriom.

He sat up, dwelling upon the fading scene of nightmare - Knygathin Zhaum; the black phantom.

The former Headsman's eyes narrowed. "Zhaum," he muttered angrily, "so, this is your doing."

~*~

A mid-afternoon treat of carro-nuts and foum-wine was all that Athammaus required to put him in a frame of mind to resume his journey to Commoriom. He was well on his way down the old road, further than he had expected for his advanced age.

The vegetation was dark and dense, a myriad of colors, all tending to a strange ethereal dark mixture in the faded light and shadows beneath the towering trees; the vegetation gave off fragrant appealing aromas pleasing to the smell, playing with one's senses, and tending to make one forget the passage of time.

Overgrown boughs clung to one another high above, creating a tunnel in which to pass. Tall grasses pushed up between the flagstones in the road, separating the ancient construction, many of the stones cracked or split with age and weathering.

Again the voices spoke to Athammaus as if from afar. Strange and ethereal voices, musical in tone.

The black phantom that guided his steps had returned unbidden, floating amidst the trees, darting about the thick underbrush like a child playing games in the olden days of Commoriom's city park.

The aged former Headsman glared with distaste at the phantom. Such a strange thing it was, a shadow of black emptiness.

This phantom so much like Knygathin Zhaum in form, so much like the nightmare…

And the voices…so serene…

The scent of the vegetation acted like a drug; it dulled the old man's senses. Dimmed his awareness.

On the road to Commoriom...

He walked dreamily, the world around him now faded, distant; beyond his touch and understanding.

But he cared not.

The voices were there, speaking to him. Ethereal. Dream-like.

*One last task to be performed*, they whispered.

*One last task...*

"Are you too but phantoms of my mind?" he muttered in a brief moment of clarity. The question quickly faded and was forgotten. His thoughts drifted aimlessly.

He continued on from day into night, walking until he could walk no more. Then he sat before a campfire and listened to the night.

There were strange cries in the dark and the nearby rustling of underbrush. The moon had risen long before, still full, but very little light shown through the thickened canopy, just enough to cast strange elongated shadows that writhed across the worn and cracked flagstones of the narrow road.

Athammaus watched the shadows claw and twist as though they were alive, trying to gain some form of foothold to rise up and stand before him. But they failed and finally lay still.

The moon moved on with the night.

The softness of the warm air and the fragrant scent of the strange vegetation overwhelmed Athammaus. He curled up before the dancing flames of the campfire and spiraled happily into a drug induced sleep.

Even in his sleep the former Headsman heard the voices whisper to him.

*One last task for Athammaus*, they said.

*One last task.*

Then they fell silent.

Such a pleasant day on the road to Commoriom again gave way to a night of terror in the dream world of his mind.

~*~

*A dark cavern beneath Mount Voormithadreth.*

*Campfires dotted the cavern floor; their flames licked the darkness above, and cast writhing shadows low on rough stone walls.*

*There had been a long day and night of celebration among the gathered Voormis. They had taken four people captive, three men and a woman, Hyperboreans, no doubt come to the mountains from Commoriom.*

*They were of high standing by their manner of dress, and by their arrogant tone of voice and demeanor, having demanded their immediate release.*

*Instead, the three men of Commoriom were stripped of their clothing and bound to towering poles of wood, while their female companion was dragged away to another part of the cavern; her screams escalated to shrill shrieks that lasted long into the night.*

*The Voormis danced around the three bound men while some abominable travesty of priesthood stumbled forward with a small bowl of paint and brush. The Voormis priest painted strange signs and symbols on the flesh of the captives. No doubt something that represented their god, the horrid abomination they called Zhothaqquah.*

*There was a pounding of drums, wooden shells with human skin stretched across them, and frenzied dancing that reached a fevered pitch before everything suddenly stopped. Only the terrible shrieks of the woman could be heard echoing through the dark.*

*One by one each of the men were untied and brought forward. Forced to their knees, each in turn had their heads torn from their shoulders by the Voormis and impaled upon pikes that had been struck into the soft earth of the cavern floor. Their bodies were eaten, freshly gnawed bones discarded in a dark corner.*

*Only the female, Atalana, adviser and confidant to King Loquamethros, remained alive, shared in a most hideous and vile manner by a number of Voormis, and in the course of time she gave birth to numerous hybrid abominations.*

Athammaus awakened. Sat up. "Abominations," he muttered angrily, and shook his head.

The day had come, the fire long dead and cold.

The former Headsman of Commoriom sat for a moment and thought of the nightmare still fresh in his mind. Yes, it had been a nightmare. But more than that, there had been some truth to it.

Many years before a Commoriom delegation had been sent to Mhu Thulan to discuss depredations of the Voormis in the mountain passes of the Eiglophians. The delegation had disappeared and was never found. Their fate was a mystery though many secretly whispered the name Knygathin Zhaum.

Athammaus sighed. It was a long ago memory.

"Knygathin Zhaum," he muttered, eyes dark and staring.

~*~

The light of late afternoon was like dusk the closer Athammaus came to Commoriom. The vegetation was thicker, the fragrance more pungent, a cachet that took away the senses, made one see and hear things.

Real?

Perhaps. Perhaps not.

It mattered not to Athammaus.

He merely smiled, and continued toward the crumbling ruins of the once mighty capital of Hyperborea.

Twilight deepened; shadows grew long. The black phantom lurked amidst the thickening vegetation. The whispering voices told their stories to Athammaus, strange stories of places and times the former Headsman had never known, told in tongues foreign to the old man, yet, strangely, he understood.

They were tales of victory, pleasing to the ear. Tales of love, adventure, families, and conquests; of great wizards and sorcerers from faraway lands and the magic they performed, and of great kings and their courts and the ladies of the courts and the jesters that made everyone laugh; and of dreams that were real, and of those who had ventured to those Dreamlands and had stayed.

Amidst the cacophony of whispering voices, there came a single voice that told a different tale, a tale of foreboding, pain, agony, death, and resurrection to the world of the living dead, a tale of Black Rites and the blasphemous toad god, Zhothaqquah.

Then the whispering voice that had spoken of the dead fell silent.

Athammaus stopped; his thoughts had wandered, and the voices had slowed his pace.

Dusk was quickly turning to night. He would not make Commoriom before nightfall. Best to wait until the morn.

He kindled a campfire, spread his bedroll, sat and stared.

There were strange sounds there in the dark, and black shapes on the edge of the firelight. And somewhere nearby there was Commoriom.

His eyes and thoughts clouded with the night and fatigue...

~*~

The former Headsman peered across the blasted landscape at the crumbling gate of stained marble entwined with creeping vines.

Commoriom, a haunted ruin bathed in the light of the moon.

Here was the great gate to the once majestic city, fabled former capital of Hyperborea. Now mere tarnished stone, crumbled and collapsed, entombed in vines, vegetation, and towering trees.

And here where Athammaus stood was the blasted waste dump, a land spoiled and scarred as though blighted by some horrific pestilence, where Commoriom's executed criminals lay buried in nameless graves, executed by Athammaus on orders of King Loquamethros.

The earth beneath the former Headsman's feet trembled, barely perceptible. A slight crack; dust billowed, a small spiraling cloud unseen in the shadowed night.

Athammaus turned an eye to the gate. The strange black phantom stood there; it motioned for the former Headsman to follow. He did, and stepped lightly across the waste dump, trod on numerous unseen and unknown graves. The earth turned. More cracks snaked through the waste dump, more clouds of dust billowed in the dark. Athammaus paid no heed.

The blasted waste dump split, tore open. Earth crumbled into widening crevices. Decayed fingers of headless corpses clutched at the earth, pulling themselves free of their graves to follow Athammaus into the city.

Athammaus walked the ruined and vine covered streets and alleys; behind, unseen and unheard, came a horde of headless dead. They made their way to the public square that so long ago had served as the place where the king's justice had been meted out.

The Executioner's Square.

Where the eighon-wood block lay affixed to the flagstones, long weathered, aged, and stained with the blood of countless dead.

Where the horror that was Knygathin Zhaum waited. But not Zhaum as Athammaus remembered when he had fled the city so long ago.

They turned into the square and stopped.

The headless dead gathered behind the former Headsman.

The moon shown above.

An eerie incandescent yellow glow issued from the mottled flesh that glistened wet and churned like ocean waves under the light of the moon. Knygathin Zhaum had changed yet again. No semblance of humanity remained.

Here was a huge bloated black and yellow protoplasmic mass that had wrapped itself around the square, blanketing nearly everything but for the eighon-wood block and a narrow exposed line of flagstones upon which Athammaus stood.

The pulsing and hissing mass clung to the sides of buildings, slithered into cracks in walls. Black hair-like filaments danced along its rippling edges while tentacles writhed across the square, then retreated to disappear into the churning mass of flesh. A thousand yellowed eyes without pupils floated in the mass, turning their gaze upon the newly arrived former Headsman and the headless dead that gathered behind him.

Athammaus caught his breath. The scent was terrible, worse than the decaying flesh of a thousand fresh corpses.

"Why have you called me back to Commoriom?" Athammaus said, his eyes narrowed, voice angered.

"I have not," Zhaum hissed. The words echoed through the night air.

"I called you back to Commoriom," came a strange, familiar voice.

A hush fell over the square. The liches, victims of the Headsman's ax, crowded in. Across the square something dark moved in the Temple of Zhothaqquah.

In the silence, Athammaus turned a half turn.

And saw himself, Athammaus, the former Headsman, clutching the ancient copper colored and blood stained executioner's ax.

"What manner of sorcery is this?"he said. "I do not believe such things!"

"Our own thoughts and conscious brought us here," his double replied, ignoring the question.

"Our…?"

"You and I; yes, we are the same. Athammaus, Headsman of Commoriom. You and I. The same." He stepped forward and held out the ax. "Take it and execute me. Only in this way…"

"…can the city be saved and the people return," he completed his

156

own thought while reaching for the ax.

A brief pause, and he smiled. They smiled.

"We know this to be true."

Athammaus watched as he saw himself lean over the eighon-wood block.

One last task, he thought, and smiled.

There was a flash of copper. The blade arced, an instant of time, and the severed head, his own head, rolled.

So strange, this feeling of death…

"So strange, this feeling of death," Athammaus echoed the thought. His voice was torn, the words forced, strained. He opened his eyes. Morning had come, a gray overcast dawn.

Athammaus found himself in the public square.

He turned, and peered about through clear eyes.

The dead were gone, and the shadows, and the pulsing mass that Zhaum had become. All were gone.

The square was empty. Just the crumbling ruins and creeping vines and towering trees and shattered flagstones remained.

And the Executioner's ax embedded in the eighon-wood block, the blade and block awash in fresh blood.

The former Headsman's fingers wrapped tightly around the ax handle and pulled it free of the block. He slung it over a shoulder and started across the square, back from whence he had come. His severed head, tied by his long silver hair to his belt, bounced against his thigh.

Blood trickled. Athammaus grinned.

Something dark moved in the shadows of the Zhothaqquah Temple.

# The Beauties of Polarion

## By Don Webb

In the century before the coming of the glacier, the wise folk of Iqqua sought to stop the coming of the ice through sorcery and sacrifice. Kard Gha Vin, a wizard of great standing, counseled the Queen of Iqqua that the ice hungered for beauty. One need but watch the Northern Lights play over the ice at night to see the need the Ice had for things of beauty.

"Perhaps Queen Voorla, if we find the most beautiful woman in your kingdom, we can sacrifice her to the approaching ice and stay its advancement for years, perhaps decades."

"But surely Ri Kard Gha Vin, you jest, for I am the most lovely woman in Iqqua, perhaps in all of Polarion."

It had never occurred to Gha Vin that the queen might still consider herself beautiful. In fact her wrinkles upon wrinkles would surely have made her hate younger, more beautiful women. He pondered her well-known policy of retiring government officials to the foul smelling torture pits beneath her ancient castle as he sought for a politic answer.

"Of course, my liege, we would need to hide your loveliness for a season, so that we could fool the ice demons into thinking they had found the loveliest woman. We could not expect to buy time with any second-rate beauty."

"It would pain my subjects not to see their queen in her lovely form."

"Well, we shall do it thus: you will disappear the night of the contest, and the second loveliest women shall be proclaimed the winner and we shall sacrifice her and return you to your throne a fortnight later. The kingdom will be doubly happy. Its beautiful queen restored and the danger of the ice adverted at the same time. It will be a source of bardic empowerment for years to come."

So the word went forth to the towns and villages of Polarion, even to the huts of the auroch hunters, that a beauty contest was to be held in Iqqua, and the winner given a spray of ice diamonds, and crowned Queen of Winter. The duties of the Queen were not made clear, but certainly such a role in a land that had been marked by colder and more fierce winters for the last three hundred years, it must be a powerful position as well. Besides, the ice diamonds could buy many things.Many women sought the role, but three were early on seen as the most likely contestants. One was Rentha, daughter of the mayor of Iqqua, a blonde beauty with grace and charm. The mayor had been hoping to marry off to one of the richer households and the winning of the contest seemed a sure way to increase his daughter's market worthiness. Another contestant was Leetha, a raven-haired beauty whose father was a poor but honest hunter of mammoths. Leetha's slanted purple eyes gave rise to a rumor that her mother had been some sort of nymph or sprite, and her wild and uncouth ivory jewelry was much remarked upon. The third seemed the least of a threat, yet the red haired Zinoë, whose father dealt in rubies, had her champions as well. The names of three beauties were on all lips, and gold and orichalcum were wagered.

Queen Voorla was unhappy at the attention the three girls were receiving, so Gha Vin sagely suggested the Queen enter the contest. He knew that her entry would bring fear to the other contestants. In truth, everyone would assume she would win, and speculation as to whether the dark-haired girl of the wild or the blonde daughter of city life would come in second. The Queen was gratified. Gha Vin suggested that because of the Queen's beauty, she could be kidnapped the night of the contest. It would add great fame to the proceedings. Then her return, ostensibly back from another kingdom, would stay with her legend for years. Voorla was delighted.

"How will we manage the kidnap?"Various stratagems were suggested. Black robed monks from the south, red toga-wearing pirates from across the Hyperborean Sea and a doorway to another world were suggested and dismissed. Finally, the Queen's son Prince Haalor made the most interesting suggestion. The Queen could be made to disappear into a glowing mist. It would seem that the Northern Lights had formed a small cloud and sent it to earth to seize her majesty.

"That would make a delightful saga," said Voorla, "but how to arrange such a thing?"

"I know a sorcerer, a familiar of the toad god Tsathoggua, who is quiet adept at summoning various mists. He is well known at calling up the purple mist that is kind to dreamers and carries them off to the dreamworlds. He could easily summon something that shimmers with rainbows of beauty, mother. But do not mention this to Gha Vin, whose is a vain man."

"Who is this sorcerer?"

"Ommum Vog… someday he will no doubt be as renowned as the flying man of Mhu Thulan."

Prince Haalor desired the throne, and had been cultivating the friendship of the ruthless Ommun Vog for six years. Ommun Vog assured him that such a mist could be called. It is a sort of vampiric being that haunts the ruins of the world past Mars. It is easy to call it into the human world. One need only have the victim to drink a rather sweet tasting wine made of certain dark herbs. As the wine makes the eyes flutter and the brain grow numb, the vampire mist is called from the sky. It carries the drinker away from this world to serve at the altar of the Black Pharaoh for a thousand years. In many ways, they would be doing the elderly queen a great service. Her years on earth were destined to be few – though far too many for ambitious Haalor. Ommun Vog assured him that the iridescent vampire mists brought a great and wonderful intoxication, and by the time they had transformed the body of his mother into a temple servant that needed no air, Voorla would actually know greater happiness than any human being. Indeed, Ommun Vog assured him, he hoped to summon such a mist to carry his own body away from its deathbed.

So it was arranged that a yellow-skinned servant of Ommun Vog would visit the amphitheater where the contestants were to show themselves in various costumes  and portrayed their talents. The servant would present Voorla with a bouquet of roses that concealed the vial of the vampire-summoning drug.

A few days before the event, Rasul Menthag, the mammoth hunter, visited his lovely daughter.

"He had made a great sale of mammoth ivories to a wizard of Oggon-Zhai, Miluw Gupmire, who specialized in potions and philters. Rasul Menthag had traded a season's worth of ivory for an aging potion. If Leetha could induce her rival to consume the drink, Rentha would age some sixty years in the course of as many minutes. The wrinkled beldame would be awarded boos and cat calls, while second place would be awarded to the lovely Leetha.

Leetha, who shared her father's craftiness, immediately hired a one-eyed hunchback Zever Bepas to offer a magic potion to the charming Reentha. The toadlike Zever visited the Mayor's home. Because of his resemblance to Tsathoggua, the Mayor quickly believed that the short one must deal in true potions. Certainly his ugliness was proof of the paranormal. If the god could make one of his followers so ugly, great beauty must likewise be in his power. So the Mayor filled the hunchback's hands with gold, and bought the aging potion for his lovely daughter.Gha Vin had begun to distrust the Queen. She insisted that she had taken care of her dramatic disappearance the hour before the crowning of the Queen of Winter. He know that her vain nature would keep her in the contest until the end. She truly believed that the portraits she had painted over the mirrors of her palace were her true appearance. Of course, the judges would find in her favor, and the pronouncement of her as the loveliest woman of Polarion would invalidate the sacrifice of the second-place winner. Naming had a great effect in magical exchanges. The ice demons would never accept a second-rate sacrifice. As he pondered his dilemma, he was approached by the exotic Leetha.

"Oh wise man that reads the cold stars," she purred, "can you tell me who is the loveliest of all the women?"

"It is not my part to judge such things," said Gha Vin. "Judges far more perceptive than I say that her majesty is the loveliest woman in the kingdom."

"But you, my lord, who are not so intelligent, must see that the loveliest women of the contest are the Mayor's stunning daughter Reentha, the red-headed Zinoë... and some would say I -- if I may be so immodest as to speak plainly."

"Indeed, I think you speak truthfully. If unintelligent I were a judge, you would win."

"Sadly, I have heard that judges have been bought by the ruby merchant. Zinoë shall be our Queen of Winter."

"But she is not as lovely as you!"

"If only I could be the most lovely woman in the world that night!

Then the judges would vote for me."

"What would you give to be the most lovely woman in the world that night?"

"Anything, oh wise magician."

Surely the ice demons had no need of a virgin sacrifice, thought Gha Vin. So his worries over the Queen's actions were driven away by the clacking sounds of heavy ivory necklaces for at least a few minutes.

"I will send a potion to you just before the judging. Drink it quickly—it will only last for two hours at most, but you will be the loveliest woman in the world. Zinoë will have no chance, despite her father's gems."

The last night of the contest came round, and the stage blazed with light spells and gentle warm breezes blew at the command of Gha Vin. The lesser beauties were pressed into a songfest, while the four most beautiful women in Polarion prepared backstage. Each trusted in their beauty, and the evils wrought in their name. Zinoë thought of the handful of rubies that would buy the crown for her. Reentha greedily drank the bitter potion that her father had bought from the toadlike hunchback. The yellow skinned servant waited in the wings to hand the bouquet to Queen Voolra just before she was to step on stage. Gha Vin called his slave.

"You must deliver this to the lovely Leetha."

"How will I know her?"

"She is of brown skin and her eyes are violet. I think she is the loveliest woman in the contest, and after she drinks my potion she will be the loveliest woman in the world."

The slave headed to the amphitheater, but as fate would have it, he arrived at the same time one of Queen Vorla's serving woman had arrived. The serving woman would have been the winner of tonight's contest, if the poor could be thought pretty, but Iqqua had no such egalitarian notions. Gha Vin's slave looked upon the beautiful serving woman and thought only of her.

"Radiant one! I surely have a potion for thee! My Master told me to give it to the loveliest woman in the world, and that must be you." He held out the vial.

The serving woman snatched from his hand. "Then it is for my Mistress. Indeed, it would be foolish to speak of any woman as lovely as she." But her smile showed that she bought the slave's compliment. "Let me take it to her straightaway, and perhaps we can sit and enjoy the contest."

"Go then, my sweet, but truly. I say to you that should be the Queen of Winter."

So the beautiful serving woman ran to her wrinkled queen.

"A man brought this potion for you."

"A yellow-skinned man?"

Truth to be told Gha Vin's slave had a touch of jaundice. "Yes, my lady, he was of yellow skin."

The Queen said, "Tell no one that you gave this to me." "Yes, my lady," and off she ran to join Gha Vin's slave to steal away from their masters an hour's pleasure.

Queen Voolra drank the potion that Gha Vin had compounded. His knowledge of the art was great, for the potion removed the hard years and cruel winters from her face, softened her curves and brought a sparkle to her eyes that rivaled the Northern Lights themselves. She admired herself in a real mirror – one not painted with her face from long ago. She thought her loveliness must be what would call the iridescent mist. She proudly walked to the stage.

Behind her came Reentha, aging with each step. A yellow-skinned servant thrust a bouquet of roses toward her. "Drink the potion quickly."

Reentha asked, "Another potion?"

"I know not what you speak of, but the sorcerer said you must have this." So Reentha drank the second potion.

Behind her came Leetha, furious that Gha Vin had not provided the magic drug. She would have her father hunt him like a mammoth. She was already picturing one of her father's long spears thrust through him like a spit. Lastly came Zinoë, confident that her red hair would remind the judges of the rubies in their pockets.

Prince Haalor and Ommun Vog sat in the audience. There was something odd about Haalor's wrinkled mother. Haalor did not recognize the jewels or the dress.

"Be at peace, young prince," said Ommun Vog, "She has bought new things for tonight; you can't mistake those wrinkles. Look, the mist draws nigh."

Indeed, a shimmering eddy began to form in the air above her. Queen Voolra ran toward the mist, but it swirled down around an old woman, certainly not someone fair enough for a beauty contest.

As the mist began to lift Reentha into the air, she moaned in ecstasy. Queen Voolra leaped up toward the fog of dazzling colors, but fell back on the stage. Some of the judges ran forward to catch her,. Astounded by her beauty, they raised her up on their shoulders. Queen Voorla knew that she had been wrong to try and cheat the ice demons. Beauty such as hers belongs to the gods. She accepted the crown of ice diamonds. Gha Vin came forward. "I have given you what you wanted. Forgive me."

The Queen replied, "It is the fitting end."

Soldiers came onstage as an escort and carried Voorla away. She was placed in the back of a chariot and rushed toward the glacier. Of course, the two days' journey removed the dweomer of enchantment and she arrived as a plain and ugly old woman. The soldiers, who know nothing of magic, carried her out on the ice and staked her there. She called the Ice Demon to her.

As the soldiers left, one remarked that ice demons must not be very picky. The others agreed -- such creatures must be rather terrible, for look at the world they chose to inhabit. That year, the ice moved further into the kingdom than ever before, and King Haalor and his wizard Ommun Vog prepared to make their own magical assault.

Second place went to Zinoë , who not only gained the title but became the wife of Haalor within a year. Leetha's father did seek to kill Gha Vin, but a battle between a mammoth hunter and a wizard is rather one-sided affair. Within a hundred years, all was ice, and only Reentha dwelling in ecstasy on an airless asteroid remembered the night of the Beauties at all.


(for Chris Jarocha-Ernst)

# The Frigid Ilk of Sarn Kathool

## By Marc Laidlaw

The wizened and sagacious wizard Sarn Kathool had put behind him all the whims and errant passions of youth, and in his estimation it was time the Earth did likewise. He had seen an end to the warm spring days of Hyperborea's juvenescence, and knew the coming age of glaciation would unavoidably curtail this early flowering of man's innate capacity to fling forth what all agreed were the highest achievements of civilization (never counting those ruins of prehuman megaliths occasionally excavated from the ancient lava fields of Voormithadreth as anything more than the uncouth, accidental conglomerations of mindless ophidians). Humankind's autumn was inarguably upon it; winter would be harsh for the species; and Sarn Kathool squandered no opportunity to instruct his captive acolytes and inform his squirming visitors that none but he were prepared for the grinding doom that at this and every moment bore down upon them from the northern reaches of Polarion: a demonic glacier.

The sage's servants nodded mutely—even those who still possessed their tongues—while his voluntary visitors quickly found a reason to absent themselves, leaving the old mage, with his shocked white brows and thin ichthyic whiskers, lost in what they took to be rheumy recollections of a youth they supposed he fantasized as idyllic.

In this, however, Sarn Kathool's peers were mistaken. His youth had been a harsh and in most respects miserable one, in which any advantage he had gained for himself came only with the greatest expenditures of energy, dedication, perseverance and the steadfast application of a ferocious intelligence. Much of the authority he now wielded was his by virtue of having outlasted his rivals. This was a source more of worry than of nostalgia, or even of pride; for the great colleges of arcane investigation were poorly staffed and even more meagerly attended, and no longer matriculated skilled gleaners of esoterica with anything like the force and variety he had taken for granted in his youth. Few graduated from the remote monastic eyries of the Eiglophian Mountains, and cold were the kitchens of the Mhu Thulan lamaseries.

Sarn Kathool had witnessed the near total decline of civilization, and of man's civilizing urges, in the course of his lifetime—a paltry few generations on the scale of men less practiced at managing their mortality. And seeing now the relentless, remorseless approach of the glacial age, he felt that the burden was on him to arrest and if possible, reverse humanity's declining course. The ice would be his unwitting ally—which was well, as it had come to Sarn Kathool from various accounts that those who opposed the advancing sheets of crystalline cold rarely profited thereby.

His plan was to embrace and accept the course of nature, and navigate to an ideal destination of his choosing, rather than allowing blind fate to steer the species. It had been foretold in multiple oracular utterances, and in his own febrile visions, that the great demonic glacier would level the rich Hyperborean landscapes like a razor dragged across a whiskered cheek. Where mighty mountains crumbled and gave way before the blinding advance of frost, flimsy human structures stood no chance. No monuments of the great Hyperborean kings would survive to dazzle distant ages beyond the ice's reign; few memories would persist even in oral form.

But there was one thing Sarn Kathool relied on to survive the ravening chill, and that was man himself: vulnerable as an individual, but wily and adaptable as a race. Therefore he bent his still keen intellect to devising a scheme for the improvement of the species. The ice would give humankind the chance for reinvention. Sarn Kathool conceived a new beginning, a new race, with all the depravity, evils and ills of this degenerate age bred out of it for good!

No one understood better than Sarn Kathool the audacity and enormity of such a proposition, but his finances were equal to the endeavor. He planned to invest every last pazoor in his creation, and no matter the extravagance of the undertaking, he intended to use all of his resources to their utmost.

From the tip of his tower, set well back in the interior of Mhu Thulan, Sarn Kathool could peer out with a spyglass on a clear, still day and see the proud although abandoned spire of the sorcerer Eibon at the edge of the distant sea. Eibon had vanished from Hyperborea just ahead of a scourge of religious persecution cunningly avoided by Sarn Kathool, who diplomatically kept fanes to both Yhoundeh and Tsathoggua symmetrically installed in the depths of his own citadel.

He daily observed the rituals and offerings appropriate to each god, to ensure that no deity would thwart his aspirations. This also meant he could not count on either one for assistance. To prefer one over the other, to beg a favor of bat-featured Tsathoggua while spurning the elk goddess Yhoundeh, was to invite catastrophe. Therefore magic could play no part in his designs. He turned instead to the far more arcane study of technology, long out of favor in Hyperborea, even though its first seeds had sprouted there, as demonstrated by the occasional discovery of vast clockwork cities beneath the crawling sands of the aural reaches.

Far and wide he sent his scouts and acquisition experts, to retrieve volumes from the rare tome repositories of Mu and the archives of Atlantis; and gradually his own library, already overflowing with rare manuscripts of illuminated pterodactyl skin and vast books cased in yellowed horn of mastodon, became Hyperborea's most concentrated seat of scientific learning. The incenses and enchanted braziers, reeking of tradition and ceremony, were put aside for strange polished lenses, outré fuming glassware, miles of curved tubing that kept the glasswrights of Commoriom busy for years on end. Along with books and secret manuscripts, there flowed into his vast manse a steady procession of youths, bought from orphanages, salvaged from the streets, acquired from slave traders either by exchange of coin or the wholesale raiding and looting of transport ships. Multitudinous were the experts and specialists in Sarn Kathool's employ, putting all their ingenuity to work on his behalf, while never suspecting the role they played in his grand vision of humanity's great purification, preservation, and restoration, in hand with the great cold cleansing.

Fighters, merchants, mariners, moneylenders, healers, magistrates, sharp-dealers, assassins—all occupations figured in his plan. For at heart it was simply a matter of people. The Hyperborean people were his responsibility, and he felt it deeply; they were what he sought to preserve, after all; they were reason enough to persevere.

Sarn Kathool was a keen observer and lover of people; and in a way, late in his life, he found his true calling as collector and creator of the same. The techniques of breeding, the basic principles of hybridization and the concentration of desirable traits within a population, along with the elimination of those undesirable, were known to all but the most willfully ignorant. By such rules were fine aurochs bred into prized stock, through generation upon generation of gradual improvement. The ferocious dimetrodons, so popular as guardians of the wealthiest estates, had been bred through the ages for their lurid sails of toxic pigmentation and their loud sibilant bark. The same principles could be seen at work in human breeding. But never before had anyone thought to apply them with the relentless rigor and enthusiasm of Sarn Kathool.

He selected only the sturdiest females from among his growing stock, and those unworthy of refinement he established as their handmaidens and servitors. A similar program was instituted among the males, although toward an entirely different end. The males were set to fighting and rivalry, with all manner of duplicity and martial cunning encouraged, so as to thin the ranks as efficiently as possible and inculcate the most effective predators. The females were not set at each other in open combat, but the winnowing process was no less rigorous. Sarn Kathool reviewed them daily and received the reports of their overseers, in order to evaluate which possessed the most desirable demeanor, the greatest evidence of compassion—the qualities, in short, that one would wish the mother of the coming race to possess.

When the determination had been made, and Sarn Kathool had selected the most promising virgin, she was given a strong narcotic draught and carried immediately to his laboratory, where Sarn Kathool set to work at the heart of an extravagant mechanism fashioned of ranked lenses which permitted him to peer at the inner workings of the corpuscles and animalcules that drove the animate engines of fleshy creatures and vegetative life alike. More, the mechanism was an intricate manipulator of these cells, with meshed gears and serried levers declining into ever finer forms, so that the wizard's gross physical gestures were translated across great chasms of scale, permitting him to flex a frail index finger and thereby score a precise incision over the surface of an organelle, deploying an edged instrument a thousand times as fine as an ice-flea's proboscis. With a delicate touch, the ancient sage delved into the prenatal labyrinths of the chosen maid, and therein made infinitely delicate adjustments to the ranks of half-formed homunculi that waited to be summoned forth in service from their mother's womb.

By methods of manipulation now as lost to us as the graven records of Sarn Kathool's experiments, the maid was then induced to carry several of her inborn homunculi to term, to parthenogenetic birth, and the issue of this birth was then herself surrounded by her slightly less perfect sisters, and raised among only those influences certain to inspire the flowering of the finest feminine instincts. The girls were kept in secluded chambers, where every sensory experience was carefully designed in advance by Sarn Kathool, in accordance with a strict regimen of his devising. When this maid had ripened to the perfect and prescribed age, then just like her mother before her, she was brought to the workroom, where Sarn Kathool labored over her with pride and not a little dread, for great was his sense that time was running short, and deep was his fear that he would not complete his life's greatest accomplishment in time to do the Earth any good.

For through all his labors, the demon ice advanced. From Polarion the blue-green sheets crept at a rate previously inconceivable, singing with a low ominous moan that never faltered as the monstrous crystals formed. As the ice clawed ever closer to his tower, laying claim to all the cities of the realm, and began to sizzle and quench the four blazing craters of Voormithadreth, the glacial sheets emitted weird emergent surges, casting subauroral flickerings brighter than the sun—so that even at midday, the summer skies surged and sang with a haunting glow that had been associated previously with none but the midnights of midwinter. Soon, he knew, it would all be midwinter—winter with no end, ice with no edges. And he bent himself to the minuscule razors and gleaming armatures with renewed dedication and purpose.

What gave him some hope of success was the progress he had made with the males of the experiment. In contrast to the maids, he selected the finest fighters, the most wicked and deceitful, and from them removed their half-formed homunculi. Ice here played its first role as partner. For upon removal from the male fighters, he placed each homunculus in a crystalline vial, which itself he set in a block of ice hollowed for the purpose of preservation. Here it waited in a frigid stasis while he summoned one of the rejected maids and prepared her womb to receive the warrior's spawn. The maiden's own progeny were scoured so that there could be no possibility of contamination, and then the male homunculus was implanted. Unlike a child conceived by normal means, the offspring of these efforts were not a mixture of mother and father. The males were purely male—bred for speed, size, aggression, violent disposition, tenacity, utter fearlessness, ruthlessness, cunning. Sarn Kathool knew which qualities he wished in a protector, and such were these. For Sarn Kathool's plan was deep and complex, and extended through the ages. He had few illusions about the world that was likely to greet his progeny.

As the ice thickened around the base of his spire, his shipments of new subjects slowed to a trickle and then failed completely; but he scarcely noticed, for by now he was fully stocked on specimens; he had all he needed. He was many generations into his plan, locked in a deadly race with the advancing glacier, which moved with a restlessness that betrayed its demonic spirit, closing white claws around his tower like an evil god seizing Earth's last scepter.

His daughters, the mothers of all future men, were pure and noble and worthy—worthy to receive the final gift that he would give them. They were the ideal bearers of Sarn Kathool's own seed—for this it was that he intended. Parthenogenesis only to a point, and then a final conjunction, in which his own homunculi would make the short journey from Sarn Kathool's loins to the waiting womb and the receptive, incomplete homunculi of the perfectly created maiden. And in her womb, their offspring would sleep, utterly frozen, the glacier's greatest power used to thwart and undermine its depredations. And in the ultimate thaw, whenever after unaccountable ages it would come, that child would commence to grow...and Sarn Kathool himself, merged with this specimen of perfect motherhood, would live and lead the way in that future age—the first of a perfect breed that he himself would continue to refine after its creation.

But still he feared, for he knew his own vulnerability. He easily pictured what could befall even the most carefully concealed tombs of the great kings. The vast estates of the dead that skirted the edges of Commoriom were a waste of plundered crypts—and in all the eons of ice that lay ahead, there was no telling what manner of greedy cold wretches might come in search of the fabled lair and resting place of storied Sarn Kathool. Therefore, the warriors, bred to protect the mother and her handmaids—and to do so with all their wiles, with every trick of ruthlessness and cunning their vicious nature could devise. Any thaw, any disruption to the frozen vaults sufficient to disturb the maiden's rest, would also stir the warriors, and in this way bring on the certain death of any violator. But Sarn Kathool could not shake the foreboding, sharpened by the incipience of ice, that this was not enough—that the maiden herself had need of innate defenses.

After much consideration, and convinced of his design's foolproof nature, he began to make certain alterations to the maiden homunculi, although nothing that could express itself without the proper triggering conditions. In the presence of threat, at the danger of rape for instance, the maiden mother would find herself possessed of all the cunning strength and violent power necessary to exterminate her assailant. It pained him to compromise the creature's innocence, but dark ages lay ahead. What if the warriors did not wake? What if the maiden was left alone and at the mercy of her violators? Who would protect the sanctity of Sarn Kathool's homunculus then?

No, the female must be permitted some subtle yet potent means of defense.

And so, more generations of maiden mothers were bred, refined, and from their selfsame stock bred again. Within the wombs of his select matron, a lineage of perfect mothers waited as if queued to receive the seed of Sarn Kathool, prefiguring the perfect race that one day would venture forth. While this program wended on, Sarn Kathool neglected not the furtherance of the warrior breed, and with all he learned from his practice on the maidens, the male lineage was also improved. From the inferior yet no less fertile wombs of the subsuperior parti-matrons, he hatched males of inarguable ferocity, continually eliminating the weak or hesitant, honing the protector until he felt he had a specimen that could protect his mother from any future harm, no matter how unimaginable.

At last there came a stretch of howling whiteness, a plunge of temperature so cold and penetrating that its menacing ache could be felt in the deepest vaults of Sarn Kathool's redoubt. On what promised to be the last morning of Hyperborea's fleeting age of glory, the old mage, weary beyond belief yet elated by his success, mounted to the highest turret of his grim frost-locked citadel and permitted himself a final glimpse of the world he had labored so strenuously to save. The program had cost him the final centuries of his life, and in that time he had scarcely allowed himself to be distracted by the encroaching of the glacial horror that had claimed the Earth while closing around him slowly, as if saving Sarn Kathool for last.

From where he stood, it was no longer possible to see the peak of Eibon's lofty tower, for it had long since been buried beneath the hungry blue-green waste. Weird lights glowed through the ice at that spot, and that was the only clue that Eibon had ever existed. Wherever else Sarn Kathool looked, there was not even a memorial glow. All the works of man were locked in ice. The glacier itself possessed a demonic soul, a spirit that remorselessly sought the extirpation not only of Sarn Kathool, not only of all intellectual accomplishment, not only of Earth...but of *all*. The fiend's disregard for the greatest of minds was the ultimate insult to Sarn Kathool, and yet he had met it full on. His victory was a feat to be flung in the demon's howling maw. It had not defeated him, nor would it outlive his progeny.

As if sensing his moment of gloating as a challenge, the winter-thing sped at him, wielding an ice-edged sword of wind—the blast that through some irony would come to be known as boreal, even though through all the ages of Hyperborea's existence that phrase had evoked balmy cosseting breezes and green, sweet-scented zephyrs. Sarn Kathool cringed back inside and sealed the outer portals. Frost burned through the walls, rendering them searing to the touch, turning the lush and colorful arrases hung there to brittle grey wafers that shattered at a breath.

He turned to the spiral stairs and wound his way quickly down into the depths, and the cold chased him, icing over the steps as he descended. There could be no return. The passages were choked with crystals of ice; his very exhalations solidified and fell crashing around his feet, while the air in his chest threatened to transform into sharp shards that would stab his lungs from within. The demon howled! And Sarn Kathool repressed a youthful exuberant laugh, so narrow was his sense of escape. A joyous exhilaration quickened his steps.

And then he was in his final chambers: His workshop, his lair, and in the last and deepest room, the nuptial laboratory. It crossed his mind that the laboratory was perhaps a degree warmer than it ought to have been—as if the ice had not yet reached these depths; as if it had exercised restraint. As to why the uncalculating ice might have let a spark of warmth remain, his suspicion was so faint that he scarcely troubled with it. It was time to put aside all thoughts of restraint.

His maiden bride awaited, locked in artificial slumber. He gazed upon her beauty and saw that he had created perfection. A suitable mother in some distant age, but for now an irresistible and alluring mate. She had been prepared for him by her handmaids, themselves now locked away in secure adjacent galleries to which the demonic cold had been cleverly diverted. The warrior breed had also been frozen into their holding cells; with the chiefest of them, and her most perfect protector, cast into stasis in this same chamber, nearest to wake should she require protection.

All was utterly, completely still. The demon's howl was inaudible.

Sarn Kathool, despite the elderly gasping that his hurried plunge had elicited, felt a youthful quickening in his blood. And as he beheld his maiden matron, primed to receive him, the quickening came to a point.

Erect, flush with his life's masterwork and the pride of his achievement, he advanced on his maiden receptacle, the vessel who would carry him into whatever future awaited, and entered her like an old man easing himself gingerly into a rocking boat.

That was not quite the last sensation he felt, nor quite his last awareness of existence. For although his spine broke instantly, there was enough life left in his eyes to see the grinning face of the warrior protector as his fierce creation twisted the wise old head entirely backwards on its neck; and with another half-turn, continuing the revolution, he was able to gaze into the wide-awake eyes of his no less ferocious maiden-but-not-mother, who was pleased beyond measure by what she saw in his expression. And even as their laughter rose in his ears, and as the obscene noises of their twinned passions commenced, to intimate exactly what form of race he had visited upon the future as the mother and father of mankind's newest iteration, there came a storm of deafening white sound flooding his awareness, boastfully and wordlessly, mindlessly gloating— informing him how in all ways he had failed: the insane, incomprehensible, and purely witless tittering of the ice.

# The Debt Owed Abhoth

## By Robert M. Price

A mong the hoary pterosaurian leaves of the addenda to the fabled *Codices of High Uzuldaroum* one finds a legend, deemed apocryphal and spurious by those few scribes who even know of it, but which is, nonetheless, of some interest. It may indeed contradict most other accounts of sacred saga, but perhaps it is the more famous and fully attested narratives which are in error. There is no way to know for certain, at least as the question presently stands, and it is likely to remain in doubt till someone chances to unearth (or fabricate) a seminal manuscript either confirming or condemning the episode.

For the tale concerns an invasion long forgotten, and a hero who came from Outside in that hour when all seemed lost, and how he stemmed the tide of what seemed irrevocable doom.

Even in the early days of the first frost, how ancient was the internecine enmity between the squat and hirsute Voormi savages— scarce evolved beyond the pitiful state of ape-men, for all their cruel cunning—and our own forbears, who proudly walked upright with clean, straight limbs and partook of the written word, and yet had little sense of their own self-preservation. None recalled the origin of that feud, whether it was the lustful coveting of our females by their drooling, tusked troglodytes, or a petty dispute over territory, or some dim, ill-remembered insult. But the old argument had come to an unsustainable boil with the fall of the northern reaches to the breath of the White Worm. And the kings and barons of the surviving Hyperborean realms had reason to shiver with fear, for the very civilization of which they were so proud proved a mortal hindrance in the impending crisis. Cultured men are ever soft and porous, susceptible to corruption and ambition. The congregated worthies found it a near-insurmountable labor to set aside their petty interests and claims to primacy and privilege over each other, and thus they could never easily forge a bond of cooperation.

Their semi-human foes, by contrast, had precious little to lose by combining their forces. When Zurazgha, the chief shaman of the Voormi clans, issued a summons to amass and go forth from the stygian precincts which tradition had assigned them, and to sweep down upon the pastoral provinces of the Hyperboreans, there was no room for argument. Simple instinct provided clear purpose, even if none of the skulking, noisome devils was capable of articulating what it might be.

It had taken an unseemly amount of time even to negotiate a war council in which all the Hyperborean potentates would agree to participate, for there was much haggling among sub-ministers over the proposed site of such a meeting, which prince or baron should be accorded the honor of hosting it, what shape the table should be; and who should have the honor of building it; what variety of wood of which it ought to be built; and who should supply it. And all the while, the slavering Voormis marched steadily and tirelessly into the defenseless heart of Uzuldaroum, impeded only by the despoliation of such small villages as they found along their way, looting and pillaging them and making kindling of such scientific and spiritual treasures, goods and artworks as they could not use to wipe their matted, monstrous hindquarters.

As scarcely sensationalized reports filtered in of the mayhem and chaos rampant across the land, the assembled princes of Hyperborea shivered, though they had long been acclimated to the creeping frost-iness of their continent. Several of the individual nobles had fielded batches of defenders, but they had at once been swept away by the advancing hordes. The lords of the beaten kingdoms of men came together by rally at the same spot, a crumbling keep on the desolate plains adjoining the eastern face of the Eiglophian Mountains.

As the days passed, with the princes and barons exchanging half-hearted and useless stratagems, the castle and the serfs' hovels within the collapsing outer wall rapidly filled up with refugees who had blindly followed their fleeing rulers. It was a small and sorry assemblage. And no one had reason to believe there were any other such enclaves in all of Mhu Thulan, so great was the animal fury of the half-men headed their way.

~*~

All the men, women and children left of the great cities of Hyperborea huddled close and shuddered around their meager fires. And as time ticked away and provisions dwindled and the priests composed new rituals of expiation to new gods whose names they invented with dice, a strange rider appeared within their desperate defenses. He was mounted on a griffin, its chimerical anatomy replete with wings, though none could attest to having witnessed it in flight. Ignoring the curious throngs whose bleary eyes followed him, the stranger rode confidently through the camp and into the castle. He dismounted, leaving his beast in the care of a threadbare squire who gaped, agog and overmatched by the remarkable creature. For his part, the squire knew not which was the greater wonder, the griffin or its stately rider.

The grand rulers of Mhu Thulan stopped their bickering at the sound of his footsteps, looking at him as with a single eye. At first they supposed him a fellow royal, arrived too late to the ill-starred war party. Nor were they altogether wrong. A tall, slender man with finer features than the relatively gnomish, beetle-browed folk of Hyperborea, swathed in an ebon cloak against the eternal cold. Beneath it could be glimpsed black links of chain mail. His polished helm at first appeared to be the skull of a small styracosaur, cleverly forged of some glossy black alloy into a regal diadem of lethal horns. Once he removed his headgear, his true visage looked scarcely less outlandish, for the unmarked skin of his hollow cheeks, aquiline nose and high forehead all but glowed in the dim-lit room with a silvery, bloodless pallor. Was this, too, a mask? Heedless yet of the awe and desperate hope he'd already ignited in them, he brushed back his snow-white tresses and began to speak to those awaiting his word.

"My true name must never be spoken in your tongue, though I am possibly known to some of you as an agent of Disorder, and to others as a champion of Law." And he withdrew from its jeweled scabbard a great long sword fashioned of black volcanic glass. "Some of you may know of me as a sorcerer. And it is true: I am both. I count myself no man's slave. Certainly not yours. And yet I am here to serve."

One of the faded princelings—unnamed in any version of the tale—spoke up. "Do you mean to say you have come to our aid, to the aid of Mhu Thulan? What gods do you serve, O stranger?"

"For many years did I serve the Old Ones until the day I realized there was no profit in self-destruction, for they offered no better reward than eternal chaos. From that day I have reversed myself and now serve the Elder Gods, though hardly as an acolyte. Sometimes they serve me. They did not send me here to you, but it may be that I must needs send for them."

These words puzzled the company, nor was their bafflement at an end. The least cowed of the aristocracy asked, "Does an army follow you, O Prince?"

"Not such as you, or the Voormis, imagine. Yet I am not alone." At this he raised the black sword before his eyes as if no more answer, nor any more of an army, was needed.

The oldest and most wise of the priesthood of Yhoundeh forced a break in the crowd and hobbled up to the stranger. "What will you require in return for the sorcery you mean to work on our behalf?" Suspicion dripped from his raw-throated words, for the priests were not yet convinced they were not interrogating a menace as great as the savage Voormis themselves. His talk was oblique, enigmatic, and it might be a trap.

"You need not fear me, mortal cousins. I seek no reward beyond the survival in this world of humankind capable of recording the stories in which the other gods sleep and dream. Your presence is, I confess, an affront to me, so imagine a world in which my only company is such a herd as those amassed outside. It is no pleasant prospect. The future will need races possessed of your peculiar talents, cowardly buffoons as you are."

Still unsure if the haughty stranger was friend or foe, the collected aristocracy of Hyperborea watched silently as he took his leave—without, the priests jeeringly observed, partaking of any of the sacrifices left out for any hedge-deities as might stoop to play the savior. What would he do for them and for their world? What could anyone do? For even in these late, decadent days, there were wizards with considerable powers, but they had achieved nothing, no doubt because the prevailing fashion in enchantment depended upon beguiling the minds of those on whom one cast one's spells, and the Voormis had among them so little in the way of mind that they were not easily enchanted.

~*~

Though most were too busy foraging for whatever greasy scraps they could find, any who cared to look overhead might have beheld the sight of the strange, ivory-skinned rider ascending into the clouds on his griffin. He was headed west to the Eiglophian Mountains, and the great, secret-riddled summit of Voormithadreth.

The sword-bearing sorcerer clearly knew what lay buried within the darkness of the inner caverns, and he knew the secret paths of access. A kind of infernal Olympus, the peak crested above a hive of ancient, largely dormant entities. The sages of later eras would surmise a subterrene realm containing the ghostly archetypes of all material objects, living and unliving. But they would dream of what they did not see. Or rather, their inner eyes saw them, but their inner eyes deceived them. The white-locked warlock out of primordial myth had seen with his fleshly eyes the living creatures that served as both specimens and progenitors of all terrene lifeforms.

As he passed unseen through many noisome catacombs and their dreadful yet intangible inhabitants, the ghostly likenesses of monsters that would remain stubbornly lodged in the ancestral night terrors of mankind, he heard peculiar sounds like the snoring of Things with respiratory apparatus utterly unlike our own, perhaps designed to circulate something other than air. No sunlight or moonlight ever penetrated here. There were no torches, since only visitors from without would require them and such visitors were never welcome. He strode with certainty, though carefully, guided by the peculiar purplish radiance of his unsheathed, rune-encrusted sword, until he arrived somewhere beneath the foot of the terrible mountain, at the echoing cavern of the one that is called Abhoth the Unclean.

A world unto itself, Abhoth (whose name means "father" in the Shemitish tongue) stretched out as far as any mortal eye might see in the pitch-black void. It had the appearance of a bubbling lake of abhorrent slime. Men call Great Abhoth the "Unclean," for the Old One's essence was the primal substance of all life as yet unformed, though its infinite fertility had been stilled with the fall of the stars into disharmony.

Of old, the stranger knew from the sorcerous lore of his eldritch race that Abhoth was the last living remnant of Ubbo-Sathla, the Unbegotten Source from which the First Forms of all living creatures emerged in the dawn of the cooling earth. For all its abominable fecundity, Abhoth moved the stranger to pity. It was a diminished orphan of Ubbo-Sathla, even as the stranger was the last survivor of a race lost to history and that might only ever have existed, in this realm, as figments of legend.

But it was this legendary sorcery that he meant to conjure against the rampaging Voormis: he would awaken Abhoth and restore it to its ancient glory, cause it to expand once more so to regain all that it had lost, to reabsorb all the grand-spawn of the Unbegotten Source, and so become Ubbo-Sathla again. For it was written that, at the end of days, all would return to the primal Oneness from whence it came, and those days had arrived. The stranger's role was merely to supply the catalyst, and with his dire sword plunged into the shore of Abhoth, did he finally do so.

The terrible, unholy words he spoke have been lost, as has the alien text from which the silver-countenanced mage read them, though some sages hold that he intoned the now-forgotten *upposatha* ritual. In any case, who would be foolhardy enough to record his words of power here? In any case, the incantation did not take long. Soon, the stranger was retracing his footsteps by the light of his keening, hungry sword. He could hear the snaking, liquid tendrils of the bubbling pit following him toward the surface, as well as by other routes and cracks and fissures too narrow for him to have taken. He did not fear the universal absorption that should overtake all who dwelt upon earth, for, not being native to this world himself, he owed no debt to Abhoth, to Ubbo-Sathla. He merely hoped to avoid befouling his garments from contact with the viscid stuff.

~*~

The tactics of the stranger transcended the understanding of those whose cause he championed, for they found themselves utterly nonplussed when the black-clad stranger shortly returned to their enclave, not with any glad tidings of victory or of rescue, but with his crackling sword unsheathed and a command to prepare to march into battle. Every face registered shock and betrayal, if it registered anything at all. If all that their savior meant to do was deliver him to the tender mercies of the beasts at their door, then they were better off with no savior at all. None of those on whose behalf he fought survived to witness his victory in their name. Swiftly and silently, he fed them all to his terrible, insatiable sword.

As soon as the stranger took his leave of the last, unmanned outpost of Uzuldaroum's survivors, he took to the blood-hued skies once more and made for the vanguard of the Voormis horde.

He landed and dismounted in full view of the surging tide of flyblown beast-men, who halted to gawp in puzzled wonder at the spectacle before them. Many fanged muzzles foamed with drool at the prospect of devouring the griffin, though none possessed the courage to attack the mighty steed for fear of its rider.

At some length, a lone figure, slighter of build and taller of fore-head than his fellows, perhaps a modicum less hairy, elbowed his way through the packed and snarling crowd. This almost-human, accoutered in colorful rags, caparisoned with strings of finger bones, his muzzle crudely ochred, was Zurazgha, the shaman who had urged his brutish flock to undertake their mindless crusade. When the colorful witch doctor approached with empty paws upraised, the white-haired sorcerer delivered his tidings.

"Hail, high priest of the Voormi clans! I bring you news of your enemies and of your victory! Just now I have saved you the trouble of bearding the aristocrats of Uzuldaroum in their lair, and likewise their servants and their heirs. You may see the aftermath with your own eyes. For all I care, you may fill your bellies with their remains, while they are fresh. But I must forewarn you: you have first a debt to repay. The debt is yours, not mine, but I will see you again there once you have fulfilled your glorious destiny."

Though the grunting shaman, filmy eyes open wide, offered no articulate reply, the stranger felt sure he had understood the rudiments of the message. Withal did he vault once more into the saddle on his griffin and take to the air currents again.

~*~

Atop the summit of Voormithadreth, he waited, lost in medita-tion. Eventually the chaotic horde came in sight, converging with their shambling gait upon the plain below.

Below him the stranger espied the brightly painted figure of the shaman Zurazgha, standing upon the burly, hunched shoulders of his acolytes. The apish conjurer seemed to be awaiting a new command from his erstwhile ally. And the stranger did speak, though not to him. Instead, he incanted the tongue-punishing syllables of the notorious First Sathlatta, and when he was finished and had plunged his soul-glutted sword into the rocky soil, the earth rumbled in reply.

The first sign that the Voormis suspected something amiss was the universal wrinkling of flat noses and almost canine howls of disgust. To offend such palates as the ghastly proto-humans possessed, it must have been unearthly, indeed. They turned to retreat into the caverns beneath the mountains from what they knew must be some terrible abomination of fell human sorcery, when, from out of the bowls of numerous craters surrounding Mount Voormithadreth, there began to flow a queer and disgusting ooze. From narrow cataracts in the earth, hissing jets of the foul stuff shot out, while from other pits with wide-open mouths the noisome stuff surged with leisurely dignity like lava flowing from a volcano. Little understanding what they saw, the Voormis nonetheless sensed terrible danger and searched frantically for any path of egress. But they found none, for the oozing mouths surrounded them.

What torments, yes, and what wonders, must befall mortal flesh when touched by the questing pseudopods of a god of fecundity? Even the stranger was touched by a morbid curiosity to witness whatever might follow. Each Voormi, and their "human" cousins, too, should at last pay the debt owed Abhoth, and to the unborn of the Earth.

Each fleeing form howled with pain when the viscous flood touched and tasted and digested shaggy pelt and mottled hide, until immersion in the gelatinous tide drowned their last, gargling shrieks. Reunited with their primeval progenitor, they dissolved and informed the swirling unborn abominations percolating within the myriad rejuvenated wombs of Abhoth the Unclean.

In less than no time, Abhoth again became Ubbo-Sathla, for no terrene life would escape its cloying embrace. The dark stranger from some far, unguessable kingdom, stood in pensive contemplation. Compared with the great eons of silence surrounding the brief span of life's career on this new-made earth, the fledgling human races were not promising in either their longevity or their evolution. But he disdained the prospect of cutting short their time on earth as the successors to the once-lordly races of decadent crinoids and torpid, mind-stealing trilobites. And there was something he could do about it. Indeed, something he must do, for it had already been done, or else—

He snapped the reins of his griffin and mounted up into the cloudy heavens, where he circled, taking in the sight of the expanding mass of the renascent Ubbo-Sathla far beneath him. As the primal land mass of Gondwana had once broken up and drifted apart, destined in the long evening of the failing sun to reform into the ultimate continent of Zothique, a vast circuit was now being completed. How is it, mused Thasaidon, in his own realm a god of evil, that it fell to the future to continually repair the past?

He unsheathed his obsidian sword, gleaming with the energy of the souls it had lately devoured, and lifted it high as he caused his beaked and winged steed to plunge earthward. As by some latent instinct, the quivering mass retreated from the descending hoofs of the griffin, leaving a circle of dry tundra about the god and his beast. The rider dismounted, spread his feet apart to plant himself firmly on the ground, and then he plunged the sword into the steaming lake of protoplasm, a placid sea of potentiality no more. The stuff heaved as the blood and souls of the kings and peasants of Mhu Thulan flooded directly into the mass of Prime Matter, and the cycle began again. Serpents and salamanders detached themselves in the first moments, followed by larger and more complex creatures as the hours passed and the mass spent itself in new invention, even as it shrank down to become the remnant Abhoth once more.

The population of the earth had not yet grown great enough to surpass the coasts of the polar realm of Hyperborea, but it would still take very many years to replace it, from the pitiful tribe that lay upon the shore like a pack of breach births in the afterbirth of the Great Old One.

The result was little better than he'd feared, but they would thrive where neither the Voormis nor the gnomish, milk-blooded proto-men of Mhu Thulan could survive the cold, hard ages ahead. Bodies wrenched erect in distress at the cold winds, these new ones were taller and stouter and uglier than either of their parents, but their brows were higher and promised a bit more brain than the last batch. Thasaidon trembled with fatigue and even a trace of sorrow, that he had to destroy so many, to achieve something that would only fall, in the far end of the future. But as he took his final leave, even if there was not a word of worship to mark his departure, neither did he hear any of them complain.

# Return of the Crystal
## By Charles Schneider

The child played in the ruins of an ancient city of Mhu Thulan. He was reenacting an ingrained drama of the Gods, using the dry, broken bodies of iridescent snow-beetles as surrogate deities. Close by, a sun-bronzed hag scratched weird sigils into frozen tundra, watchfully keeping an enlarged and filmy eye upon the small one.

Though aged hardly a handful of years, this lad, so the crone's witcheries revealed to her, was secretly surrounded by a shimmering cloud of silver and violet flames. These lapping, singing tongues of unknown occult power enveloped him as if within a mandala of protective salamanders. One day he would be a man of great power and greater destinies. He would become a great sorcerer, and die a strange death. He would be reborn, as he already had been, countless times over many aeons, and take many diverse and grotesque forms. Today, however, he was a mere child, and she would let him play for some time longer as the day waned.

The youth wore a bracelet of dried infant toads and deadly snake rattles, strung together by the gut of vermin. He had received it at an eldritch ceremony, as a mighty priest sprinkled him in hyssop. He would wear this until the chain of animal parts would break of its own accord, the contents dispersing, perhaps unnoticed.

The moon, dead but still mighty, hung pendulously above the entire landscape, afflicting all below with strange influences and unpredictable insanities. The very landscape was changing, for it was the end of a gilded world of fable. A new age of malignant decay had begun. One day, the vast and exotic blossoms, which filled the enormous vases that lined the great temples, were found to have wilted overnight in a sudden and unexpected freeze. Exquisite lichen

187

and delicious moulds glazed over the grotesque carvings, and water rotted the very clay of the monstrous statues of the land. Everything was breaking down, as iron in water, as flesh in sarcophagi. Once the very art of a world begins to decay, the death of the weary soul of the people shall soon follow.

The red and fiery orange, velvety leaves turned brown and wet overnight, infused with deathly frost. That was the beginning of the Great Change – the end of a world beyond dreams.

~*~

The child lifted his tiny leg up high and brought his foot down hard upon the pile of fragmented husks. They exploded into a small cloud of glittering, metallic greens and deep, golden blues. In the same manner have gone the very Gods themselves. When men stop believing in the Gods, the Gods no longer believe in men. Their great godly hearts, as big as the center of any sun, plummet into icy depths. The world turns into monster-engorged oceans of shadows.

Fissures upon the humid mountains surrounded the snow-capped plains. Frozen and pale-blue geysers of crushed ice erupted from these frost-volcanoes, locked and time-lost.

In the distance an entire village of grey figures traveled, part of the diaspora precipitated by the change in the land. It was growing so cold that the people had no choice but to attempt to outrace the encroaching Glaciers of the Gods.

The travails of doomed and desperate mortals mattered not to the small boy as he played godling in the deadly polar wastes. His young mind tried to forget the sound of the snowy avalanche into which his parents had vanished. He was fortunate that the village beldame took an interest in him. He was consumed by the tasks at hand, the games and secret machinations of a child grown far too wise. Any observer would have noticed in the lad's wisdom a sparkle of glinting energy and the sort of enigmatic smile that only an old man, learned in the strangest arts and steeped in the most decadent of tastes, might possibly have possessed.

The boy poked the frozen earth with a hard, grey stick, looking for things to make into strange toys. Into God-toys. The vegetation was sparse. Freakish grasses stabbed through the snow, denuded of color. The ragged children always had to use their imaginations to create new games here, unlike the spoiled youth beyond the white wastes, who might find all of the latest puppet creations of city-craftsmen in the glittering marketplaces. New pastimes or near-forgotten ceremonies, both had to be reenacted here in the far reaches, with naught but snow, animal bones, stones, scraps of leather, cast off and rusted metal bits and the occasional ice-worm to play with.

Is there any more ideal locale in which to set a demoniacal magician's den than within the ghoul-crypts and lich-caverns of ice? As the boy played above, not far below his feet began the systems of ancient, endless tunnels, built by the long-vanished serpent men. Many an unfortunate traveler had inadvertently begun the descent, had found the forbidden entrance and, thus, faced untold, invisible and nameless horrors in fathomless depths of crystalline ice and ruins inhuman. Those villagers who dwelt close by spoke fearfully of these ancient shafts of reptilian origin, and shunned them.

The boy was well aware of many hidden entrances to such subterranean grottoes. If he could have, he would have spent all of his time exploring the secret, inner worlds and lost, forgotten ruins of the land. He had grown bored with this sport of making new gods out of old sticks and older pebbles, then destroying them. Seeing that the hag was distracted, he wandered toward a deep blue rent in the earth. He swiftly descended a few hundred feet into the ice tunnel. He slowed his pace as it began to grow dimmer. He studied the frost-kissed earth at his feet, studded with odd stones and shards. He kicked at a few rocks. It was at this very moment that he dislodged a milky crystal from the cold earth. He had never beheld its like ere this. As he picked it up, the boy found that it filled his small fist like a stunted piece of fruit, being round in the center and flatly tapered at the edges.

Excited, he hurried back to the entrance of the tunnel. Once outside, he held the weird crystal up to the white sun and was puzzled by what seemed to be a shifting within the orb. There appeared to be an angry miniature world within the crystal, a place of dark clouds with sudden, bright pulses of crackling lightning within. The young one had witnessed such things as one ten times his age would go mad to recall, and this might give reason for the disturbing premonitions he felt as he held the faintly glowing, translucent orb. Or was it just the late afternoon sun hitting one out of an endless expanse of pebbles and weird stones?

"Gaze into me!"

Had he imagined the ancient, croaking voice, thick with power and suggestion… and insistence? Was this strange crystal speaking to him through some unknown sorcery? Or was it a madman's lost soul piping into his ear, as it drifted upon the ghostly, boreal winds?

He raised the crystal to his eye, and hesitated. He seemed to hear the murmuring of distant voices. One exhorted him to gaze into the crystal's depths… but another interior voice loudly urged him away from any such inspection. Such resistance he found as difficult as passing by those sweet, candied syrups that ooze out of the sacred Notash tree like the liquid, ruby-blood of a dying god, without partaking of the rare delicacy.

~*~

The shadow of a dreadful but inchoate threat flitted before the lad, and he now found himself powerless to resist the siren call of the crystal.

He held it up to his face and took a peek within. He beheld a tiny figure, then another, and then still another changing form, each replacing its predecessor in turn. Like ripples of flesh in an ancient ocean of fetid creation, the visions of these shifting figures slid like oil into his brain. He had seen more interesting things that had beached themselves upon the shoreline, flopping, multi-limbed things of pink and blue transparency.

Despite his newfound ennui, it occurred to the boy that the befogged, glass-like stone might smash apart wonderfully. It had been such a good day of making and destroying things. This lump of glass would be a grand ending to this game. He grabbed the strange stone in his fist and raised it aloft in the chilled air.

At the very instant he was about to bring the crystal crashing down upon another rock that jutted out of the earth, he heard the hag call his name.

"Zon Mezzamalech! Enough playing. It is time to return home."

~*~

So began the long walk back to the tiny ice-cave wherein they sheltered themselves during these days of the dying land.

He thoughtlessly dropped the milky white stone and ran to the hag's side. After all, when your grandmother says it is time to stop playing, 'tis best to heed her.

As it lay upon the ground, the crystal dropped in temperature. Within three heartbeats, its temperature fell below freezing. A translucent lizard scurried from a fissure, searching for sustenance. Its side glanced against the crystal, instantly turning black. The malignant ice-rot slowly and terribly consumed the flesh of the reptile. The foul, bubbling remains were devoured by a vulpine scavenger who was, in turn, destroyed by the sloughing horror.

Boy and hag sojourned to their squalid dwelling where a meager fare would await them. As he walked through the snow, listening to it crunch beneath his roughly shod feet, the boy could not help but think upon what he had seen within the stone.

Flashes of reflected visions flamed in his mind's eye, fragments and glimpses of the Yet-To-Be. So many twisting, bobbing heads, screaming dolls of blood and bone who came and went, mere shapes, splintered forms. It seemed to him that he should know them, yet despite their troubling familiarity, they remained strangers.

Why was one figure coming into strange and wild focus? The form was in a room, surrounded by... were they books and all manner of old and strange objects? At first distant, then coming closer with alarming speed, the figure was looking right at him! Or rather, the figure appeared to be staring with unbreakable focus at him through a stone of identical form and substance! The ever widening eye was staring, it seemed, back at him and beyond with magnetic fascination and awe. A burst of blasting white, as the death of a star, and the vision was gone.

With a half-shudder, the boy hurried on, walking beside the crone. There was a stomach to fill and a night of studies. How was he to become a mighty sorcerer if he did not apply himself to the hag's lessons, the crumbling grimoires, the powders and liquids? A good thing he had tossed the idiotic crystal. It would never trouble his thoughts again.

# Rodney LaSalle Has a Job Waiting in Commoriom

## By John Shirley

atching Oddney Rodney walking off in that oddball way of his, Hezza whispered, "You know what he said? 'Riches and freedom await me there.'" Hezza ran the back of his hand across his damp nose. It was cold in West Oakland that evening. "*That's* what he said, Skrog."

Skroggy shrugged. "So? He says all kinda weird shit."

"So these riches 'await' him...where? His uncle's got the only riches Rodney'll ever get near. And his uncle's house is right directly flat-out that way. No other place he could be going. His mom's house is the other way. I know this dweeb. Lived on the block with him all my fucking life. He doesn't go anywhere but the library and his mom's house and school—and that way. Why now, tonight, when the old loon is dead? Maybe 'cause there's a pile of money there, dude."

"His uncle's dead, yeah, last week," Skroggy allowed. "Don't see it means nothin." Skroggy shrugged again.

Skroggy was getting on Hezza's nerves. He always was a dumb ofay, just greasy red-haired, trailer-park white trash. Slow on the uptake. Hezza's sister asked like once a week, *Why you hang with that dumb white boy?* "Skrog—listen. Rodney Lasalle *fucking knows* where the cash is. He's gonna get that cash and get outta town. You see? Riches and freedom!" He started off after Oddney Rodney, who was almost a block ahead.

They'd catch up, but not too fast—they'd have to hold back some.

Oddney moved slowly, due to that fucked up left leg; it seemed to lean toward the other leg at the knee, tilting him over to one side, making him walk in a kind of step swing, step swing.

Hezza—known to his moms as Hezekiah—had been keeping an eye on Rodney Lasalle since their first term at Laney community college in this cracked and much-tagged corner of Oakland, California, because he had this weird second-sight feeling that he and Rodney were entangled in the sneaker shoelaces of destiny. Hezza's mom said the second sight ran in the family, and Hezza had always thought he might have it. He wanted to use it in the Emeryville casino but they wouldn't let him in there, because of that incident in the parking lot...

Anyway, he figured if there was a tangled destiny involved, that involved money. To Hezza, *destiny* and *mo' money* came together like a Fitty Cent half-rhyme.

Skroggy, on the other hand, never figured anything, he just bounced from one event to the next like a pinball. So he slouched passively along with Hezza. The red-haired lunk was bigger and stronger than Hezza, and that came in useful.

"I'm telling you, Skrog," Hezza muttered, as they paced along slowly behind Oddney Rodney, "I can feel it coming. Laney going to take away my school loans and shit. I'm one of the best students at that damn school, too." A slight exaggeration, but he did have a 3.1. "So what I'm going to do? Got to go somewhere. Got to connect with destiny, dude."

"What you mean, *destiny?* I heard people say that, never know what they mean."

"It's like a story where you know how it's gonna end, man. Destiny, for you and me."

"End with mo' money?"

"Fuck yeah. What else? I swear I can feel it. Oddney there, he knows where that old crackpot's money is..."

They walked through the early evening's mist; this muggy October night the fog was like some kind of sour belch from San Francisco Bay. Up ahead lurched the ungainly figure of Oddney Rodney, with his heavy lower half, his narrow shoulders, his crooked leg, his unkempt, curly brown hair; the diamond-patterned sweater he never seemed to change.

"Boring, walking this slow," Skroggy grumbled.

"We can't go faster yet," Hezza muttered. "Don't want to catch up to him, clue him we're here."

~*~

Rodney knew full well that The Dolts were there. That was how he thought of them. The Dolts. Philistine dolts like so many others in Oakland. Once, Oakland and Berkeley had hosted great writers, like Jack London and Ambrose Bierce. Now the East Bay was a tatterdemalion, was the creeping grounds of beggars, of the worst sort of drug fiends and licentious professors who seduced nubile students; it was the abode of "hip hop stars" and part-time rappers and full-time Occupation protesters, and punk rockers and Phish heads. When Rodney heard of Phish heads he'd hoped they might have something to do with Lovecraft's Dagon. Sadly, no.

Those in the East Bay who'd heard of Lovecraft and Howard and Clark Ashton Smith were like to smirk at the supposed "campiness" of the old Weird Tales writers; their bookstores were prone to selling stuffed Cthulhu dolls, and the fake, mass-produced Necronomicon some enterprising oaf had concocted.

The fatal day of transfiguration would come. The mockers would have their comeuppance. Uncle Jonathan had told Rodney so. As unwholesome and half mad as the old man had been, Rodney had not known him to be wrong. Uncle Jonathan had reverently showed him the yellowed "Clue Books," as he called them: decaying, pulp-fragrant magazines in which the Hidden Magicians had carefully inserted traces, had tucked away their prolix encryptions: the keys to the hidden realms; to Uzuldaroum and Commoriom and other morbidly magical abodes in long-frozen Hyperborea.

Uncle Jonathan, on his death bed, had given Rodney a sickly yellow-toothed grin and said, "Employment, Rodney! Yes, a job awaits you! You shall count the treasure, the riches of Eriphodes of Commoriom will glitter under your hands, if you come to this house on the appointed day and at the appointed hour! Riches await, and destiny!"

This...this was the appointed day. And very nearly the appointed hour. It didn't matter that The Dolts were trailing along behind him. Let them come and have their share of the golden destiny—what did it matter?

No one had mattered to Rodney—not since his father had stormed across the living room, kicking toys aside; had shaken the floor with his footsteps as he stalked to the door that day, years ago, when Rodney was but eight years old. Rodney had tried to block his drunken, brawny father from the door, for he'd heard him vow to walk out and never return. For all his father's faults, Rodney loved him. The boy stepped into his father's path and cried out, "No, Daddy! No!"

In an icy fury, his father picked him up and hurled him across the room. Rodney had struck the hearth in just the wrong way—as if the Fates, with cruel glee, had arranged for his left leg to shatter in three critical places; had seen to it that he splintered his left knee. Bone had to be removed; cartilage was liberally excised. There was no money for special surgical reconstruction. Rodney was lucky the county had given him the steel leg brace.

Soon after that day, Rodney's Great-Uncle Jonathan had asked his weary, despair-ridden mother if he could watch the boy while she was at work. "Uncle Creepy," his sister called Jonathan. But after all, he was an older relative who wanted to give Rodney some care, so Mom was for it.

Soon after Rodney arrived at the old man's creaking Victorian house—where not even his father had been admitted—Great-Uncle Jonathan took him by the wrist and led him through mold-reeking hallways into a dusty, untidy library.

*Now, boy, your education begins,* Uncle Jonathan had said. *First, the Clue Books. Then...the decryptions! And the fragments of the true Book of Summoning...*

Rodney had at first thought the scrawny, white-haired man raving. Clue Books? Summonings? Jonathan was the elderly father of Dad's uncle; his hands were gnarled with arthritis; his eyes as yellow as his teeth; as yellow as his wrinkled suit, with its padded shoulders. "I am king here, in this house!" Jonathan cackled. Then he'd chortle to himself, almost inaudibly: "The King in Yellow! The King! In yellow!" And indeed, most of his clothing was yellow.

Rodney had learned to read at two; at nine he was already bookish, and more drawn to the company of a decaying volume of *The Red Fairy Book*, or *The Arabian Nights*, than the companionship of other children. So he turned eagerly to Jonathan's strange old volumes, some of them gawdy pulps, some hoarily ancient tomes bound in a peculiar pinkish-brown leather.

The old man's ravings had turned out to be founded on reality—or perhaps, on *realities*. Jonathan had been right: the dead four-coned volcano Mount Voormithadreth indeed still looms over the obsidian peaks of the Eiglophian; and somewhere in mountain range's labyrinth of lava tunnels the Spider God Atlach-Nacha, wrapt in its own white silken bedding, lies dozing yet—waiting for the return of worshippers long since perished. While in Commoriom, one of the last surviving sorcerers brooded, even now; kept alive these long ages through his arts and the devotion of his servant. A servant, however, now lost to him...

And so it was, that when Rodney discussed the Hyperborean cycle of Clark Ashton Smith with his English teacher, Mrs. Gamble, in this, his second year of community college, he told the bemused woman, "Clark's Hyperborea was real! Commoriom itself is real! Oh, to be sure not every tale he imagined taking place there was true. But much of it was true: it was transmitted to his imagination by a sorcerer whose name I cannot speak aloud. I tell you, Mrs. Gamble, riches and freedom await me there, in ancient, brooding Commoriom..."

Mrs. Gamble had smiled condescendingly and looked at the costume-shop cape Rodney wore to school. "Is this a rehearsal for some of that cosplay stuff I heard about, Rodney, where fantasy fans get costumed up and play roles?"

"Just as you like," Rodney told her coldly, his voice ringing with unspoken portent. "Just as you like, madame."

"Madame?" that blonde in the class laughed, hearing that. Melissa, that was the blonde's name--she sat beside the staring dolt Hezza. She slapped her forehead like someone from a sitcom and said, "You don't have to always come off so *nerdy scrub*, Rodney, I mean, God, take a chill pill."

Rodney turned to the eye-rolling blonde and calmly informed her. "The Judgment of Yhoundeh will be upon this world, and upon the like of you, girl," he said. "The Elk Goddess is displeased with the poisoning of the natural realm. The time of punishment will come soon enough, and consume you all in choking heat..."

Mrs. Gamble sighed. "That kind of rant kept you out of the universities, Rodney. It sounds threatening! Ease up, please, if you don't want to be excluded from here too."

Threatening? They had threatened him! And now The Dolts supposed themselves a threat too. But, according to the old pewter pocket watch Great Uncle Jonathan had given him, the time was almost upon him. Any moment now...

Then first wave of transfiguration struck. So far, it affected only Rodney's perceptions. He walked painfully along past the tenements, trudging with his usual difficulty—yet he began to feel lighter. And there was a glow, a gleam to things. The telephone poles, that rusty old mail box, the stoops, the parked cars—they seemed to shimmer. Then, up ahead, they became ghostly—and were replaced by another vantage, another scene entirely.

*Commoriom!*

Up rose the crumbling terraces, the soaring cracked spires of ancient Commoriom, bathed in a strange light—a diffuse blue light that came through a distant ceiling of ice. For this was Commoriom today, in the twenty-first century—almost deserted, and hidden beneath a camouflaging sheath of ice, in the far North. The ice was gradually melting, as the planet warmed—Greenland's hidden land-scape, and unknown cityscapes, would eventually be revealed. The long lost capitol city of Hyperborea would be spoiled by outsiders—unless the sorcerer Eriphodes could prevent it. Though steeped in the lore of countless centuries of study, Eriphodes would need help to keep Commoriom's secrets.

What was that ahead? Cast in some unknown metal stood a ti-tanic statue of a warrior, sword in hand, slashing down at a cringing beast-man. The massive statue of the warrior and his cowering enemy towered over an ice-puddled square. Judging by illustrations Rodney had glimpsed in his grand-uncle's books, the statue showed some forgotten warrior king of Commoriom slaying the chieftain of the Voormi—a king who led an army that drove the Yeti-like creatures to their hiding places in the most remote fastnesses of Hyperborea.

*It had begun.* Rodney was being given a vision of Hyperborea.

Rodney knew that, physically, he was still hunching along in Oak-land, California, on a misty autumn night; past liquor stores and a shuffling wino. He could discern the ghostly outlines of the city block beyond the luminous loom of Commoriom—so far, he was only be-ing granted sight of his goal. But he knew that soon enough, when he reached his great uncle's house, the final transfiguration would happen, and he would be given all that he hoped for.

~*~

"What the fuck is he staring at?" Skroggy wondered aloud. "Scoping around all over like he's on acid and never saw a liquor store before, bluh."

"Man's crazy," Hezza said. "We knew that. His uncle was crazy. But story is, the old man squirreled away a big stash o' cash in that old house of his. So Crazy Like a Fox Oddney, here, is gonna sniff it out for us."

It seemed to Hezza, then, that Oddney Rodney looked back at him and Skroggy, for just a moment, with a knowing sneer on his face.

"You think he's wise to us?" Skroggy asked.

"Hell, Skrog, he don't know if we're just walking the same direction as him. Anyway another three blocks and we get into that old part of town with all the Victorian houses and shit. And that's where his uncle's place is. We could follow him and walk past like we were going somewhere else, just let him go in, then follow his crazy ass inside...And take whatever he's dug up in there."

"If there is anything much. Maybe it's just full of old junk."

"No, dude. Remember what he said—riches. Treasure. It's gotta be there."

~*~

The gray lineaments of Oakland seemed more and more ethereal as Rodney made his aching way to the old house, whereas the soaring towers, the crusted battlements, the shadow-haunted doorways of old Commoriom seemed increasingly solid, quickly becoming far more corporeal than the city in which Rodney had grown up.

But had he indeed grown up here? Oh in this body, yes; but in fact his true genesis, his true arising, had been in another body, and in another place long ago. Centuries ago. He only remembered it in a scrappy way, now, but he knew he had been Pnom, loyal scribe and factotum to Eriphodes the Arch Sorcerer of Commoriom. He and Eriphodes, and the wizard's bestial retinue, were amongst the few who stayed while all others fled the capitol city for decadent Uzuldaroum; they had fled for fear of the vicious thugs commanded by the brutal Knygathin Zhaum, and as a result of dreadful auguries, the bleak portents suggesting that Tsathoggua would arise once more; arising to demand sacrifices in the thousands. *Your newborns will the Toad God feed upon...*

But Eriphodes had sent Pnom to the city's enemies, with a rat in a bag; the rat's fleas carried a sickness, a plague that struck down Knygathin Zhaum and his men; while the supposed portents of the return of Tsathoggua were the cunning sorcerer's own invention. He was glad to have Commoriom to himself. Its gold, its silver and gems, rising in dusty but precious piles like a dragon's hoard, were his to savor—long had the love of treasure been his weakness.

And so centuries passed as the ice advanced over Commoriom, and as Eriphodes enslaved ever more shades, more of the elementals and demons who thronged the outer darkness, making them his servants too. But the time came, long after most residents of Hyperborea were dead, when the restless shades of the outer darkness demanded payment.

Rodney remembered it all, now. As the transfiguration proceeded, the memories came flooding back: Pnom had been sent by the Eriphodes on a mission, about a century earlier, to misdirect a certain great ship into an iceberg. The *Titanic* struck the iceberg just as the sorcerer intended—as his dark servants had arranged—and hundreds of passengers took to lifeboats. Some passengers were rescued but, as Eriphodes had planned, two lifeboats were drawn by the minions of Dagon farther north and west. Those who survived the journey were summoned to the icy shore by Pnom—who now knew himself as Rodney. The castaways followed light of a swinging lantern, made shore, and willingly accompanied Pnom to what they hoped would be warmth and succor. Instead, they were taken through a tunnel of ice that curved and twisted down into the bone-strewn galleries under Commoriom.

Here they were seized by the half-men whom Eriphodes had bred from Voormi and human women. Some of the lost survivors of the *Titanic* were dragged by the half-men to the Chamber of Sating, so that certain demons might be fed in return for their allegiance to the ancient sorcerer. Other survivors, a few handy maintenance men and several women, were kept for Eriphodes' special purposes. The men would be set to work; the women...

But it didn't matter. What mattered was that Pnom had done well, in procuring this fresh flesh, and expected to be rewarded with another thousand years of life as the sorcerer had promised.

Then—he made a mistake. He failed to watch the prisoners closely enough. One of the men, doughtier than the rest, had caught up a flame-sword, and used it to fight his way out. Pnom rushed to stop him...much as Rodney had rushed to stop his father...

And Pnom had been struck down by the sword-wielding bravo. He had died, with fire consuming his heart.

Pnom's spirit, unwillingly released, went howling up in confusion, mad with fear, lost to Eriphodes, at least for a time.

Pnom's spirit wandered the upper airs for decades until, suddenly, it was reincarnated into the body of an ill-fated boy born in 1993. One Rodney Lasalle.

Rodney had forgotten it all—until Eriphodes, magically fore-seeing Pnom's predestined incarnation, prepared a return for him. Working through suggestive writers like Smith and Lovecraft, the sorcerer had planted hints and secrets in certain publications favored by young Jonathan Lasalle. Most of these hints and secrets were for none other than Pnom. Deciphered, they explained themselves, and they indicated a time, and a place. They led...

Here.

Rodney stood in front of the wind-scoured Victorian house, with its broken porch posts, its darkened windows. He could scarcely see the teetering old Victorian itself—he saw, instead, its parallel: the entrance to a temple, its facade shaped rather like this old house, but in stone, and windowless; the temple yet stood, somewhere in Commoriom.

The door of the temple stood open, inviting; just as the door of the house swung open for him now...

*I have opened both doors for you*, came the familiar intonations of the sorcerer. Eriphodes spoke in a language that Rodney Lasalle had never heard. But Pnom knew it, and Rodney understood it now.

*Two there are who have followed me here*, Rodney warned, in his mind.

*Do not be concerned, Pnom! I have summoned them here. I have planted certain enticing ideas in the mind of the one capable of holding ideas.*

Rodney nodded, and struggled up the creaking old steps, walked to the open front door, and stepped within...

Suddenly he felt as if he were walking through thick, gelatinous fire. And with each step the fire was eating away at the impure body he'd been trapped in all this time: The body of Rodney Lasalle. It was killing Rodney's body--so that the trapped soul of Pnom could be set free.

Rodney had to force himself to take the last few steps. The pain was unspeakable, the resistance gigantic...

He staggered to the basement door which awaited him, just behind the stairs. He opened it and looked not at the basement stairs--they were there, but he couldn't see them. He saw only the secret shaft within the temple, in Commoriom. The stone shaft that led down into the depths under the temple. He saw, now, only the temple...the house had quite vanished. He couldn't see the basement stairs.

Pain fountained up in him, consumed him. He could no longer stand. Rodney collapsed--and died.

~\*~

"Whoa, Oddney's all collapsed," Skroggy said, as they stepped through the open front door. "Maybe he's drunk or stoned or something."

"Maybe," Hezza muttered. "Maybe that's why he was looking at stuff that wasn't there."

Inside the thickly musty old house, illuminated in the streetlight shine spilling through the open door, Rodney Lasalle's body lay half sprawled down the cellar steps.

"Help me with this..." Hezza reached down and pulled Rodney's ankle, Skroggy took the other one, and they dragged him into the light near the door. Motionless, Oddney Rodney was staring...and grinning. But his eyes had been burnt from his head. Only blackened sockets remained.

"That's fucked up, man!" Skroggy burst out. "Where are his eyes!"

"I don't know. Maybe he ran into an exposed wire or some shit." Hezza felt Rodney's wrists, then tried the neck. No pulse. He shook his head. "The guy's dead! Flat out dead!"

"Hezza--maybe we oughta get the fuck outta here!"

"We didn't kill him, dude. Anyway..." Hezza got up and looked through the door at the street outside. There was no one nearby on the street. He quietly closed the door. "...He was trying to get down those basement steps. Makes sense that's where the money is. Down there somewhere." He reached into his pocket, took out his keychain, which had a small flashlight on it. "Come on."

"What about the electrical wire shit?"

"We'll watch for it. Gotta be careful. We're not going to be stupid like he was."

He led the way to the basement door, started down it, slowly, flashing the light down the unpainted wooden stairs. Looked like an ordinary old basement, down there, mostly stacked with old magazines of some kind. *Thrilling Wonder Stories*, stuff like that.

They were halfway down the steps—and the flashlight sparked, jumping from his hand. "Ow!" A flaring blue light coalesced around them, spinning like water going down a drain.

The basement stairs vanished under their feet--and they felt themselves falling into the spinning light. Screaming, spinning into darkness into a tunnel in space. Hezza waited to hit the basement floor. He never did hit it. Not that one.

Hundreds of miles passed below them in seconds...They had glimpses of city lights, passing beneath them; of a sea unfurling below...of a frozen landscape. They rocketed toward a tower, jutting through the ice--a tower missing its roof. They were plunged down, into it the gaping mouth of the tower, down, into a brooding gloom...

~*~

Sheathed now in comfortable ectoplasm, Pnom—who'd once called himself Rodney Lasalle—floated over the great sparkling heap of gemstones in the vault as gold-robed Eriphodes turned to gaze up at him. Eriphodes smiled, showing sharp-filed teeth as he stroked a beard like Spanish moss. "There you are, Pnom! Back at last! You don't have your old body, it's true, but I think you'll find this apparitional modality a satisfying replacement. It's far more mobile. And certainly better than the one you've been trapped in more than twenty years. You have had enough dallying about with the unclean ones, yes? Ha ha! Now then--I have found a new clutch of treasure stones and would have you count them...after you and I take care of one other matter..."

"Certainly, Golden Master."

Eriphodes went to the door, humming to himself, and strode through it, along a stone corridor lit with fluorescent gems ensconced in the high, platinum ceiling. Pnom floated along close behind his master, content to be free of the damaged body and equally damaged feelings of Rodney Lasalle.

They came to the Chamber of Sating—where two groaning, bruised and bloodied figures twitched on the stained granite floor, feebly trying to rise: Hezza and Skroggy. But they could not stand, they could even crawl; most of their bones were broken, for after falling through the tunnel in space itself, and down through the shaft into the temple, their impact on this cold stone floor had been considerable.

"Help...help me..." Hezza said hoarsely.

"Dolt!" Pnom jeered. "There is no help for you! Your physical suffering is about to come to an end. Your psychic suffering—that is just beginning."

Then he and Eriphodes spoke the words, together, that opened the doorway between planes, and the hungry ones came swiftly to be paid for their service...

The hungry ones took their time in feasting. They did so enjoy a good meal.

# The Winter of Atiradarinsept

## By Zak Jarvis

is sword smoldered on the table between us. It terrified me that he did not care about the value of wood, now that winter had come.

"This," he said, gesturing to my inn as though it were his. "Is my victory. This land destroyed, the waste of my every dream. Gather your people and anything you have to record my story."

He put his armored hand palm down on the glowing metal of his sword. The room filled with the smell of his flesh cooking on the blade.

I pulled my skincoat close and stepped into the cold.

Our only ingenite lay in steaming pieces, its milksac ruptured. We would not survive long without it. My anxious, thrumming heart blotted out the sounds of the world so that even the crunching of snow under-foot went unheard. Our home, joined to but separate from the main inn, glowed golden in the nighttime ringlight.

The moment the door opened Gematra clasped me and held my eyes with his weird stare.

"Do we need to flee?"

I looked past him to the children, their eyes nearly luminous in the dark, all turned to me.

"No," the stranger's voice said behind me. "Gather up your things and come in the other building. I have right of laniation. Obey."

I heard his footsteps recede behind me.

"That was the crest of the Interdiction, but what in the name of Mnos-tia and all the eternal heirs is a right of laniation?" Concinnity whispered.

"Who knows, love," I said. "But we're ruined even if we obey. The ingenite is dead, and that man killed it."

They gasped.

Gematra pulled away and turned to the children.

"Hurry! Do as he said! We might still find hope so long as we're alive."

"We're to record a story," I said, feeling the cold bite my skin.

With my family herded into the main inn, I began to write what the stranger told me.

The following is as it was told to me, Sough of Ge'sqnul, owner and records keeper of the Way Home at the border crossing.

~*~

I am Atiradarinsept, fourth Cicurator of the Magisterial Interdiction. My masters chose me to lead an army and crash down the wall between our world and the strange place that our fathers, Eibon and Morghi, abandoned.

Can you imagine the honor? The terror?

There are few of us, we humans, who are allowed to speak with Intercessors, and only in the bondage of what you might call matrimony.

Your triune marriages are an echo of this, but the Intercessor's mercy bears little relation to what a husband and wife do with their trennel. Even the most pious do little more than carry semen in hand or mouth from husband to wife.

A very long time ago I was pledged to a zeugma called Heptanquirra. It took me months to learn how to manipulate her glands, to stroke the ciliated ridges just so, in order for her to open herself to me. That I did not lose my manhood to those early experiences should be proof enough of my loyalty, but the Interdiction needed far more. I had to train myself to penetrate Heptanquirra in front of a royal audience, to do so while my head was immersed in the viscous fluid the Interdiction uses to breathe, to fulfill congress in full armor, while being flogged.

Only when I could perform all of that to the satisfaction of my masters was I allowed to even to see an Intercessor.

In all Cykranosh I had seen no being so powerful.

She towered above me like a garrison. Plates of armor moved with her body like river ice in spring. Her lashing hands clattered against my armor. Her musk burned my nose and left such an ague in my lungs that I thought they'd cracked a mnechtun seed. Heptanquirra, gulping furiously around my manhood, folded back her sheath and unfurled the organ that would join the three of us together. Never in our solitary couplings had she shown me this part of her. Innumerable tongues of the Intercessor mopped over the grayish organ, each slathering Heptanquirra with a sizzling, catheretic mucus.

In a great press she pulled the three of us together, bucking hard enough to bruise my iliac crest.

Her ten arms pecked through my armor in a hundred places, moving like the probing limbs of a kultern spider until my flanks burned with tiny punctures.

Just as her exculpatory mandibles opened to bathe me in imperative fluid she dislodged Heptanquirra, the aperture gaping open and pouring glair in lumpen strings. The Intercessor slowly withdrew into the darkened chamber from which she'd come.

The zeugma's conjunctive organ pulsed in the open air, turning violet as their combined fluids oxidized.

I had passed the final test.

My Intercessor was Analepsis. To bind me to her, they took one of her eyes and let it burrow into the base of my skull. Then, after a joining much like the previous Intercessor, she soaked me in her imperative fluid. The orders seeped into me. Like dreams or madness they invaded, pushing my thoughts aside.

From that day onwards I conquered for Intercessor Analepsis and the Magisterial Interdiction that guided her.

The obstreperous sciapodes of Pnul watched in awe as I dismembered their patriarch.

The once glimmering mineral forests of Opsiun fell before me.

Hundreds of lesser gods took my offered yoke of slavery.

My army grew from a small squad to a land-shaping mass more beholden to the foodgoods I could procure than even the will of the Interdiction.

Any peace you've known, or prosperity, has flowed into your life through the wounds I've left on the world.

For most of a year I labored. As I warred, the infants of my sisters and brothers grew, from swaddled dependance to successful adults. My days were marked by scars. The cicatrices of my service are a map of our age.

My defining mission came at the height of my power.

At the end I lay coated in the glut of her influencing rheum. I felt her intent becoming my own. The shape of the mission, the eidolon of it rooted itself to everything. It was in the convulsing throat of the zeugma as she milked me, in my own cataleptic explusion, even Heptanquirra's thirsty grunts as she gulped down the product of our union.

The Intercessors chose me to return to the world of humans.

~\*~

Concinnity caught his attention.

"Where did you serve before the Intercessors?"

"I was among the war chattel in the Battle of Three Moons. My life before that is erased."

Gematra ignored the children for a moment only to be accosted in their strange language. It made me ache for the day when they learn to speak like proper adults.

"I don't understand," I said. "How did you know you were chosen? You said the idea came from inside you. How can you be sure that you aren't mad?"

He smiled at me, broad and wavering. It was not the smile of a sane man.

"That's always the question, is it not?"

He leaned over the table and grabbed the skins that kept me warm.

"How can you ever be certain what is inside your head and what is real?"

As quick as you please he brought the sword around behind my head. It burned my neck.

"A finger's width of this into your spine and the inside of your head begins the transition from personhood to slop. I assure you though, the world outside your head goes ever onward."

I felt sure that I defiantly held his gaze, but as I enrich this transcription of his story I cannot be certain. Could I *really* have looked that man in the eye?

He relaxed back into his chair, the sword returning to the char it had left on the table.

"It is very perceptive of you to ask," he said.

Gematra caught my attention briefly with a tiny raise of his eyebrows. He had a plan, but I could not know what.

~\*~

Over four hundred years have passed since our fathers Eibon and

Morghi lived. Thirteen thousand generations of men and women, stilli-cidious births, a defluxion of lives, and serein deaths uncountable. As best I knew, none since had set eyes upon their Mhu Thulan sea. We humans of Cykranosh have only the stories of our fabled home. Until the moment I knew I was to return, I discounted the stories as myths of a race denied knowledge of its origin.

Intercessor Analepsis gave me a hoary incunabula from the defiled Blemphroims. It detailed a portal, crafted from common metals and imbued by the will of wayward gods. While most of the Blemphroims died to purge their heresy, a few, I learned, escaped to Hyperborea some hundred years ago.

I made a new portal, large enough for armies.

The first scouts reported trackless ice. Truly, none of us expected a world unchanged by the vast years between Eibon's crossing and our time, but no one expected desolation. Again and again our sorties found only ice, featureless and expansive. So I ordered them to look down. I procured a mithridate key from the Interdiction's stores, gathered my best soldiers and stepped through the portal.

The hyemal wind wrapped me in a thousand stitching pains. Its arescent howl flayed away all my purpose and left me with the fearful certainty that all my effort would end in smoke.

I steadied my nerves as I'd been taught, as though I were preparing to meet an Intercessor. The fear pulled back and I grasped the hilt of my sword.

The sky above us was black. No ring lit the land, only a wan and gib-bous moon. The land, such as it was, stretched into hazed obscurity. Gelid dust drifted in curls and strings, prickling my nose and skin.

That pale, miserable satellite glistened across the icy powder as a long line, like a bridge or a beam reaching for the sky.

I ordered my soldiers to dig pits. They filled them with naphtha and we burned snow. Beneath hard-pack waited monumental serac like sharp and numerous teeth. As that ice melted its surface became pellucid. Ir-reconcilable blackness stretched beneath us as blank and terrifying as the Kulgness at high tide when the megapredators have sunk deep to feast.

For hours we flensed the rime from that distant world, spiraling out-wards to always leave a path to the surface.

When the unnaturally huge sun rose it turned the landscape into a blinding emptiness, endlessly luminal. The blinding disk mocked us with its failure to bring warmth. Though we did not benefit, its rays heated the atmosphere above us enough that a thick fog rose from the ground. That terrible sun crept across the sky with agonizing slowness. We made a base camp with our return portal.

The Hyperborean sun circled us again and again as we worked. We burned deeper, finding at last some stones bearing extra-telluric metal, but no sign of hands, human or otherwise.

At the surface of the submerged mountain I ground a tiny portion of stone and let the mithridate key make its decoction. A sour drink, from the glacial ice and these otherworldly stones, but in a moment the visions came.

I saw the ice ebbing and flowing against the mountain, carving it into a vertiginous tooth. A city sprang up and crumbled, then another and another, like crops in harvest. Roads stretched and stunted, pulsing and radiating away from the habitations. The ice, for its part, had imperceptibly retreated from my view. The cities grew and merged, involuted by roads and metallic beams, rivers of tiny metal and glass cells flowed between them and all around them.

Then came the ice. Resolute and imperdible it crouched, pulsing against the movement of the city. Men and women uncountable surely looked up at that wall and despaired.

The end came quickly. A single flexion and all the city's movement stopped. That brumal mass rolled between the towers, it thickened and grew, filling every space with neve and serac.

With the vision fading, I pointed toward the entombed city and we set the fires anew, pumping naphtha down from the surface in long pipes.

The tunnel work went much faster than the dig.

Our reflections writhed inside the ice, the movement giving illusory life to the vile stillness of that world. My soldiers busied themselves behind the boring crew. They ferried supports to shore up ice we did not trust. The world outside the tunnel appeared liquescent and ghoulishly blue, rent by fractures and inclusions. From time to time that disconnected fear would return to me, squeezing on my chest like failure, but we pressed forward.

I had to know.

What happened to these people? If we could achieve footing on the city, the mithridate key could tell me. I called back through our supply line for equipment to remove the melted ice, to dig into it faster, to clean the air of choking naphtha fumes.

At first I could not tell what the shape was, glinting green and distorted through serac bulb and facet. It hulked low to the ground outside our tunnel. I ordered it excavated.

As we got closer I recognized one of the glass and metal cells I had seen pulsing between cities. It bore a thin metal shell and rhomboidal apertures sealed with mineral glass. The form of the thing was almost like a predatory desert tresk, its sharp edges flowing over a smooth, elongate mass. With the ice carefully melted away I knew it as a conveyance. Its interior, though filled with ice, housed a soft bench and two shaped cathedra. The textiles that wrapped the seats sagged and ruptured as the water poured out, revealing thick sponge beneath, the ugly orange color of fungus or rot. It would have seated five in its day.

I ordered my soldiers away but for a guard and I settled in to devour the history of the Hyperborean device.

It had conveyed one of many duumvirate families from a residence on the distant shores of the city, to a larger transportation center at the interior, and sometimes to disparate places across the continent. The device itself was supremely clever, being a distillation of extra-telluric metals and attenuated mineral elixirs. The motive force came from a fiendish arrangement of ritual magics that ultimately combusted and relied upon a strange draught. An entire subclass of men scoured the Earth, as it had come to be called since Eibon. They extracted the residue of a vast sacrifice, many millions of years distant. A sacrifice of unimaginable proportion. All this arranged against a foe that I could not see. The sacrifice permeated everything about the device, an event so singular, so vast that none of the people in its wake could see it. I had glimpses of an ancient cult guiding events, but the mithridate key could find nothing more than a few meaningless names: Good Walkers, Phoebus, The Oculists. All opaque to me.

We tunneled on toward the city. There I hoped to learn more. As the days cycled, the sunlight filtered through the ice came to be more and more ominous. It made shapes move when there was stillness, made me see soldiers that were not there. The tunnel once contracted in my view like the throat of an enormous beast swallowing its prey.

In their fear, my soldiers attempted to rebel, but ultimately I was the more fearsome.

We continued on.

The city massed above us as a vast darkness concealed within the evil blue of the ice. There our tunnel found caries within the ice, and within them the mummified remains of people. The air in those pockets came in stercoraceous gusts. My less-trained soldiers retched at the smell and retched again when I used the mithridate key on the dead.

Then did the magnitude come clear.

~*~

"Bring me spirits," he said, interrupting himself. "The memory does not bear sober recollection."

Gematra stood so suddenly I thought he'd been waiting for the opportunity. "Does ignis wine meet your needs, sir?"

Atiradarinsept looked us over, a smile grudging its way to his mouth. He nodded slowly.

"I've only understood half your words, but it is all faithfully recorded," I said.

That brought him to full smile. The expression suited him and I felt a flicker of admiration.

"You've never been among people more important than your village elders, have you?"

I shook my head.

"And you think I'm going to kill you."

I nodded.

This time he laughed. "You're coming with me after the story is committed," he said. "Do as I say and I'll keep you and yours far from the sear and yellow leaf. If I'd left your beast alive, you'd have wanted to keep it. It would slow us considerably."

My muscles instinctively pulled taut at the idea of going with him, as though my whole body wanted to refuse. I had felt myself a knot of tension before, but after his proclamation I was a storm-pulled mooring. Concinnity's hand squeezed mine. Instead of comfort, I felt only pain.

The children clustered in, making their nonsense sounds.

He looked at us all.

"The three of you. What are your names? And the children."

Concinnity told him.

"The three of you love each other, yes? You perform your sacraments and make holy any union intended to be fruitful?" He looked at the children.

My pride got the better of the fear. "We perform our sacraments always."

"You know what it is, then," he said, tilting his head down to look at us

212

through his bushy eyebrows. "To give and see your gift given, to take what has been taken before you. You know that delicate trust. The tiniest thread that can hold everything."

At which point Gematra returned with our best carboy and a chrysoprase tazza.

With his considerable dignity, he placed the tazza in front of our guest and poured it full. The wine perfumed the air, that smell whose mood seems always to counteract your own.

Atiradarinsept gave us the most cursory nod and took the tazza in both hands, filling his nose with its smell then his belly with its liquid.

"Now then."

~*~

The ice was the world's tomb.

Hyperborean, or Earth years are vastly shorter than our own. It had taken only ten for the ice to overwhelm them, and ten of their years is barely a third of one for us. While ten of their years is a brief time in the span of history, it is ample time for a people to be broken by cachexy.

Bizarrely, they welcomed the ice in the beginning.

When glaciers blockaded trade routes, the enthusiasm waned.

A singular moment catalyzed their fear. A group of polar explorers became lost in the ice. Their markers vanished, landmarks shifted. Voices came to them in the wind. All signals of dementia, of course. But these things existed in their documents for anyone to see. Everyone saw. Not dementia, but truth.

After that, an increasing portion of industry was devoted to the problem. Each brief year brought further encroachment until finally their seasons held no respite from the marching walls of ice.

They huddled around fires, burning the last sticks of wood in their desperation. As you have done.

All were swallowed.

Near the very end, the cult made itself clear, hoping wide support could reverse the tide.

They had called themselves Phoebus for some time, and that is the name they used then. Presenting as burgraves of industry, luminaries of might and politics, they promised that worship of Bhinendrosz would cicatrize the world. Bhinendrosz had left them, though, millions of years previously, and his worship did little but encourage the worst excesses, assuring that humankind on Earth died with no remaining dignity.

My soldiers *mined* that city under the ice. Months we spent there, horripilated and pruinose, our refuse frozen in troughs and caves carved for the purpose. Some days the air warmed enough that our midden thawed to stink.

I consumed the lives of thousands in my search, I charted their relationships, learned the patterns of employment and dissolution as the end came, until finally I wormed my way into the trail of the Phoebus cult. Almost all of them were human or close to it. The one I found who was not, however, opened a chasm of time beneath me.

I dove through epochs. Their buildings becoming smaller, made of cruder material as I went, until the cult ruled over not humans but hairy men, then bird-like men, saurians. Still backwards I went, back to that great sacrifice, thirty million of our years ago, and still the one I investigated had lived.

The later humans of Earth believed many things about the sacrifice, but none guessed at its truth.

Yes, volcanoes choked the air with reechy clouds, much as the people believed. What they did not guess at were the inquinate gods of the abyssal sea, lashing apart clathrates with their operose pedicles. That clathrate boiled the seas and filled the entire air with irremedicable clouds. Even as all life on the planet ground to a valetudinarian parody, the beings of the Phoebus cult marched to the union of one mind, murdering themselves as they went, in order to exterminate every living thing in their path. A selected few cultists remained, encysted in deep caverns and untouched by the toxic air.

They sacrificed *life itself* to defeat their enemy. The lost gods of the Phoebus cult did not know its name, nor where it came from. It seemed to them to come from everything. You might call it entropy, or nihil. Perhaps even death, though death regularly brings new life and thus hardly seems applicable. They called it a demon, and the demon loricated itself in ice.

For millions of years the sacrifice kept their Earth warmed and proof against the demon. The early humans built great civilizations only to be toppled by an epoch of returning ice, reduced from cultures to creatures. They rose again with the help of the Phoebus cult, but were soon beset once more. It was then that Phoebus began burning the long-dead sacrifices of the world that had been, and that strategy, they felt, was unbeatable.

They thought so until the very end. The last of them now lies clutching her mummified flesh in perpetual horror.

And I have let that demon loose here. This strange winter you suffer, the winter that came while I was away. It is the only thing that could be taken from Earth. I was tasked to return with Mhu Thulan's treasures. Winter is my victory.

Now then, I command you to imagine this scene.

My triumphal return in the dark of night, near-to-day compared to what I had become accustomed. My soldiers sent to their homes, my armor donned, I entered the chamber of the Intercessors.

At the zeugma pens I called for Heptanquirra. She came to me in delight, her junction awash to see me after the long absence. We embraced and traded affections.

I had to tell Intercessor Analepsis what happened to Earth; what was *happening* to Cykranosh. As I organized the story before her, I could feel her contractions through Heptanquirra, but Analepsis withheld all her fluids from me, leaving her mood unreadable. Her arms tapped the joins in my armor as though she wanted me to denude myself before her. Heptanquirra burbled soothingly to me, but there was no hiding her fear.

The Intercessor wrung the last words out of me, piercing my armor in a hundred places, bleeding me until the air hung thick not with the smell of her excretions, but only my blood and Heptanquirra's fear.

Then there was the interpellation.

Everything became vast around me. Sounds went on, the taste of blood overwhelmed me, the tiny movements of the zeugma and the intercessor magnified.

Analepsis slashed Heptanquirra.

Pink flesh peeled back, I felt her muscles relax around me and then blood boiled from the wound. The zeugma's sensory nodule fell onto my thigh. It rang the metal of my armor as beautifully as a musical instrument.

The Intercessor strode above me, Heptanquirra's body releasing me to wet exposure. Her arms rose above her, Analepsis, the integuments stretching to reveal fine traceries of vessels under her skin. The zeugma dangled from her body.

Only then did Analepsis anoint me, her fluid black and angry. It burned my wounds and filled my head with rage-thoughts.

I drove my sword through her.

As I fled from the outer decretal chambers I felt her inside of me. No one was meant to know what I had done. She wanted me dead and silent.

Intercessor Analepsis intended to simply deny the truth of what returned with me, as though turning away from the threat would defeat it.

And I could not be certain, as I hastily dressed my wounds, whether the urge to kill her had come from me or her. For hours my thoughts chased and worried at the possibility that I had killed her, or worse, that I had not been in control of myself.

There was not much time to worry. Shortly after her death, the Intercessor's chambers filled with ice.

That ice has filled the government center.

It will cover our world.

But I know everything that the Phoebus cult knew, and if I can find the wizard Jelhrhelnuilgusehtnh, there is hope.

~*~

The words had scarcely left his mouth when his eyes rolled back. Pink-tinged foam dribbled from his mouth.

Gematra grabbed Concinnity and me by the hands and pulled us away, urging the children to follow.

"The poison took far too long," he said, letting the winter cold in through the open door. "The strength of a madman, truly. Whether he intended to kill us or not, the children would not have survived the flight he commanded."

"He came from the Interdiction," Concinnity said. "I am certain. If we can reach the coast my cousin will take us beyond their reach."

"But the story," I said. "What if it's true?"

Concinnity took my face in her hand, her skin almost hot after the icy rasp of the outdoors.

"Everyone knows the government lies to us," she said. "We will have to find our own way."

I looked back into the firelit room where Atiradarinsept, fourth Cicurator of the Magisterial Interdiction lay dead. I reassured myself that such a tale could not be true. Only lies would need such labored speech.

# The Door from Earth

## By Jesse Bullington

I

When Pipaluk, the chief engineer of Hiurapaluk's Peril Containment Plant, together with twelve of her most well-armed and efficient underlings, came at flickering, artificial dusk to seek the infamous Professori, Laila, in her amphibe-chanical facility on the lower-most substreet of the city's underlevel, they were surprised, as well as disappointed, to find her absent.

Their surprise was due to the fact that Professori Laila had made much to-do about her expedition not taking place for another fort-night; all of Pipaluk's plots against the Professori had hinged on there being sufficient time to gain the rest of the Quorum's approval before confronting the rabble-rousing academic. They were disappointed because their formidable warrant, with symbolic fiery font glowing on an antique digital tablet, was now useless; and there seemed to be no earthly prospect of wiping the smug expression from Laila's hairy face, to say nothing of confiscating her domestic warrens for the use of the Engineers Guild.

Ingeniøri Pipaluk was especially disappointed, for Laila was her chief rival in the Quorum's science bloc, and was acquiring altogether too much fame and prestige among the Voormis of Mhu Thulan, that ultimate peninsula of the Grænland subcontinent. Pipaluk had been glad to receive certain evidence corroborating her suspicions that Laila's expedition through the Eibon Gate could be catastrophic, and not just in terms of heightening the Professori's already-dangerous popularity.

This evidence suggested that Laila was not, in fact, a devotee of the state-god, Tsathoggua, whose worship was incalculably older than the Voormi race. No, it seemed that the Professori instead paid tribute to Tsathoggua's paternal uncle, Hziulquoigmnzhah, with whom the *true* god of the Voormis had suffered a falling-out sometime in the previous millennium or three. This schism, which had something to do with the fall of Humanity, or perhaps the rise of the Voormis of Grænland and sundry other peoples in sundry different places, had resulted in the sealing of the Eibon Gate.

Walling up the entryway between the worlds of the benevolent, bat-furred toad-god Tsathoggua and that of the much-less-attractive demon prince Hziulquoigmnzhah seemed a surefire means of reaffirming Tsathoggua's favour. The Quorum's vote on this matter had been unanimous, and so the pit where the portal was located was closed off using a variety of fail-safes, and then the whole area was surrounded in a series of airlocks, cultural heritage be damned. Until Professori Laila started in with her insane theories of interstellar harmony and pan-theological unification, no one had given any thought to reopening the portal of ultratelluric metal that lay buried in ruins of black gneiss beneath Mhu Thulan's capital city.

Pipaluk had suspected the worst as soon as she discovered the Professori's new laboratory was directly adjacent to the outermost airlock housing the gate to Cykranosh that the warlock Eibon had used to escape Earth in ancient times, if the mytho-historical record was to be given credence. Alas, the Quorum had dragged its feet, despite Pipaluk's warnings, and now it was too late - she would have given her musk glands to kick the Provost in the kanaaks for postponing his vote as long as he had.

Pipaluk's subgineers bustled about Laila's laboratory in their glistening salamander-suits and, behind a tarp, they discovered where the Professori and her team of graduate students, clone servitors, and formless spawn had hacked into the municipal pipe that made up one of the facility's walls and plugged in their plasmaborers. The tunnel they had excavated led - surprise surprise - out of the lab, through a mega-support column, and directly into the first airlock bay, the dull-metal doors towering some thirty meters tall over Pipaluk's team.

"Airlock initially opened, Aggusti Second," the voice of one of the subgineers crackled in Pipaluk's pulsing, yellow bio-helm. "Breached on average twice daily each day since."

"*Hymirbjarg*," Pipaluk cursed, and several of her underlings grinned to themselves to hear their normally unflappable superior use such strong language. "I trust this is sufficient?"

"Fall back, Ingeniøri," Provost Ole answered over the Quorum channel. "We'll hold an emergency meeting. Politibetjent Chief Malik is on his way up, so extract your team and - "

"Wha - shhhack?" Pipaluk held down the garble button she'd installed onto her com-panel as she addressed her subgineers on their private channel. "Right, we don't have time to deal with more dawdling by those kanaaks. Ane and Nuka, with me. The rest, seal this airlock after us and don't open it, no matter what. I trust you all remember what happens when you open airlocks, yes?"

They did. It had been Pipaluk's team, after all, who designed the last batch of svataarsualiartartoq-suits for Mhu Thulan's formless spawn commandos - space stations tended to lack many gaps for the polymorphous spawn to flow through, so infiltrating the interstellar strongholds of those Yig-worshipping Valusians and Ithaqua-kissing Gnophkehs necessitated finding another way to get the formless spawn inside. Spacesuits that matched the design of those used by the targeted station, save with opaque helmets, did the trick quite nicely - fill a few suits with the spawn, trigger a rescue beacon on the station's frequency, and float the formless commandos through the void until they were retrieved by drones and taken inside the airlocks. Then, total havoc as the deadly children of Tsathoggua swept through the station, a sentient tidal wave of ichorous death.

"How will we get back, Ingeniøri?" subgineer Nuka asked, his voice cracking.

"Have some faith, son," said Pipaluk. "We'll recode the locks as we go. Things were built by your ancestors; think their primitive programming is beyond your skill?"

Nuka straightened his shoulders, his three-toed foot snapping up in salute. Through the faceshield of his bio-helm, Pipaluk could see the lad's umber fur bristling straight out from his face in embarrassment. Good, he *should* feel like an idiot.

" – stunt," Provost Ole was saying as Pipaluk relaxed her finger on the garble button. "Is that clear?"

"Perfectly, sir," said Pipaluk, and quit the channel altogether. "Right, let's go."

Nuka whined, long and low; Ane prayed, fast and loud; and the other subgineers all saluted as the ancient airlock opened into the deep.

## II

There were three airlocks in total, and the trio had reached the control panel beside the second by the time the first had ground shut behind them. Before advancing any further, Pipaluk had Ane explore to the left and Nuka to the right - the Ingeniøri had been over the schematics a dozen times lest just such an emergency entry become necessary, but it never hurt to confirm what the blueprints had already told her.

"Dead end," Nuka reported through the bio-helm's thrumming com-membrane. "Basalt. Dry. No cracks."

"Same here," Ane said, as she hiked back across the bay.

"Good," said Pipaluk. "Everything matches up. The reports state that the Eibon Gate was interdimensional, so they were able to completely surround it. Basically, they built a giant basalt box around the thing, with only an airlock leading in or out. Around that, another stone box with an airlock, and then another. So, through this door is another bay and across that is the final airlock, which opens into the ruins where the Gate is. Professori Laila and her team are either in the bay beyond this door, working on the last airlock, or they've managed to breach it and gain the ruins, which could be bad. Very bad."

"'Bad'?" said Nuka. "'Very bad'?"

"Depends," said Pipaluk, hoping against hope that her quarry was still fiddling with the last airlock and not beyond it. "Even with the feeble half-lives they were capable of producing, back when this was all built, the fail-safes in the ruins should still be operational. So, in a best-case scenario, the fail-safes will have arrested the Professori's advance. Worst-case scenario, Laila will have somehow gained the Gate."

"Fail-safes?" Nuka whimpered. "*Issi*."

"Act like you've got a quad," Ane snorted, petting the slimy muzzle of her microwave spitter as she sidled up to Pipaluk. The weapon purred at the subgineer's touch and Pipaluk made a mental note to invite Ane over for a soak in her breeding bath when they were safely home - the Ingeniøri's whiskers needed a serious stroking and she had a feeling this was just the Voormi to give it to her. This wasn't really the time for such concerns, admittedly, but stress always made Pipaluk's glands overproduce.

"Remember," Pipaluk said, as her fingers danced over the airlock's panel, "we need to stop Laila at all costs. Alive to stand trial is preferable but by no means necessary. The main thing will be avoiding the fail-safes, if those idiots have opened the airlock, and the Professori's formless spawn if they haven't. We may already be too late, so from here on out, we move faster than fast, got it? Now, let's get this heretic."

"Oh *yeah*," said Ane, and her weapon shivered in anticipation.

Nuka whinnied and made the sign of Saint Toad.

Pipaluk opened the airlock. A rush of cooling, semi-congealed blood poured out over their feet.

## III

The bay between the second and third airlock doors glowed a faint turquoise from a K'n-yan luminance system, and before the Voormis' bio-helms could tint out the blinding, pale light a fail-safe leapt on Ane and bit off her head. The thing's gears screamed and spat puffs of rust as it thrashed atop the decapitated subgineer, a blur of slick, amphibious tails and bluish metal pincers. Nuka panicked, his high-pitched howl nearly blowing out Pipaluk's com-membrane, and the Ingeniøri had to force herself not to attack the subgineer before taking out the fail-safe. She spat out the immolation code for Ane's suit, even as she leapt out of the way of the imminent blast. Even through her own salamander armor, she felt the wave of heat buffet her like a solar flare.

The fail-safe was still alive, but its metallic components had melted to the point of incapacitating the thing. Nuka had managed to avoid the worst of the blast, but was still crying like a Gnophkeh, sitting in the tacky, smoking blood that had flooded the bay. The bio-helm filtered out everything but the smell, the bouquet of burnt hair and engine oil making Pipaluk's eyes water. She didn't look down at the fused mass of mewling fail-safe and gorgeous, dead subgineer. Instead, she yanked Nuka to his feet and fired a cold-shower code down his channel - the result was instantaneous, the coward straightening up and shuddering as his suit doused him in a psychoactive chemical spray.

"Subgineer Nuka," Pipaluk barked in his face while he was ripe for imprinting. "Ready your weapon and follow me. Those hymirbjarg-brained academics have obviously breached the last airlock. Hurry!"

The subgineer saluted and snapped his olid-pistol off his belt. It was no microwave spitter, but it was better than the ceremonial gladius that Pipaluk had brought - had she known Laila wouldn't be in her lab, ready for arrest, she obviously would have brought something more substantial. At least there weren't any more fail-safes between them and the final airlock. Probably.

They cautiously entered the final bay, splashing in puddles as they moved through the cobalt twilight. Judging from the oily whorls of colour in the blood, the team of grad students, servitors, and spawn had taken out a fail-safe, as well, but there was no sign of the fallen guardian, nor, for that matter, any of Laila's crew, beyond the blood. That was ... odd. Holding her hand up to the last panel, Pipaluk saw her talons were shaking. She gritted her fangs, willing herself to enter the code, when Nuka nickered excitedly behind her. She lowered the volume on his channel before turning to see what was bothering him now.

A pillar of blood had flowed straight up into the air behind them. Pipaluk went into a roll, just as the formless spawn crashed down. Of course that was why there were no bodies - this must be one of Laila's, injured in battle with the fail-safe and left behind to heal itself on the corpses of the fallen. It probably couldn't have hid from the fail-safe for long, trapped alone with it in this bay, which meant they might be just behind the blasphemous Professori ... unless she had died in this place, too. Well, no sense being optimistic just yet, Pipaluk reasoned, as her reflexes carried her backward, up, down, sideways, flipping away from the relentless, deadly ooze.

"Stink it!" Pipaluk panted, as she lured the pursuing wave back toward Nuka, who sat with his back to the final airlock. "Stink the thing, already!"

Nothing came over the subgineer's channel and, cartwheeling up to his splayed body, she saw he was not simply lying down on the job; he had quit it altogether: His neck had been twisted almost completely off when the spawn had hit him, only the suit keeping it attached. Gross. The pistol in his hand seemed intact, however, and all she had to do was -

- Go spinning across the bay as the formless spawn caught her foot and hurled her away from her prize. It was on her before she stopped sliding over the slick basalt, but a low heatburst from her suit drove it back, the thing hissing as it smoldered. Before it could throw itself atop her again, she was on all fours and dashing back to Nuka's corpse. It tried to put itself between her and the gun, but another suit-pulse let her slip past it, then the bony handle of the stinker was in hand. The spawn tried to hide in the pools on the ground, but her bio-helm filters picked up the creature immediately and she blasted it into oblivion with the foul little weapon.

"For Ane," she caught herself saying, as she depressed the trigger a second, superfluous time, which surprised her - she was not one for redundancy or sentimentality, as a rule. If anyone found out she was going soft, they might make a move for her position, try to hit her with the old bump-and-shuffle. But there was no time for politics, not now. Giving the bay another scan, just to make sure she hadn't missed any of the spawn in her haste, she turned and opened the final airlock, praying she wasn't too late.

IV

The ruins of Eibon's tower retained their five-sided design but little else, at least that Pipaluk could recall from the blueprints. There certainly hadn't been any mention of mineral cacti, molten streams of metal crisscrossing the floor, or a perpetual ashy cloud in the toxic air. A yellow moss coating the walls and fallen blocks confused her, for it was surely a close relation to the squamous fungus that grew only in the most hallowed temples of Tsathoggua, and yet she could not imagine a place less-favoured by the god than this foyer to his uncle's realm.

The moss also carpeted the floor wherever the mercurial creeks did not, but was trampled down so thoroughly that she could make no estimate of who had passed this way, or when. Everywhere she looked were wet scraps of Voormis, oily hunks of fail-safes, and puddles of deconstructed formless spawn, but nothing seemed alive in the ruins. The grotto was cramped, dark, and malodorous; it immediately put her at ease.

Pipaluk crossed the bizarre chamber, ducking beneath acid-dripping stalactites that whispered to her in a foreign tongue as she methodically searched the area. She paid them no mind, for she made out the name 'Hziulquoigmnzhah' amidst their stony gibberings and knew them to be heretical deposits. Then, at last, she saw a florescent reddish panel set in a spit of black gneiss that rose from a pool of the liquid metal – the small plate had a crack at its base, and from this fissure issued the iridescent fluid that dribbled down the ebon rock to feed stream and puddle alike. There was no sign of Laila, any member of her team, or even an active fail-safe. Pipaluk had failed.

"Pipaluk!" Provost Ole blared in her ear, the Quorum channel forcejacked back on. He sounded upset. "We've been monitoring everything. You've failed."

"Impossible," she sneered, too tired and disappointed for diplomacy. "You're bluffing; you can't - "

"Subgineer Refn here sneakpatched us into your bio-helm before you even reached the second airlock," said Ole. "He's also filled us in rather *thoroughly* regarding the *numerous* infractions you have committed in the course of your tenure. Effective immediately, you are to return to the first bay, where politibetjents are waiting to relieve you of your government equipment. Thereupon, you will stand trial for putting your subgineers in harm's way instead of using spawn, *as is basic protocol.* And *then* there is the matter of your refusal to obey my direct order to return to the Quorum for further instruction, and –"

Pipaluk couldn't deactivate the channel anymore, but she found she could still mute it. Subgineer Refn, eh? She hadn't seen that coming - she'd taken him back to her warrens a few months ago, but hadn't found him particularly enjoyable or even memorable. Now she wondered if he had been researching her, probing for weaknesses, rather than probing for - well, no matter, the damage was done. She had to admit he'd made a decent play of it, going directly to the Quorum, but it was hard to admire an action that would most likely result in her being painfully sacrificed to the inscrutable god she had spent her entire life trying to serve.

Of course, there was a second option. Depriving Ole, Refn, and their cronies of the political points her public trial would bring was a proposition too tempting to pass up, interdimensional, reality-shattering horror be damned. Pipaluk smiled to herself, shaking her head, and stepped into the shallow pool of shimmering metal. Just as she put her hand on the portal, however, a cry came from just behind her. Spinning around with the olid-pistol primed, she saw Professori Laila rising from behind a softly-chanting stalagmite, the camouflage of her suit falling away as she willingly revealed herself.

"Wait!" Laila repeated. "Don't!"

"Fancy seeing you here," said Pipaluk, dialing the gun down to Reek. She wanted Laila alive and sane enough to stand trial, after all. Pipaluk might be going down, but it wouldn't be alone. Then she

remembered the portal just behind her, her potentially suicidal reso-
lution of moments before, and she cocked her head curiously. "What
*are* you doing here? I thought the whole point was to go through the
Gate, not get your team killed just to skulk about some ruins."

"The point was to determine *if* the Gate could be safely used," said
Laila, crossing her arms. "Just as I always said. You were the one who
insisted I was trying to enter the damn thing."

"Right," said Pipaluk. "Sure. So, you're telling me you didn't have
any of your team go through?"

Laila winced. "Most of them didn't make it this far. Those fail-safes
were –"

"Most. But you made it. And so did ...?"

"A couple of grad students." Laila shivered. "Their names aren't
important now. They'll come up at the trial, I'm sure, and –"

"What happened to them!" Pipaluk barked. "You crazy kanaak,
what happened to them?"

"They went through." Laila looked down at the blurred shadow of
her reflection in the metal pool. "Dorthe went first. She was supposed
to return immediately, if she could. When she didn't, after a day, Nivi
went and –"

"'A day'," Pipaluk groaned. "Those toe-dragging fools on the Quorum."

"More like two," Laila said sheepishly. "No sign of either of them.
Which, well, isn't surprising - the portal is older than we could date.
Even if it still leads to Cykranosh, there's no telling what might be on
the other end by now. Maybe the Gate projects you into solid rock, the
bottom of an ocean. Maybe the planet's shifted so much it just dumps
you into space." The Professori shuddered. "None of the probes we
sent through came back, observation cables were severed as soon as
they crossed over, remotes failed, blah blah blah, and so those two
volunteered. And now we know – it's not safe, anymore. If it ever was."

"Maybe," said Pipaluk thoughtfully. "Maybe not. Surprised you
didn't take your chances with it when you saw me coming. Surprised
you warned me off it."

"Despite your slanderous campaign of character assassination, I'm
a devout Klarkash-Tonian," said Laila, straightening her shoulders. "I
would never allow a fellow servant of the Sleeper of N'Kai to unwit-
tingly fall into that devil Hziulquoigmnzhah's realm without a sure
means of escape. I told you and I told the Quorum time and again,

I'm not a heretic. I'm just —"

"Hush!" said Pipaluk, her com-membrane rippling. The second airlock had just been activated. The politibetjents were coming to arrest them. "They're coming. For both of us — I violated orders by pursuing you and got a few subgineers killed in the process. That puts us in the same bath, so let's make a break for it. I'll take a possible death of my own making over a certain one of theirs."

"Pipaluk, Pipaluk, Pipaluk," Laila chided. "Where is your faith? There is nowhere to run. We have committed crimes, you and I, and must be taken to the Eiglophian Plains for punishment. It is written that they who err in the service of the slothful ebon god shall be forgiven, so long as they are purified by a sacrificial death. I go willingly to my justice and suggest you — blargh!"

Laila doubled over in agony, retching into her bio-helm. A faint wisp of stench danced at the end of Pipaluk's pistol as she tucked the hot weapon into her belt and went to the incapacitated Professori. The final airlock was beginning to open as Pipaluk hoisted her former adversary and shoved her headlong through the Eibon Gate, the back of the hinged metal panel banging softly against its gneiss setting as the Voormi disappeared into the misty haze that obscured whatever lay on the far side. Without a backward glance at her pursuers, Pipaluk hoisted herself up and squirmed after, through the door to Saturn.

IV

The team of politibetjents and formless spawn sent to capture Pipaluk waited for days in the mossy ruins, neither wishing to follow the Ingeniøri through the mysterious portal, nor daring to leave in disobedience of Provost Ole's orders. At length, they were recalled, but the result of the whole affair was highly regrettable from the standpoint of the Quorum. It was universally believed, due to a leaked bio-helm file here and an uploaded simcreation there, that Professori Laila and Ingeniøri Pipaluk had not only escaped by virtue of the luminous science they had learned from Hziulquoigmnzhah, but had made away with a dozen formless spawn commandos and fail-safe behemoths in the bargain. As a consequence of this belief, the public's trust in the Quorum declined and there was a widespread revival of the dark worship of Tsathoggua's paternal uncle throughout Mhu Thulan in the last century before the onset of the great Solar Firestorms.

# Weird of the White Sybil

## By Ann K. Schwader

You see me as you wish, a lissome maid
Descended from some lunar race of old,
& never dream that you should be afraid.

No matter that my draperies are frayed
By tempests only glacial wastelands hold.
You see me as you wish, a lissome maid

Less prophetess than purest spirit strayed
From paradise – or legends left untold --
& never dream that you should be afraid

To follow in my footsteps.  Undismayed
As any moth hypnotic flames enfold,
You see me as you wish: a lissome maid

Who flickers at your vision's edge, displayed
Within a bower, brilliant in the cold.
O, never dream that you should be afraid

To speak your love . . . or to embrace its shade
As one more of the fortune-favored bold
Who saw me as a wish, a lissome maid
To kiss their dreams. *Too late to be afraid.*

# They Lie not Dead, but Dreaming...

*Dead But Dreaming* and *Dead But Dreaming 2*
are the new classics of modern Lovecraftian literature. Reviewed as
excellent tomes, they have been well received by fans of the genre for years.
The two books contain tales by Ramsey Campbell, Darrell Schweitzer,
Donald R. Burleson, Cody Goodfellow, Joseph S. Pulver, Sr., and
W. H. Pugmire. Explore the darkness.

*Dead But Dreaming* and *Dead But Dreaming 2* are available from
Amazon.com, BookDepository.com and other fine booksellers
worldwide.

Miskatonic
River
Press

**Horror for the Holidays**

Dark literary gifts from Ramsey Campbell, Thomas Ligotti, and H. P. Lovecraft, with new fiction from Cody Goodfellow, Lois H. Gresh, Robert M. Price, W. H. Pugmire, Joseph S. Pulver, Sr and more.

Edited by Scott David Aniolowski

"When the footpads quail at the night-bird's wail,
And black dogs bay at the moon,
Then is the specters' holiday – then is the ghosts' high noon!"
-- Sir William Schwenck Gilbert, Ruddigore, Act 1

Holidays. Special days of commemoration and celebration. Feasts and festivities. Remembrance and revelry. But what dark things lurk just out of sight, in the shadows of those celebrated days? Forces beyond our comprehension, yearning to burst into our warm and comforting world and tear asunder those things we hold most dear. As the wheel of the year turns and we embrace our favorite occasions, let us not forget that beyond the light is a darkness, and in that darkness something stirs. Some nameless thing that brings us Horror for the Holidays!

Let dark fiction from Ramsey Campbell, Thomas Ligotti, Robert Price, Cody Goodfellow, and Lois Gresh adorn your holidays throughout the year!

Available in paperback ePub, and Kindle formats!

Available Now from

Miskatonic
River
Press

# THE H.P. LOVECRAFT HISTORICAL SOCIETY

LUDO FORE PUTAVIMUS

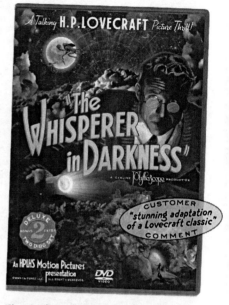

## The Call of Cthulhu

Widely acclaimed by critics and audiences throughout the world, this black and white, silent film version of HPL's classic tale has been called the most faithful and effective Lovecraft adaptation to date. Features an incredible original symphonic score, available as a soundtrack CD. The region-free DVD features titlecards in 24 different languages and a behind-the-scenes featurette that some enjoy as much as the movie itself!

## The Whisperer In Darkness

HPL's classic tale bursts onto the screen in the style of the classic horror films of the 1930s. Skeptical folklore professor Albert Wilmarth discovers a century-old manuscript describing weird creatures and demonic rituals in the remote Vermont hills — setting off a chain of events that will lead him deep into the mountains and to the very edge of madness as he confronts the true purpose of these shadowy visitors. Now available as a deluxe 2-DVD set with hours of bonus features, and on Blu-Ray disc with commentary track!

A GENUINE Mythoscope PRODUCTION
REG. U.S. PAT. OFF.

## Dark Adventure Radio Theatre

Experience some of Lovecraft's best stories in the form of 1930s-style radio drama, with great acting and all-original music. Our lavishly produced 75-minute CDs are accompanied by elaborate prop documents, photos, and maps, bringing the stories to life in your hands! Collect the whole set packaged in a nifty custom-made collector box shaped like an old time radio! New titles coming soon!

# WWW.CTHULHULIVES.ORG

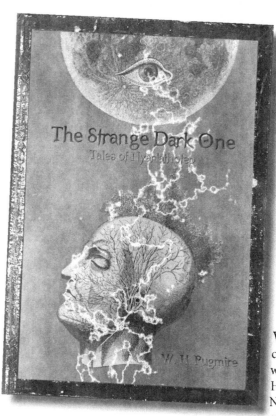

With

## *The Strange Dark One,*

W. H. Pugmire collects all of his best weird fiction concerning H. P. Lovecraft's dark god, Nyarlathotep. This avatar of the Great Old Ones is Lovecraft's most enigmatic creation, a being of many masks and multitudinous personae. Often called The Crawling Chaos, Nyarlathotep heralds the end of mortal time, and serves as avatar of Azathoth, the Idiot Chaos who will blow earth's dust away. Many writers have been enchanted by this dark being, in particular Robert Bloch, the man who, through correspondence, inspired Wilum Pugmire to try his hand at Lovecraftian fiction. This new book is a testimonial of Nyarlathotep's hold on Pugmire's withered brain, and these tales serve as aspects of a haunted mind. Along with stories that have not been reprinted since their initial magazine appearances, The Strange Dark One includes "To See Beyond," a sequel-of-sorts to Robert Bloch's tale, "The Cheaters", and the book's title story is a 14,000 word novelette set in Pugmire's Sesqua Valley. Each tale if beautifully illustrated by the remarkable Jeffrey Thomas, who is himself one of today's finest horror authors.

Thomas Ligotti is beyond doubt one of the Grandmasters of Weird Fiction. In *The Grimiscribe's Puppets,* Joseph S. Pulver, Sr., has commissioned both new and established talents in the world of weird fiction and horror to contribute all new tales that pay homage to Ligotti and celebrate his eerie and essential nightmares. Poppy Z. Brite once asked, "Are you out there, Thomas Ligotti?" This anthology proves not only is he alive and well, but his extraordinary illuminations have proven to be a visionary and fertile source of inspiration for some of today's most accomplished authors.

Also available in ePub, and Kindle formats!

Miskatonic River Press

CPSIA information can be obtained at www.ICGtesting.com
Printed in the USA
BVOW04s1259200813

328985BV00007B/15/P